The Younguns of Mansfield

The Younguns/Book One

The
Younguns
of Mansfield

❖

Thomas L. Tedrow

THOMAS NELSON PUBLISHERS
Nashville • Atlanta • London • Vancouver

Published in Nashville, Tennessee, by Thomas Nelson, Inc., Publishers, and distributed in Canada by Word Communications, Ltd., Richmond, British Columbia, and in the United Kingdom by Word (UK), Ltd., Milton Keynes, England.

Scripture quotations are from the NEW KING JAMES VERSION of the Bible. Copyright © 1979, 1980, 1982, 1990, Thomas Nelson, Inc., Publishers.

While this book is fiction, it retains the historical integrity and general history of turn-of-the-century America. Any references to specific events, real people, or real places are intended only to give the fiction a setting in historical reality. Names, characters, and incidents are either the product of the author's imagination or are used fictitiously, and their resemblance, if any, to real-life counterparts is purely coincidental.

Library of Congress Cataloging-in-Publication Data

Tedrow, Thomas L.
    The Younguns of Mansfield / Thomas L. Tedrow.
      p. cm. — (the Younguns ; bk. 1)
    Summary: At the turn of the century in rural Missouri, a rabies epidemic in the Youngun family's area threatens Dangit the dog and challenges Sherry's blossoming belief in angels.
    ISBN 0-8407-4132-4 (pbk. : alk. paper)
    [1. Rabies—Fiction. 2. Dogs—Fiction. 3. Country life-Missouri—Fiction. 4. Missouri—Fiction. 5. Christian life—Fiction.] I. Title. II. Series: Tedrow, Thomas L. Younguns ; bk. 1.
    PZ7.T227Y0 1996
    [Fic]—dc20   95-15431
                                                     CIP
                                                     AC

Printed in the United States of America
1 2 3 4 5 6 7 - 02 01 00 99 98 97 96

To my family. Yesterday, today, forever.

Contents

Foreword   vii
1   Deadly Visitor   1
2   The Younguns of Mansfield, Missouri   3
3   Big Wart and Little Wart   8
4   Preacher's Children   12
5   In the Dark   17
6   Little Wings   20
7   Bats, Bats, Bats   24
8   Silly, Stupid Pants   26
9   Newspaper Reports   33
10   Cain, Abel, and Mabel   35
11   The Cave on Devil's Ridge   40
12   Skunk Juice   45
13   Skunked Out   51
14   Bottle Brother   54
15   Redbone's Misery   59
16   Dracula?   62
17   Vampire Bat   66
18   Night Moves   71
19   Cornbread and Honey   75
20   Cody   79
21   In Sarah's Kitchen   85
22   Sheriff Peterson   88
23   Granddoc Crawley   93
24   Walk in the Woods   97

25 Bat Attack 102

26 Dr. George 107

27 The Red Shoes 113

28 Dangit 116

29 Mr. Palugee 120

30 Vaccine 122

31 Terry's Poem 125

32 J.J. 131

33 Back to the Junkyard 134

34 U.S. Angel Mail 140

35 Under Siege 143

36 Fish Shocker 145

37 Rocking Chair Wisdom 151

38 Keeping Score 159

39 Going Insane 164

40 Burn Them Out 172

41 Fever's Goin' Up 174

42 Secret 177

43 Town Meeting 183

44 Swollen River 188

45 Breakout 193

46 Gordo 200

47 Hide the Doggie 203

48 Tell the Truth 206

49 Secrets of the Ozarks 210

Foreword

When Thomas Nelson Publishers released my eight-book series, The Days of Laura Ingalls Wilder, something wonderful happened. From all across the country, cards and letters began coming in asking for more stories about the Younguns.

And not just from children. I heard from teenagers, parents, and adults I had figured were so stuffy and stodgy that I thought they'd forgotten how to really smile. How wrong I was!

These three mischievous rascals—Larry, Terry, and Sherry Youngun—touched a chord, set off a memory, or just plain tickled the funny bones in people of all ages. Then I knew what I had to do.

I set to work to create a book series about these lovable preacher's children who seem to unleash the magic of childhood in everyone they meet. They are kids who make mistakes and get into trouble but always have the best of intentions.

So here is the first book of a series that will take you to a simpler time before things got so complicated. If this is your first introduction to the Younguns and you haven't had the magic of youth starched out of your soul, then welcome aboard. All you need is an imagination, a dash of wonder, and a limber funny bone. Leave the rest up to the Younguns.

Thomas L. Tedrow

Deadly Visitor

❖

The big bat at the top of the cave on Devil's Ridge struggled to get comfortable. It wanted to sleep, but nothing felt right. Everything seemed on fire.

Thousands of smaller bats hung from the ceiling, resting for the next night's hunt. They were nocturnal hunters—night creatures—who lived for darkness.

The other bats in the cave were only inches long, but the large bat had a two-foot wingspan. It seemed like a giant hanging next to the others. While the other bats in the cave dined on bugs, the big bat was different. It thirsted for blood—as all vampire bats do.

This vampire bat stood more than eighteen inches tall when it walked on its hind legs. New to the Ozarks, it had come all the way from Mexico, burning with rabies it had caught from another bat. That was why it couldn't get comfortable. The disease wreaked havoc in its body.

The vampire bat had traveled in the hold of a cattle ship out of the Bay of Campeche from Veracruz, into the Gulf of Mexico.

Along the way, the bat never thirsted. There was fresh blood wherever it landed in the dark hold of the ship. There were men on board, but the cattle were tied in place and easy to feed on. Making a small cut in each steer's skin, the bat drank its fill of blood. The cattle never felt a thing.

Slipping out in New Orleans, the vampire bat had ridden boats up the Mississippi River. In Cape Girardeau, Missouri, the bat had been chased off the boat by a broom-swinging cook and then had managed to hide in a train car riding into the Ozarks near Mansfield.

But the rabies disease ate away at the bat's insides. It was in the final stage before death and having trouble knowing night from day, knowing when to sleep and when to hunt.

The sickness made it harder for the animal to fly and hunt the way it was supposed to. So swooping over the hills, the vampire bat looked for easy prey, like cattle and the injured raccoon it had feasted on several weeks ago.

That was the bite that brought the deadly disease of rabies to the Ozarks. The raccoon recovered from its injuries long enough to bite other raccoons and a big hound with a collar that bore the name Gordo.

Gordo had been abandoned in Mountain Grove by an old farmer who couldn't afford to feed him anymore. The big dog had joined a pack of wild dogs roaming the hills, and he fought his way to become the leader.

Now an epidemic of rabies was approaching Mansfield. An epidemic that no one knew about.

2

The Younguns of Mansfield, Missouri

❖

The keys of the scratched and dented parish piano sounded the opening bars of the wedding song. It was another living-room wedding at the Younguns's house.

Rev. Thomas Youngun stopped at the doorway to straighten his coat. *I wonder how many couples I've married over the years,* he pondered, looking around the room. *Time flies. It's hard to believe that it's already May of 1907.*

His good neighbor, Eulla Mae Springer, played the battered old upright piano with the broken key as if it were a concert grand. Her husband, Maurice, huddled in a corner on the horsehair divan, absorbed in a magazine. The bride and groom were still dressing, she in the back bedroom and he upstairs.

When Rev. Youngun's wife, Norma, died he had needed someone to play the wedding march on the piano. Eulla Mae had volunteered, and Rev. Youngun always paid her a share of the wedding fees. That was five years ago, and now she had played more weddings than she could remember.

Rev. Youngun hummed along, waiting for Eulla Mae to hit the dead note. It was a private joke between them. He chuckled when she hit the broken key. "That's the same wrong note you always hit," he whispered.

"Not a wrong note," she said, "but it sure is a broken key. When you gonna get it fixed?"

"Can't get it fixed until the church approves it." He shrugged. "And you know how Sarah Bentley can be."

Eulla Mae nodded. "That woman sure has it in for you and the kids. But that's no reason not to fix this piano . . . and your leakin' roof," she said, nodding her head toward the pot on the floor in the corner. It was filled to the rim with rainwater from last night's storm.

"Maybe the Spirit will move her to be reasonable." He sighed, not really believing it.

Eulla Mae chuckled. "And I'll turn white and you'll turn black long before that happens."

"Why does it all come down to money?" he asked.

"Most everythin' does," she replied. "I sure hope you get a nice weddin' fee today."

He nodded. "We need it."

Rev. Youngun loved Mansfield. Though it was considered a time of opportunity, the widowed Methodist minister had never made much money. Saving souls was supposed to compensate for the pitifully low wages normally paid to men of the cloth. Raising and feeding three kids and all those animals on his small salary was difficult, which was why Rev. Youngun needed the "gifts" that the couples he married gave him. Though payment wasn't required, most gave Rev. Youngun two or three dollars, which was enough to help buy groceries and clothes for the children.

His children nicknamed them all COB couples—"couple of bucks." COB couples were like money from heaven.

Shiny Wilson down at the marriage license bureau was a member of Rev. Youngun's congregation and knew that the Younguns needed all the extra money they could get. So he sent him anyone getting married without a church, whether they were Catholics, Protestants, nonbelievers, or eloping young couples on the run.

This was the only wedding that had come to Thomas Youngun this month, so they really needed the money. There was only one dollar and two cents in the money box. The wedding tomorrow would bring in another few dollars. That would see them through for a while.

His three children, Terry, Sherry, and ten-year-old Larry—had complained about having to eat cereal and "chewed-up" meat (what they called ground beef) for the past week. He thought about his promise to

Norma on her deathbed, how he'd keep the kids fed, clothed, and churched.

Norma wouldn't have given them chewed-up meat and church hand-me-down clothes. But raising them by myself hasn't been easy. He shook his head. The week before, one of the wealthy children had pointed out that Larry was wearing the rich boy's old shirt. Rev. Youngun remembered the pained expression on his son's face. Larry had held his head high, but his father's heart almost broke for him.

From the second floor, he heard his seven-year-old son, Terry, teasing his five-year-old daughter, Sherry:

"Roses are red,
Violets are blue.
Cabbage makes me sick,
And so do you!"

Rev. Youngun went to the stairs and shouted, "That's not nice! Stop it!"

"Sorry, Pa," Terry answered.

"That boy's a poet." Eulla Mae laughed.

"And that boy may end up driving me crazy." Rev. Youngun smiled, shaking his head.

"Just give him time." Eulla Mae smiled too. "He'll turn out all right."

"Reverend, it's about time, isn't it?" "Mom" Carter called out.

Rev. Youngun nodded. "Yes, Mom, it's almost that time."

Today "Mom" Carter and Hambone Higgens were getting married. They were an odd-looking couple. Mom was just under five feet and round as a ball, while Hambone was at least six feet six inches and had to duck when he came through doorways.

Mom owned Mom's Cafe, Mansfield's only restaurant besides the fancy one at the hotel. She'd earned her nickname from the way she mothered and watched over her customers without families.

Hambone was Mom's cook. He'd earned his name working as a cook for Teddy Roosevelt's Rough Riders, when he'd fought off a group of hungry Cubans using a ham bone from the soup pot at the battle of San Juan Hill.

"Straighten out your tie," Mom ordered, as they made their way down the hall to the living room.

"Yes, Mom," he mumbled.

"Now, Hambone," Mom whispered loudly as she tried to straighten the only tie he'd ever worn in his life, "don't go sayin' somethin' dumb out there."

"You know I won't." Hambone sighed.

"You just say 'I do' when I tell you to. Now say it."

"Do . . . do I?" Hambone nervously stammered.

"No . . . no . . . that's the same way you don't listen to how folks want their eggs. You give 'em sunny-side up when they ask for scrambled, and I have to refund their money." She gave Hambone a stern look. "Just say 'I do' when I tell you to . . . ain't that right, Rev. Youngun?"

Rev. Youngun nodded and excused himself to find his tardy flower girl and ring bearer. *For better or for worse,* he thought.

In the kitchen, Terry Youngun studied the stereoscopic picture cards donated to the church. Dangit the dog licked water from the drip pan under the icebox, which held a fifty-pound block of ice to keep their food from spoiling. Beezer, their parrot, sat on the back of the chair screaming, "Bad dog . . . bad dog!"

"Hush up, Beezer," Terry said.

"Bow-wow . . . woof-woof," Beezer screeched.

"Beezer," Terry said, glaring at the bird, "you're botherin' me."

"Dummy-dummy," the bird squawked and flapped his wings.

Wish I hadn't taught him all that, Terry thought. He didn't like to be disturbed when he looked at the stereoscopic picture cards. Especially cards of pretty dancing girls that had been left in the stack by mistake.

He scratched his head, trying to read the description written under the picture of the skimpily clad women. "The naughty dance ca . . . called the hoo . . . hoo . . . ."

Beezer screeched out like an owl, "Who-who."

Terry took a peanut from Beezer's food bowl and threw it hard at the parrot. He just missed. "Shut up!" He looked back at the card. "Dance called the hoo . . . chie . . . koochie—"

His father came into the kitchen. "Terry, I thought you were upstairs dressing."

Terry looked down at his play clothes and shrugged. "Just wanted to finish lookin' at these cards," he said, putting the viewer back up to his face.

Rev. Youngun looked at his watch. "What's so interesting?"

Terry smiled. "They're pictures of the Chicago World's Fair. Thought knowin' 'bout city life would help me in school." He looked at a few more cards, then asked, "Pa, what's the hoochie-koochie dance all about?"

Rev. Youngun's eyebrows raised almost to his hairline. He grabbed the viewer out of his son's hands, looked at it, then turned to Terry. "Go up and get dressed, young man. Right this instant!"

"But Pa . . . what's the hoochie . . . " Then Terry noticed the dark look on his father's face and skedaddled from the room.

3

Big Wart and Little Wart

❖

Ratz, the tattered calico cat with the white face, looked up from his warm spot on the dilapidated sofa at Eulla Mae who sat at the piano, then at Mom and Hambone talking near the doorway. The cat stretched, coughed up a hair ball, then left the living room for a quieter place to sleep.

"Oh, Ratz," Rev. Youngun whispered, looking at the mess on the floor. The cat meowed back at him from the hallway.

Rev. Youngun took a napkin, cleaned up the floor, looked at his watch, then at the pictures of his three children on the wall above the sofa. *I wonder what's keeping them?* It was something he wondered about constantly, since he had three rascals on his hands who certainly earned their "preacher's kids" stripes.

He tried to keep them in line with firm love, believing that sparing the rod didn't spoil the child. But he shook his head, weary of saying, "One day you'll thank me for this," as he disciplined them in every way he could think of without striking them.

Then he saw Sarah Bentley speeding up the driveway in her new 1907 open-air Chrysler. Sarah was the wealthiest member of his congregation by way of inherited money and marrying William Bentley, the timber and land baron of the Ozarks. She parked her car and stormed toward the house with her eight-year-old son, William, Jr., following right behind.

"Uh-oh, here comes the witch," Eulla Mae whispered.

Rev. Youngun nodded that he'd seen her arrive. She was upset about something again. He shook his head. *Anger is such a destroying force. I should do a sermon on turning away from anger.*

"Looks like she ain't comin' here to fix the piano." Eulla Mae sighed.

"Nope. Don't think this is a social visit."

Rev. Youngun looked at the battered piano, raggedy sofa, and pot full of water under the leak in the roof. *Guess it'll be a cold day in the devil's den before these things get fixed.*

Upstairs, Terry Youngun looked out the window and closed his eyes. "Big Wart and Little Wart just came flyin' in on their brooms." Terry eyed Willy Bentley. "I bet he blamed what happened at Mr. Palugee's on us."

Larry came over to the window. "Us? It's you that's in trouble now. I *told* you to stay away from Willy. He's a rat."

"I just wanted to get a look at Palugee's two-story outhouse."

"And I told you we should stay off his property and stay away from Willy Bentley, but oh no, you wouldn't listen!" Larry exclaimed.

Terry shrugged. "I didn't believe Willy when he said he'd light that bag of dog doo-doo and put it on that old man's porch."

"You know Pa said to stay away from that man's home," Larry continued his lecture.

"I was just lookin' 'round at all his junk." Terry grinned, as if it was no big deal. "You liked lookin' at the crazy man's stuff too!"

"No, I didn't," Larry said. "I was just tryin' to keep you out of trouble." Terry reached over and suddenly grabbed his brother's nose. "What you doin'?" Larry asked.

"Just wanted to see if your nose was gonna grow like Pinocchio's for tellin' that fib."

Terry had to smile, thinking about what Willy Bentley had done. It would have been even funnier if he hadn't blamed Terry for it.

Mr. Palugee was the town's pack rat who saved junk. His house and yard were stacked with anything and everything, and he spent all his waking hours either tinkering around in his rusted kingdom or scouting the back roads and hills for more "treasures" to add to his mess.

People were as used to seeing him carrying his burlap sacks around as they were to seeing the abundant wildlife of the hills. But unlike the animals of the forest, Mr. Palugee didn't keep his nest clean.

From the road you could see broken-down wagons, a wrecked car, hundreds of tools, washtubs, and enough odds and ends to start a junkyard. This didn't account for the stack of newspapers inside his house, a five-foot ball of string, and a room full of flattened cans, which he couldn't remember why he'd saved for the past thirty years.

The people of Mansfield considered his property an eyesore and his two-story outhouse, salvaged from a burned-out rooming house near Branson, an embarrassment. It wasn't so bad that the privy was a double-decker. What people didn't like were all the gewgaws and whatnots he'd nailed to the outside. On some days, when the sun was high in the sky, it could almost blind you.

They also didn't like the sign that had been nailed onto it by some prankster: "Ol' Watch Out Below." It horrified the church ladies. They whispered about it every time they passed by his property.

To the citizens of Mansfield, Mr. Palugee's home was an eyesore. But to the kids, it was a tempting place to trespass. Sneaking through the stacks of junk and broken equipment without being seen by Mr. Palugee was one of the more daring things to do in the sleepy rural town.

The day before, Willy had dared the Younguns to knock on Mr. Palugee's door. Larry had refused, but Terry took the dare. The three of them hid in the bushes, giggling to themselves when the old man came out and looked around. He was annoyed to find no one there. He finally went back inside and closed the door behind him.

Then Willy got another idea. "I'll do something better," he whispered. "I'll light this bag and put it on his front porch."

"Why?" Terry asked.

"'Cause when Mr. Palugee comes to the door, he'll see the fire and stomp on the bag."

Larry stood back, knowing it was all wrong. "What's in the bag?"

Willy snickered. "Doo-doo."

"Doo-doo?" Terry said, shocked. "But when he stomps on it he'll get . . . "

"That's right," Willy said, raising his eyebrows. "You dare me?"

"No," Larry said.

"Yes!" Terry screamed, not really thinking that Willy would do it.

But Willy ran up to the porch before Larry could stop him. He lit the bag, knocked on the door, and ran. Mr. Palugee opened the door and panicked at the sight of fire. He stomped on the burning bag and . . . needless to say it was quite a mess. He was furious.

The boys hadn't counted on Willy getting caught and blaming Terry, which was what they heard him do as they scampered away. And now Willy, Little Wart, was downstairs.

Larry knew his brother was in trouble this time. "Willy's a rat. He tattled and lied to Mr. Palugee to protect himself. And his mother believes everything he says."

Terry spit out the window. "If they weren't so rich, it wouldn't matter what she said."

"Can't change what's God's way." Larry shrugged.

Terry frowned. "Wish God would let loose with a little money in our direction. I'm tired of eatin' chewed-up meat and old bread."

"Hamburger's better than starvin'," Larry said solemnly.

"Barely," Terry replied, wincing at the sound of Sarah's footsteps on the wooden porch.

"What are you gonna do?" Larry asked.

"I better get down to tell Pa my side," Terry said. "It'll be my word against the wart's."

Larry shook his head. "No, it'll be his word and their money against your word and Pa gettin' the roof fixed."

Terry thought about the drip pot in the corner. "Guess we all might get used to wearin' raincoats to bed."

Preacher's Children

Sarah banged on the door, her cheeks red with rage. "Rev. Youngun, I want to talk to you!"

Mom glared at the door. Another interruption in what should have been her special day.

"What's she want?" Eulla Mae whispered.

Rev. Youngun shrugged. "Just wants to complain about something . . . just like she always does." He winced as Sarah pounded on the door a second time. "I'm coming."

Rev. Youngun straightened his coat. In the hall, he heard Terry whisper, "Psst, Pa, I didn't do nothin'."

Rev. Youngun turned to see his auburn-haired scampster vigorously shaking his head back and forth.

Sarah pounded on the door again. "Rev. Youngun, would you open the door, please?!"

"Tell me quickly what this is all about," he ordered his son.

Terry rattled the story off quickly. "Willy lit a bag of burning doo-doo and put it on Old Man Palugee's porch, who got his feet kind of dirty when he stomped it out."

"Is anybody home?" Sarah called out sarcastically.

"What?" Rev. Youngun exclaimed, flabbergasted. "A burning bag of what?"

"Doo-doo," Terry said, blushing.

"Why'd you do it?" Rev. Youngun asked.

"Rev. Youngun, open the door!" Sarah called out.

"I didn't do it, but I think she's comin' to say I lit the bag of doo-doo and put it on the porch."

"Were you there?"

"I was walkin' by when it happened."

Sarah banged on the door again.

"Did you have *anything* to do with what happened?" Rev. Youngun asked his son.

"No, Pa. Honest. I just happened to be walkin' by and got tricked into watchin' that no-good Willy doin' it. I didn't do it. Ask Larry. But Willy got caught hidin' behind Palugee's house and blamed it on me."

"Are you're telling me the truth?"

"Swear, Pa. Swear to God, cross my heart and hope to die, stick a needle in my eye."

Rev. Youngun knew that when his son said that, he was telling the truth. "Go on back upstairs. I'll handle this," Rev. Youngun said to Terry, turning toward the door.

Lord, help me through this, Rev. Youngun asked as he opened the door. Then a line from Proverbs came to him: "A soft answer turns away wrath." *Thank You, Lord.*

When he opened the door, Sarah's eyes flared with anger. She proceeded to read him the riot act. "Rev. Youngun, your children are uncouth, disgusting little monsters!" she screamed.

"Please calm down, Mrs. Bentley, and tell me what the problem is," he said gently, trying to maintain kindness and good manners in the face of her hostility.

"Preachers' children are all alike!" she fumed, scarcely trying to control herself.

"Mrs. Bentley, please, start from the beginning."

Her face was red with anger. "They set a fire to a . . . "

Rev. Youngun held up his hand. "Who did what? Please, just calm down."

"Well," she said, catching her breath. "William said that your son Terry set fire to a . . . to a . . . "

"A doo-doo bag?" Rev. Youngun asked with an innocent expression on his face.

"Yes, and this is what happened," she said, as if discussing a disaster of catastrophic proportions.

As she related Willy's side of the events, Rev. Youngun's eyes glazed over. *Her money will buy the truth as she wants it. It'll always be a losing battle as long as the church needs their money.*

Sarah Bentley was head of the Methodist Ladies Aid Society and had the final say when the church provided the Younguns money to repair the house. She had the final say because she and her husband were the largest contributors to the society and most of the charities in the county.

Money was Sarah Bentley's power over the Younguns. And lately, she'd been in a running battle with Rev. Youngun over the discipline of his children. With the parsonage roof leaking, the stuffing coming out of the sofa, and the paint peeling off the outside walls, she tried to force her views on him. Sarah was a stubborn woman who believed her money made her right.

". . . and I won't authorize the repairs for your roof until your boy confesses the truth," Rev. Youngun heard her conclude. She turned and patted her son on the head. "William, Jr., here, would *never* do such a thing."

"He's a wart," Terry called out from the top of the stairs.

Rev. Youngun spun around. "Terry, I told you to stay upstairs."

"The wart's a fibber," Terry snapped back.

"Mother!" Willy protested. "Are you gonna let that brat get away with that?"

"Terry, apologize to William," Rev. Youngun said.

"No," came the response.

"Terry," Rev. Youngun said in a gruff voice.

"Okay," Terry said, thumping down the stairs on his rear end. "I'm sorry I called the little wart a wart . . . but he's still a fibber."

Sarah put her face up to Rev. Youngun's and wagged her finger under his nose. "You need to spank some sense and manners into that boy . . . matter of fact, *all* your children could use some firm discipline."

"I don't believe in spanking children," Rev. Youngun said calmly, pushing her finger back down to her side. He imagined what the next rain would do to the roof, but there was principle at stake here.

"Rev. Youngun, I guess you don't know what the Bible teaches."

"The Bible has nothing to do with this."

Though Sarah Bentley had never spanked her own son, she did believe in spanking others—especially the Youngun children. "You need to take a hairbrush to their behinds every morning and every evening for good measure, until they learn respect!"

"How you raise your child is your business," he said.

She pretended to slap the palm of her hand with a brush. "You've got to beat sense into a child . . . just like you housebreak a puppy."

"They're kids, not animals . . . and they're *my* kids, thank you," he said softly.

Sarah tried another tack. "You need to learn the value of money. My husband and I own a lot of land around here . . . think about it."

Rev. Youngun steamed inside. Her threats were not very well hidden.

Mom interrupted the tense conference. "Let's start the weddin'. I wanna marry this man before he gets away."

Rev. Youngun nodded, then turned back to Sarah. "If you don't have anything else to say," he said, "I have a wedding to perform."

Sarah eyed him closely with a thin, tight smile. "You shouldn't bite the hand that feeds you, Reverend."

"You might be very rich, Mrs. Bentley, but all my riches come from God."

"Ask God to fix your roof then." She chuckled.

"I do every evening before I go to sleep," Rev. Youngun said, looking her in the eye.

"Think carefully about what you're doing. Spare the rod on these kids of yours," she said coldly, "and I guarantee you'll reap what you sow . . . and the birdseed ideas you believe in will produce nothing but jailbirds."

"I don't need to think about it. I don't believe in beating children." Tempted to tell her to leave, Rev. Youngun instead said, "Mrs. Bentley, why don't we join hands and pray about this. I'll discipline my children in my own way when they deserve it." He tried to defuse her anger with soft words and a kind smile.

She would have nothing of it. "Then my prayers with you would be wasted."

Mom called out impatiently, "Are you gonna marry me, Reverend, or do I have to go down to see the justice of the peace?"

Rev. Youngun looked at Sarah. "Please stay for the wedding. We'll talk afterward."

Sarah looked over at Mom, and nodded. "I'll stay for Mom's sake. But just keep that Terry away from my precious son, William."

Willy smiled, and then went around the corner toward the kitchen to get a glass of water. From the stairs Terry whispered over the rail, "You're a lyin' tattletale, no-good, wart-rat, doo-doo burner."

5

In the Dark

Up on Devil's Ridge, just outside Mansfield, Sammy Lester woke up and wondered where he was. All he could remember was that he'd spent the night before drinking at Tippy's Saloon.

Now he was in the dark and his hands hurt. He felt the cuts and scratches on his wrists and fingers, wondering how he'd gotten them. He had no idea he was in a cave filled with bats.

Where the heck am I? He looked around, but his eyes wouldn't focus. *I must be still drunk.*

What happened? He couldn't remember anything after the first drink. *The first drink. Seems that I'm blackin' out 'most every time I fire one down.*

The booze is gettin' to me, he admitted, trying to rub the fog from his brain. *What's happened to me?*

He thought about how his father always urged him to take stock of his life at harvest time, as winter approached.

Take stock, he moaned. *Pa would say gather your life together and check your mental and spiritual harvest. "What have you done this year with the wealth of opportunity that God has given you, Sammy?"* he'd ask.

Sammy chuckled cynically. *I'm a drunk, Pa. I've got nothing to show . . . not even my paycheck which I spent at the bar.*

He thought he heard something around him. *My ears must still be ringin'.* The big bat moved its head, turning to look down at Sammy. It was hot and sick with fever.

Yesterday Sammy had been hiding under the Willow Creek bridge, shocking fish with the old wall phone. He'd hooked up copper wires to the horseshoe magnets in the base of the phone, then cranked the handle, sending an electric shock into the water.

Though it hurt to smile, Sammy smiled anyway, thinking about all the fish that floated to the surface. He could dip them out with a net. There was really no work to it at all.

It was against county law to fish that way, but for Sammy, it was the lazy man's way to catch dinner. It was also a way to get enough fish to trade for drinks down at the saloon.

For a moment he was ashamed of himself, thinking about how hard his father had tried to teach him to be an honest, decent man. His pa had worked his hands to the bone on the prairie as a homesteader and wanted Sammy to love the land too.

Sammy tried to block out the memory of his father but couldn't. The memory of the waves of wind sweeping over the vast savannahs of wide open land caught him in an emotional tug.

For a moment he was sitting again in the tall grasses of Nebraska, a young boy picking at the prairie smoke and wild indigo plants around him. Sammy's pa had taught him how to fish and how to use a line and a trout trap on Plum Creek.

Sammy didn't like thinking about Plum Creek. That was where he and Emily Grant had been one-mile neighbors. *She turned out to be a newspaper writer, and I turned out to be a . . . a drunk,* he thought, rubbing his temples.

Sammy closed his eyes and willed himself back in time. He remembered working the trout trap with his pa and carrying the flopping fish back to the cabin. His ma would just smile and tell him to get ready for fried fish. Pa would cut off the heads and strip out the guts. Sammy would scale them, and Ma would roll them in cornmeal and fry them in fat. They tasted best if they were fried in the pan after cooking with salt pork.

Sammy laid back, trying to get the ringing of booze from his ears. *I can almost hear that creek. I can just about see Pa's smilin' face, goin' off to check the trap every mornin'. We'd carry back to Ma the buffalo fish, catfish, shiners, bullheads . . . heck, some of them bullheads had two black horns.*

Tears came to Sammy's face, as he remembered feeling good about himself and his life. *Wish I were back there again . . . wish I could start again. Wish I weren't just a drunk. Pa would disown me . . . he would. Wouldn't even want me buried next to him the way I turned out.*

He coughed loudly, trying to get his bearings. *Where did I leave my fish crank?* Then he remembered. *Oh man.* He sighed, rubbing his head. *I left it down under the bridge. Sheriff finds it, he'll know I was doin' it again. Maybe I should go find the crank 'fore the sheriff does.*

But his head hurt, making it hard to think straight. He still couldn't figure where he was or what time of day it was. It was dark, so he decided it was night and that he'd just get some more sleep, right where he was. *Then I'll go find the boys and see if one will loan me some drink money.*

Sammy looked around at the noise he thought he heard. *Wonder what that sound is?*

But it was too dark and he was too sleepy to worry. So he closed his eyes and passed out again, thinking about his mother. Her fruit preserves floated through his mind. She used to call them the sweet jars of summer.

The hills were covered with strawberries, blackberries, and wild huckleberries . . . Ma would can them up and kiss each jar. "Just to seal in the sunshine," she'd tell me.

What Sammy didn't know was that it was morning, and he was sleeping in the cave he'd stumbled into the night before as he tried to find his way home.

The noises he heard were wings, bat wings. The cave on Devil's Ridge was filled with thousands of them. And the biggest one was very sick. That big bat was hanging from the limestone directly above him, looking down at Sammy's neck.

6

Little Wings

❖

Five-year-old Sherry Youngun completed her letter to her guardian angel, then began to read the last paragraph out loud, over the sounds of Eulla Mae's out-of-tune piano music downstairs. "And, Little Wings, I want you to get me that pair of red shiny shoes that I saw in the window of Bedal's General Store. I'm gonna be in the school play next fall and want to show everybody I got store-bought shoes."

She closed her eyes, holding on to her blankey, thinking about the shoes. *They're so beautiful. They look like dancin' shoes. I'm so lucky to have an angel of my very own.*

It had all started at church. "Angels," her father had said in his sermon, "are at the center of God's stage. They are His divine messengers."

Sherry remembered feeling a tingle as her father spoke. "It was angels who told Mary to expect a child . . . and if you close your eyes and believe, you may find your own guardian angel. Just listen to what your heart tells you."

She'd taken the sermon to heart, and two days later, Sherry thought she caught her first glimpse of Little Wings, a small angel who smiled at her and said, "If you believe, then it is true."

Sherry had run all the way home to tell her father, but he wasn't there, so she told Larry about it. He just humored her, patting her head and saying, "That's nice, sis."

Then she made the mistake of telling Terry, who began teasing her with taunting rhymes. He did everything he could to bug her about the angel, like leaving horsefly wings on her breakfast plate and whispering:

"Roses are red,
And bees can sting,
There on your plate,
Is Little Wings."

Downstairs, Eulla Mae played another wedding song so loudly that Sherry didn't hear Larry walk up quietly behind her.

He peeked over her shoulder at the scribbles which Sherry finished reading aloud, "I never had a pair of new shoes before, so please get them for me like a good guardian angel should."

Larry interrupted. "How is anybody supposed to read that?"

Sherry whirled around and hid the letter behind her back, a little embarrassed. "Little Wings can read it," she replied indignantly.

"I hope so." He chuckled, as he left the room. "You better get dressed quick or Pa's gonna get upset."

She looked around and took a quick suck on her thumb. At the doorway Larry turned and smiled. Sherry jerked her thumb out of her mouth as he said, "And you better not let Pa catch you suckin' on your thumb. He said he'll put pepper juice on it if he catches you again."

"I won't let him see me," she said.

She looked at the pictures and scribbles on the paper. "I know Little Wings can read this." She sealed the letter, then looked at her starched white dress on the bed. She mumbled as she slipped it on.

Then she thought she heard a rustling sound and smiled. "I hear your wings, little angel." Though no one else had seen the angel and the bright light that accompanied her, Little Wings was real to Sherry.

"Do you like this dress, Little Wings?" Sherry asked, turning in front of the mirror. She didn't notice Terry creeping into the room.

"You're talkin' to yourself again!" Terry laughed.

Sherry turned on her heel and stomped her foot. "Get outta my room!" she screamed.

"Angel, shmangel . . . only silly thumb suckers talk to themselves." Terry laughed again, skipping out of the room.

Sherry was alone again. She stood still in the middle of her room and looked around. "Are you in here, Little Wings?" she whispered.

Suddenly, Terry came running back into the room, flapping his arms. "Here I am," he shouted.

"Get out! Get outta my room!" she screamed.

Terry just laughed, skipping around, teasing her with another poem:

"Snow is white
And roses are red.
Everybody knows
Sherry's cracked in the head!"

"Get out!" Sherry chased him through the door.

Downstairs, Rev. Youngun raised his eyes to the sound of stomping feet above him. *Please, Lord, give me strength to survive these children.*

Closing his eyes, he listened to what they were screaming about and heard Terry's poem. *They're arguing about Sherry's angel again.* He smiled, shaking his head. *Sherry really took that sermon to heart.*

Sarah had listened also. Shaking her head, she came over and tapped Rev. Youngun on the arm. "You shouldn't let your children believe in silly things like angels. Otherwise, they'll end up like Joan of Arc."

"Joan of Arc?" he asked, somewhat surprised.

"Yes," Sarah said matter-of-factly. "She listened to angels, and look what happened to her. She was burned at the stake." Sarah shook her head. "No, Rev. Youngun, I won't teach my son to believe in flying spirits . . . teach children the reality of life. That's how they live and learn."

I don't think you know what reality means, Rev. Youngun thought, frowning.

"Are you listening to me, Rev. Youngun?" Sarah asked.

"To every word, Mrs. Bentley," he responded, without batting an eye.

"So you should tell Sherry that there are no such things as angels."

"But Mrs. Bentley, the Bible says . . . "

"Rev. Youngun," she interrupted, "what the Bible says and what a child thinks she sees are two different things."

You are a wart. He grinned, thinking about Terry's description of her. *You're an old wart in a young body.*

"Whatever are you grinning about?" she asked him.

"Just thinking about warts," he chuckled.

"Warts? I don't think there's anything funny about warts."

"Neither do I, Mrs. Bentley. Neither do I. Now, if you don't mind, I do have a wedding to perform."

7

Bats, Bats, Bats

Along, thin tongue crept out from the big bat's mouth. And there was a man sleeping below it.

Sammy Lester snored and cleared his throat. He didn't hear the rustling response from around him in the cave. The bat looked down on Sammy Lester and wondered if it should drop down and sniff the man's neck. The vampire bat felt bloated with blood. It was engorged from the fat steer it had feasted on in the barn near the bottom of the hill. Dried flecks of blood hung from its fur in front. The blood from the steer should have made the vampire bat rest comfortably, but it didn't.

Spreading its wings out and flapping them violently, the bat knocked away dozens of its smaller cousins. As they dropped off and screeched, the smaller bats flew to other parts of the cave.

The big bat looked down on Sammy Lester, still sleeping below. Too full to feed again but too confused from the fire in its body to react normally, the big bat wiggled its head.

Sammy snored and turned over onto his back, exposing his Adam's apple. It looked inviting.

The big bat glided down and landed near the sleeping man. It had bitten several men in Mexico. But that was then. Before the disease.

Sammy snored and grunted. The bat stepped back, then walked on its hind legs, wagging its head from side to side, looking at Sammy's neck.

The neck *did* look inviting when the man wasn't moving. He was as still as the fat steer with the big veins the bat had tasted the night before.

Sniffing the air, the bat inched forward, not really hungry but wanting something to put out the fire in its head. It just wanted to cool down and go to sleep. Maybe some more blood would do it.

Licking at the specks of dried blood on its fur, the bat wiggled to get closer. Leaning forward, the bat sniffed at Sammy, who snorted and opened his eyes.

"It that you, Carol?" Sammy called out in the dark, half asleep and still drunk. He thought he felt his wife breathing on his neck.

The vampire bat didn't move.

"Guess I was dreamin' 'bout her again," Sammy mumbled.

The bat waited until Sammy began snoring again. It stepped forward, placing its clawed foot on Sammy's chest. Inching forward, it eyed Sammy's neck.

The vampire bat leaned forward, sticking out its long tongue. Sammy giggled, brushing the bat away with his arm.

"What are you doing, girl?" he chuckled in his half-sleep state.

The sick bat turned its head, sniffed again at the sleeping man, then silently flew back up to the peak of the cave. It would eat later.

8

Silly, Stupid Pants

❖

Eulla Mae finally began the wedding march. Her husband, Maurice, still sat huddled in the corner, reading the new magazine he'd bought.

"Maurice, come over here," she whispered, while she played.

Maurice reluctantly closed the magazine, rolled it up, and stuck it into his back pocket. "Yes, sugar." *Wish she'd just leave me alone so's I could finish my story,* he thought. Mom had gone into the back bedroom to check her hair, and Hambone had disappeared out the back door.

"Will you quit readin' that magazine! We got to get this weddin' goin'," Eulla Mae said, grinding her teeth in frustration when she hit the broken key again.

"You keep hittin' that dud key," Maurice smiled, trying to annoy her.

"And all you're doin' is readin' and not helpin'," she huffed.

"I just want to finish this Dracula story," he said. "It's good . . . it's real good."

"You finish it later. Now go see if Hambone's ready."

Eulla Mae began the chorus again. Rev. Youngun gave her a wink and picked up his Bible.

He looked at his church rummage typewriter, secondhand books, and desk chair with the cracked rung. Though material things had never been a top priority for him, he said a quick prayer: *Dear Lord, I know I should accept whatever comes, but I could sure use five dollars to buy new shoes for the children . . . especially Sherry, who's only had secondhand shoes.*

He drifted away, deep in thought. *Sherry wants those red shoes. She's just like Norma was before I married her. She had a real zest for life ... which marryin' a poor preacher didn't help.*

"You ready, Rev. Youngun?" Maurice asked.

Startled, Rev. Youngun blinked his eyes. "Are the children downstairs yet?"

Maurice Springer shook his head. "I know that Terry's upstairs complainin' 'bout havin' to wear those satin pants and Sherry's pouting 'cause she wants some ice cream."

Rev. Youngun sighed. "Just tell Terry that if he doesn't want to be the ring bearer, and if Sherry doesn't want to be the flower girl, that they can forget ever getting an allowance again."

Maurice laughed. "They're just kids. They want to be playin' outside where kids belong, not in here doin' weddin's."

"But we need the money."

"You're thinkin' too much about the money you're gonna get from Mom. Love of money's the root of all evil," Maurice said.

Rev. Youngun nodded. "You're right, but we're always short at the end of the month."

"You need me to loan you some?" Maurice asked earnestly, reaching into his pocket.

Rev. Youngun shook his head. "No, we'll make it. But thanks anyway. Your offer means a lot to me." Then he laughed. "Love of money might be the root of all evil, but it's never in my hands long enough to put down roots."

"You ain't alone," Maurice said, patting him on the back.

Mom stood in the doorway. She straightened her dress and cleared her throat. "We're ready, Rev. Youngun. Hammy and I are ready to become husband and wife. Ain't that right, Hammy?"

Hambone looked at her and nodded. "I do."

"No, no," Mom said sternly, "you say that when I give you the signal."

Rev. Youngun looked up the stairway. "Terry, Sherry, come on."

"Wish we had indoor plumbin'," Terry said, feeling the urge to go, but too lazy to walk all the way back to the outhouse. He also knew that it was snake season and had never let on to anybody how frightened he was about the snakes that sometimes hid in the privy.

He shivered with the thought of a snake crawling into his pants. *Ain't nothin' you can do when you're froze stiff and your pants are down on your ankles . . . if we had indoor plumbin', wouldn't have to go risk bein' eaten by spiders and snakes.*

Terry glanced in the hall mirror, eyeing with disgust the light gray and blue satin suit with frills and lace that he had to wear as the official ring bearer. "I wish I were any place but here."

"Remember what the teacher said," Sherry warned. "Be careful what you wish for . . . you might get it."

"Yeah, well, I still wish I were any place but here." He pouted.

"Even sittin' in school?" she teased.

"I didn't say that," he glared. He heard the piano start again and looked at himself in the mirror. *I'd rather wear these silly, stupid pants than sit in school,* he thought.

Sherry giggled. "You *do* look stupid."

"You're the stupid one!" Terry snapped.

"Yeah, those pants look painted on," she jeered.

Terry frowned at the skintight pants. "Ma made these for Larry when he was five years old. I'm seven. How'm I supposed to fit in these ignorant-lookin' things?"

Sherry, who had decided that being a flower girl today was for the birds, agreed. "Weddin's are stupid. I'm not never gonna get married!" she declared, spinning around in her stiff white dress, trying to shake the ribbons from her shiny brown hair.

"You ain't got nothin' to worry 'bout," Terry smiled, "'cause there ain't nobody dumb enough to marry you."

Terry ducked his sister's punch. Their father's voice rang out again from the bottom of the stairs: "Sherry, Terry, it's time to come down. Now."

"I hate these silly, stupid pants." Terry groaned.

"Pa says you gotta wear 'em." Sherry giggled.

"Why don't you ask your angel, Horsefly Wings, to make me a pair that fits?" he said, with a mocking grin.

"Don't talk about her . . . and her name's Little Wings."

"That's what I said, Stink Bug Wings."

"Little Wings!" Sherry screamed. "Her name's Little Wings! And she's an angel!"

"And you're a nut," he said, pushing her away.

"I'm gonna go tell Pa on you," she cried, heading for the stairs.

"If you do, I'll drop your blankey down the outhouse hole," Terry threatened.

"Pa!" she screamed.

"Hey, Sherry, wait."

She cautiously turned around. "What?"

"I just wanted to tell you that . . . " he paused, then chanted:

"Horseflies and stink bugs,
All have wings.
Sherry's not only loco,
She's a ding-a-ling!"

Sherry took a swing at his stomach, then ran for the stairs. Terry raised his leg to trip her but stopped in midair. *Rip.* He held his leg perfectly still, then tried to slowly lower it. *Rip. Rip.*

Sherry snickered and taunted, "You ripped your pants!" She danced around the hall. "Terry ripped his pants! I can see your underpants!"

Terry fumed as she skipped around in circles. "Shush up," he snapped. He wanted to jump over and knock the living daylights out of her, but he couldn't. Each inch he raised his leg, the pants ripped more.

"Children, come down *now!*" their father called.

"Last one down is a rotten turtle egg!" Sherry laughed, racing down the stairs in a symphony of starch-cracking dress crinkles.

Terry turned his back to the mirror and lifted up his coattails. Sure enough, he had a three-inch rip in the seat of his pants. "Oh Lord, don't let it rip no more," he whispered.

"Are you coming, Terry?" his father called out.

"I'm comin', Pa," he answered, walking slowly toward the stairs. *I'll walk like that woman in China with bound feet that I saw in the nickel movie show.* He kept his knees and feet together, not moving them more than an inch off the ground.

Terry looked down the stairs, wondering if he'd be able to get to the bottom without the pants ripping more. *Everyone's gonna see my undies,* he worried, trying to cover his rear with his hands.

He thought about praying but wasn't sure how to approach the Lord about his underpants. *Pa says, from your lips to God's ear.*

Terry shook his head. *Lord's got 'nough to worry 'bout without me whisperin' in His ear 'bout my undies.*

From the bottom of the stairs came Beezer, the green Mexican parrot that Uncle Cletus, the merchant seaman, had left with them. The bird came flying up the stairs like a green bat from a nightmare.

"Silly Terry . . . silly Terry," Beezer squawked, trying to land on Terry's shoulder.

"Hush up, Beezer, before I cut your wings off," Terry said, ducking the parrot's attempts to land on his shoulder. But each duck only ripped his pants further, so he resigned himself to the parrot's landing.

"Just don't do nothin' on me," he scolded the bird. "These satin duds look stupid enough."

"Silly Terry," Beezer squawked, flapped his wings, then flew back downstairs.

When Terry reached the bottom step, Eulla Mae waved for him to come over. "Child, you better get that ring tray fast to your father." Terry shuffled over, barely moving his feet.

"What's wrong with you?" she asked.

"Split my pants," he whispered, turning to show her.

Eulla Mae nodded toward her purse. "Get my bag. There's a pin in the pocket."

Without missing a beat, she took the pin from Terry's hands and pinned up the seat of his pants. "Bring those to me tomorrow and I'll sew 'em up." Then she resumed the wedding march.

Terry nodded, then tapped on the piano keys, making it sound as if Eulla Mae was playing the wrong notes. "Stop that," she whispered sternly.

Terry picked up the silver ring tray and stood beside his father.

Maurice came around the corner with Sherry, who was carrying the kitchen flowers that they'd gotten from the farmer down the road. "Still don't know why we can't use fake flowers," she said.

Maurice smiled. "Girl, most women get married just once and want this to be a special day. So they don't want to be steppin' on paper flowers as they walk down the aisle."

"It'd save money," she protested.

"We get too soon old and too late smart," he mumbled to himself.

"What'd you say?" Sherry asked.

He smiled at the pretty little girl who was like a daughter to him and took her back into the hall. "You won't believe it, but one day you're gonna be a grown-up girl and look back on these days and laugh."

"I won't laugh 'bout wastin' money on flowers." She pouted.

"But that money you save won't buy the same memories." He smoothed her hair, then adjusted her ribbons. "Go on, you get ready to walk down the aisle, throwin' those flowers like your life depended on it."

"Only my allowance does." She grinned and skipped back into the room in her starched white dress.

Maurice walked over and whispered to Terry, "What's wrong, boy? Is that your lower lip, or are you drinkin' a plate of soup?"

"I split my pants," Terry whispered.

Maurice leaned down. "You what?"

"I split my pants," he answered, turning and showing the belt-to-zipper split with the pin holding it together.

"Well, just don't start coughin' and tyin' your shoes at the same time. Mom and Hambone don't want to be reachin' for the ring seein' nothin' but your droopy drawers starin' at 'em."

Terry made a mean face. "These pants make me so mad."

Maurice looked at the silly-looking outfit. "I'd be mad too if I had to wear them dancin' pants. But it don't matter much in the long run, 'cause you'll get glad in the same pants you got mad in."

"Ain't never gonna be glad wearin' these stupid, tight pants," Terry mumbled.

Maurice said with a straight face, "You know, there's some people out there who think they can tell the weather by how tight their shoes and pants feel."

"Then we've got breezy weather comin' up, 'cause there's a draft up my undies." He winked at Maurice, making him chuckle.

"You best be quiet, 'cause Mom will be walking toward you any second," Maurice laughed.

Dangit the dog nosed up against Terry, who pushed him away. "Don't be pullin' any tricks on me out there," Terry said to the family mutt who would pull on their trousers if they misused his name in anger.

Dangit whined for a moment, then crawled under the ragged sofa to watch the wedding and wait for someone to drop some food.

Terry looked down and saw a dead cockroach near his shoe. He picked it up and looked over at his sister.

Sherry stuck her tongue out at Terry, and he moved to hit her on the arm.

Rip. Sherry giggled. "I can see your underpants."

"You'll pay for that," Terry threatened, then said quickly:

"You might laugh now,
You stupid thing,
But in my hand,
Is Little Wings."

He held up the dead cockroach by its wings and stuck his tongue out.

"I don't like you," Sherry said.

"Pipe down, you two," Rev. Youngun admonished. "Enough is enough."

"Other kids are out playin'... where we should be." Terry pouted to his father.

"I don't care what the other kids are doin'... you're both preacher's kids... and this is part of your job."

When his father turned his back, Terry silently mimicked his father's expression, mouthing, "You're full of beans."

Sherry saw him and tattled, "Pa, Terry just said you're full of beans."

Terry held up his hands with an innocent expression. "I didn't say nothin'," he said. *Nothin' out loud, Lord,* he thought, wanting to keep things clear.

"Don't press your luck, young man. Guilt is written all over your face," Rev. Youngun said.

9

Newspaper Reports

Andrew Jackson Summers, editor of the *Mansfield Monitor,* looked at the telegraph message he had received.

"Did you see this?" he asked his new young reporter, Emily Grant.

"What is it?" she asked, walking over to his desk.

"Got this telegraph message in from Little Rock. Says there's an outbreak of rabies in a couple of places."

Emily shuddered. "I hope it doesn't hit around here," she said.

Summers shook his head. "If it's down in Arkansas, it'll most likely be coming up around here. Just read it and be thinking about a story to write."

Emily sat down, scanned the message, and envisioned her story to read:

RABIES EPIDEMIC SPREADING

The horrible killer disease is again stalking the land. Rabies is haunting three areas of the country, and one is right here in Arkansas.

Rabid skunks are reported in the Georgia-Florida area. Rabid foxes and squirrels in the Maryland-Virginia border area. And in the Arkansas-Missouri Ozark area, rabid raccoons have been reported to attack farmers, hunters, and fishermen.

According to doctors we spoke with, this represents the greatest threat to Americans in one hundred years.

This horrid disease attacks the nervous system and leads to an agonizing, painful death. A vaccine is available, but it must be injected soon after the victim is bitten.

Even a house dog who has rabies can spread the disease if it licks an open cut on a human.

Beware of strange-acting animals. If you see one, call your sheriff or dogcatcher. And if you're bitten, try to catch the animal, because the only way to know if it has rabies is to have a doctor examine it.

Emily turned to Summers with a worried look on her face. "Do you think it will get up around here?"

Summers shrugged. "Probably."

"What can we do about it?"

"Nothing. Just be on guard and warn the folks, I guess."

Emily thought of how her neighbors and friends liked to feed raccoons. Raccoons often carried the disease. "Isn't there something we could do to stop the spread of the disease among the animals?"

"Short of killing them all, I think nature's just got to run its course."

"That's not much of an answer," she said.

"Either that or pray and be careful, because what will be will be."

"I suppose so," Emily said, sitting down at her desk. She took out her notepad to begin an article about the outbreak of rabies.

10

Cain, Abel, and Mabel

❖

Where's Larry?" Rev. Youngun asked. Sarah Bentley stood in the back of the room, tapping her fingers on the wall.

"I think he's down in the basement, feedin' his animals," Maurice said, not lifting his eyes from the magazine, which he had opened again.

"He needs to get up here and throw the rice," Rev. Youngun said softly. "That's part of the wedding package."

Maurice rolled the magazine up and stuck it back into his pocket. "Why don't you let the boy be? I'll toss the rice."

"Can't. You're the witness." Rev. Youngun called down into the basement, "Larry, get on up here. The wedding's already started."

Larry pushed the blond hair from his eyes. "I'm comin', Pa."

"Don't make me come downstairs . . . I shouldn't have to ask you again," Rev. Youngun grumbled.

"You don't have to, Pa," Larry answered, closing up the cage on his white rats.

Larry had started with two rats, and now he had twenty-one, which had given him a fair inkling about the facts of life. But since his father still insisted that children were brought by the stork, Larry decided to keep his suspicions to himself.

On the walls hung the overflow from the bug collection that had outgrown his bedroom. Butterflies, beetles, and odd-looking spiders were mounted in pasteboard boxes of every color and size.

Larry dropped some food to his blacksnake, then looked over into the cage where he kept his three pet skunks. He opened the window above them and felt the warm spring air float in along with Eulla Mae's barely tuned piano notes from upstairs.

"Wish someone would tune that piano," he mumbled.

A big black crow landed on the windowsill. The bird cocked his head and called out, "Rise and shine . . . rise and shine," which was the only thing it ever said. No one knew who'd trained the bird to say it.

"Edgar Allan Crow, how are you today?" Larry asked with a smile.

"Rise and shine!" the bird screeched.

Living in the belfry of the church, the bird would dive down and pull at the ribbons on the girls' hair as they left church, which always made Larry laugh.

His father was not pleased, however, when the crow flew over funerals and landed on the coffins squawking, "Rise and shine." But for the Youngun kids, it was the only bright moment on many a dull and boring occasion.

"You heard the piano music, didn't you?" Larry asked the bird.

Edgar Allan Crow squawked, "Rise and shine," and then flew away.

Larry looked down at the skunks in the cage. "How are my little stinkers today?"

The three skunks were named Cain, Abel, and Mabel. Though Mabel was a boy skunk, Larry thought having a girl's name didn't make much difference to a skunk.

Picking up Mabel, he stroked the sleek, black coat. "You hungry, fella?"

He'd found the skunks four weeks ago beside the road, sitting by their dead mother. Larry had felt sorry for them so he brought them home.

His father was against keeping them, but Larry loved their beautiful, glossy coats and the different sized white stripe that each had running down its back. Larry and his father compromised on keeping them in the basement.

Larry wanted to be an expert on skunks, so he'd gone to the library and read everything he could find about skunks. Then he'd taken them in a basket to John Wolf's cabin, to ask him about skunks.

Most folks called him John the Trapper, and some called him John the Baptist because of the Bible quotes he liked to carve on the trees in the hills around town. John was a mountain man and looked as old as the hills, though he was only sixty-two.

A lot of folks had trouble talking face-to-face with John, not because he was so gaunt-faced and homely, but because the only thing that remained of his right ear was the lobe—how he'd lost the rest of it was a secret he kept to himself. Some thought it was shot off, and some thought it was bitten off in a fight.

But John wouldn't say. The only thing anyone knew for sure about him was that he was a very religious man and had moved to the Ozarks to be friends with animals.

He was friendly to everyone, but his best friend in the world was his dog, Cody. The big, friendly, yellow Labrador followed him everywhere.

John had looked at Larry's skunks in the basket, let Cody sniff them, then took Larry over to a big tree by his cabin. As was his habit, he'd reached up to scratch the ear that wasn't there, then feeling self-conscious, pulled on the lobe that stuck out from his head.

He pointed to what he'd carved in the white oak tree and smiled. "Son, two things you gotta remember in life," he said, patting Cody.

Larry nodded, not knowing what to say to the big, bearded man. He wanted to ask him about his ear but could not muster up the courage.

"This here says that the wages of sin is death," John said, tracing the carved words with his right index finger.

"Yes, sir," Larry whispered, looking around for wherever the wages of sin were hiding.

John looked at the young boy. "And the second thing you gotta remember is that if you scare a skunk, you'll stink to high heaven. Right, Cody?" John smiled, and the dog woofed his agreement.

John's laughter echoed through the ravines. "Boy, just remember that anyone who tells you that a skunk can only send a stream of stink juice ten feet is a liar . . . a *stinkin'* liar."

"You ever been skunked, Mr. John?" Larry asked.

"When I was a boy your age, out in Indian territory, I caught a skunk with my ten-foot horse rope and got sprayed good by the durn thing when he lifted his tail high."

"What'd you do?"

John shrugged. "What could I do? I went back to the wagon, and my ma said I stunk to high heaven. Made me bury my clothes, and she said she wished she could bury me for a few days 'cause I stunk so bad."

"Then what happened?" Larry asked, his eyes wide.

John chuckled. "Made me stand naked in front of the other kids, scrubbing away on me with lye soap, old tomatoes, and corn liquor. None of it did me no good, 'cept the corn liquor fumes, which set my head to spinnin'."

John the Trapper. Larry smiled, thinking about the man. *Sure wish I could live like him. Be a mountain man . . . live off the land.*

Larry scratched Mabel until the skunk arched his back with pleasure. *They've never been abused or scared, so they'll never let loose with their scent on me. Pa's got nothin' to worry about.*

His father had warned him that if it ever happened the skunks would have to go, but Larry assured him that he knew how to handle them, saying, "If I can put up with Terry and Sherry, a couple of more skunks should be no trouble at all."

But Maurice had told them that the idea was crazy. "Keepin' skunks is just askin' for trouble . . . and I hopes I'm not around when it happens."

Setting Mabel back down, Larry fed them the insects he'd caught before breakfast. They gobbled them down, then looked up for more.

Larry surveyed his private kingdom. The basement was his special place. Here was the bug catcher's domain, which was the nickname his mother had given him. A place his sister was scared of and his brother didn't have much interest in, except to find something to take to school to scare girls with. And now that school was out for the summer, Terry didn't come down at all.

"Larry!" his father shouted from the floor above.

"Comin', Pa."

"Right now, young man!"

Forgetting to close the cage, Larry turned toward the stairs. "Can't imagine why everyone don't like skunks," he said to the boxed butterflies on the wall.

Dangit didn't like skunks, so he had to be kept out of the basement. Larry knew what would happen if Dangit ever got near them. He smiled, thinking about the time Dangit had been juiced after cornering a skunk. Pa had made him sleep in the barn for a month.

Larry scrunched his nose at the thought of the rank, sulphurous musk smell that still lingered on Dangit every time he got wet.

"Hate that smell," Larry said, looking at his skunks. "So just keep it inside your bodies and you can live here forever."

"Larry, get up here!" his father called out.

"Comin' right now, Pa." Larry ran up the basement stairs.

What Larry didn't notice was Dangit's cold, wet nose poking out from under the stairs. The mutt leered at the skunks, who lifted their tails and moved to the back of the cage in fear.

11

The Cave on Devil's Ridge

❖

Sammy Lester woke up again in the dark cave up on Devil's Ridge, still wondering where he was. *What happened after I left Tippy's Saloon?* he wondered. *Bet the boss at the lumber mill's gonna fire me this time for sure.*

Sammy didn't like thinking about work. Putting in sixty-five hours a week was bad enough, but it was better than the seventy-five hours a week his pa used to put in on the farm.

Guess I'll have to start thinkin' 'bout findin' another job, he thought, rubbing his head.

"Hello," he called out in the dark. No one answered. There was only a strange rustling sound. It sounded like the wind.

"Anybody here?" Sammy asked apprehensively, feeling along the ground.

Feels like dirt . . . and rocks . . . oh, Lord, what did I go and do now? Where in heck have I ended up?

He moved his fingers up and down. He felt the cuts and scratches on his hands, wondering how he'd gotten them. *I can't remember anythin' after the first drink. I musta blacked out again.*

"Got to stop doin' this to myself," he groaned, feeling his temples. His stomach rumbled fiercely. It must have been a whole day since he had eaten.

For a moment he imagined the sounds of laughter, and in his mind he was back at a prairie church supper with his family. Women were setting out the big, heaping plates of food. Kids were pulling candy.

I can just taste those turnips and cellar apples. The frostline is on the windows. Hams are being sliced. Jars of Ma's sweet preserves sit next to the fresh rolls. Pa is readin' from the Good Book . . .

He heard the rustling sound again and stopped his memory. *What the heck is that?* He listened again.

He tried to adjust his eyes to the dark, thinking it was still night. *There's a light comin' from the end of . . . what in tarnation am I doin' in a cave?*

He sat up and bumped his head on an outcropping of rock. "Ouch!" Then he panicked. "Where the heck am I?" he cried out. "Somebody help me!"

Then he heard the rustling again and squinted his eyes in the dim light. "No . . . can't be," he moaned, rising to his knees.

Standing slowly, he looked around the cave. Thousands of bats were packed inside, hanging like sardines. Some had babies hanging from them, but they all slept, rustling their wings every time he moved.

Sammy's eyes adjusted to the dark, and he slowly looked around. He saw nothing but bats covering the walls.

From the mouth of the cave came a shout, "Hey, Lester, you in there?" It was his friend and sometime drinking buddy, Ned Hutson.

Sammy waved his hands up and down, trying to signal for silence. "Sssshh . . . quiet," he whispered.

But throughout the cave, bats had already begun to wake up. They opened their eyes and fluttered their wings. At the peak of the cave, Sammy saw a large, dark spot. He decided it was nothing.

But it *was* something. It was the huge, sick vampire bat who had been awakened by the voices. The bat looked down at Sammy, flicking its tongue in and out.

Sammy saw two bats take flight around the cave, then breathed a sigh as they landed and settled back down.

"Sammy Lester, are you in there?" Ned called again.

Sammy crawled to the mouth of the cave, where he saw Ned Hutson and Redbone, his Irish setter. The dog seemed nervous, pacing side to side, biting at the air every now and then.

Ned slapped his friend on the shoulder. "There you are! Come on, Sammy, we all thought you'd fallen in Willow Creek and drowned."

"Did you find my fish crank?" Sammy whispered.

"That's what you went lookin' for. Told all the boys down at the saloon that you were goin' night fishin' . . . fishin' for drink money!"

Redbone barked. Ned leaned over and slapped him. "Quit snappin' at the air. You're actin' like an old dog."

Wonder if I fell in the water? Sammy felt his clothes but they were dry. Then he felt something crusty. His pants and shirt were covered with bat droppings.

"Come on, Sammy, let's go on back to town."

"Ned . . . be quiet . . . this cave's full of . . . bats."

Ned looked around and heard the rustling wings. "Let's get out of here!" he said, backing off.

"Not so loud," Sammy cautioned.

"I hate bats," Ned mumbled. "Don't let 'em get tangled in your hair . . ."

Redbone began snapping at the air again. A bat flew by the aging Irish setter, and he went berserk. In a flash, the cave turned into a black, screeching, flapping mass of wings.

"Run for your life!" Ned screamed.

But Sammy froze in place, swatting at the flying creatures all around him. Two bats flew at him, and Sammy screamed, "Stay outta my hair!"

Dropping to the ground, he crawled forward. *If I get through this I'll stop drinkin' . . . I swear it . . . I'll never touch another drop,* he pledged.

Another bat landed on his head, and Sammy swatted him off. "Get off me, you devil!"

Then a bat got tangled in his hair and Sammy fainted from fright. He didn't even feel the vampire bat land on his chest . . . or the pinprick bite on his neck.

Sammy awoke to find his friend Ned dragging him out of the cave. "The bats . . . keep them off me," Sammy cried out, covering his face with his hands.

"Sammy boy, you're okay. Them bats are all back in the cave," Ned said, stopping at the crest of the ridge.

"Ned . . . Ned . . . did any of 'em bite me?" he asked, feeling his neck.

"Let's see," Ned said, looking Sammy's neck and face over. "No, your neck don't show no bite marks, 'cept for where you cut yourself shaving," he said.

He looked at Sammy's hands and fingers. "But your hands are all cut up. What happened?"

"Think I did that last night, stumbling around," Sammy groaned.

Redbone licked Sammy's face and hands. Ned laughed as Sammy tried to push the red-coated dog away. "Redbone must think you taste good."

"Get off me!" Sammy said, pushing at the dog's face.

Ned took the dog by the collar and pulled him away. Redbone squealed out in pain. "Easy, boy, easy."

"What's wrong with your dog?" Sammy asked, trying to wipe the dog's saliva off his face and hands.

"He had a tussle with a mangy-lookin' raccoon a few weeks back. Strangest thing I ever saw."

"What?"

"The 'coon. He came rushin' toward us, howlin' like a bear. Weren't scared of nothin'."

"What'd you do?" Sammy asked.

Ned patted the dog. "Redbone charged the 'coon to protect me. Got himself bit up 'round the neck 'fore he killed it." Ned gently patted the dog's head. "Didn't get hurt 'cept where the 'coon bit him."

"Never heard of no 'coon actin' like that," Sammy said, watching the nervous dog pace back and forth.

Sammy stepped back as the dog jumped into the air, biting at invisible objects. "What the heck's he doin'?"

Ned shook his head. "Don't know. Think he might be gettin' old," he said, watching the dog scratch its neck where the raccoon had bitten it. "Thought 'bout takin' him to see Granddoc the vet, see what she thinks."

"Why don't you?" Sammy asked, wearily watching the dog roll its eyes, then pace in circles.

Sammy rubbed his hands, then remembering how the dog had slobbered all over him, wiped his face and hands on his shirt. But Redbone's germs had already entered Sammy's body through the cuts on his hands.

"Maybe I will and maybe I won't," Ned shrugged.

"Somethin's wrong with that dog, if you ask me."

"I ain't askin'," Ned said defensively. "Guess I don't want to think 'bout Redbone gettin' old. Means I'm gettin' old too." Redbone jumped up and licked Sammy again, then went back to his pacing.

"Here's your coat," Ned said, dusting off what Sammy had obviously dropped the night before. He weighted it in his hand. "Still got a couple of pints in the pockets."

"Give it to me," Sammy said, grabbing the coat.

"You don't look so good," Ned said, looking at his friend.

"Don't feel good neither," Sammy groaned. "Think I need to ease up on my drinkin'." Suddenly he thought about Rev. Youngun's Easter speech on the evils of drink. *Think I'll go see him.*

Inside the cave, the bats settled back down. The vampire bat wrapped up its large, black wings and waited for darkness.

Sammy had only whetted its appetite.

Skunk Juice

Rev. Youngun stood in the front of the room, Bible in hand.
It's time to get this show on the road, he thought, exhaling
loudly.

"Everyone ready?" he joked.

"We're so ready we're 'bout overdone," Mom answered, trying hard
to stay in a good mood.

Eulla Mae again pounded out the wedding march on the old piano
while Maurice silently wished he was out fishing.

Sarah stood to one side, wishing she had not chosen today to come
complain to Rev. Youngun. But with Mom's being one of two places
to eat out in town, she didn't want to offend her by leaving.

Willy kept his eye on Terry. Terry just nodded, silently mouthing
over and over, "I'll get you . . . I'll get you."

Larry stood at the back of the room, ready to throw the rice. As Mom
and Hambone started forward, Sherry skipped in front of them, tossing
flowers all over the floor.

Beezer the parrot started to waddle into the room, but Larry shooed
him away. "Don't need you in here," he whispered.

"You're pathetic!" Beezer screeched and flew back toward the
kitchen.

Larry closed his eyes, hoping that his father hadn't heard. "Close
the door, son," his father said.

When Larry looked up, he saw that all the eyes in the room were
upon him. Only Terry was smiling.

Down in the basement, Dangit nosed against the skunk's cage. Cain, Abel, and Mabel raised their tails and made frightened sounds.

Dangit growled, then began barking. The little skunks, who had never been scared in their lives, cowered against the back of the cage.

Their only defense was to do what came naturally. They were ready.

Dangit charged forward, barking up a storm. The skunks hopped around. With twin nozzles at the base of each tail, each with its own stink juice scent gland, and each gland having enough fluid for five attacks, the three skunks let loose with all guns blazing.

Dangit was clearly outgunned, but only barked louder. So the skunks juiced him again right in the face. Temporarily blinded, Dangit howled in rage at the fire in his eyes.

Maurice looked at Larry who looked at his father. Rev. Youngun nodded with his head toward the basement, as if to say, "Get down there and shut that dog up!"

Maurice leaned over. "Your pa looks like he's at the end of his rope. Best you shut up Dangit quick."

Larry couldn't figure out what Dangit was barking at until he opened the basement door. He stepped back at the smell.

"Oh no, I'm in trouble," he moaned.

On the first step, the air was tainted. On the second step, it became rank. On the third step it was absolutely putrid. Each step down into the stinking darkness was worse than the step before.

The heavy, rancid air made him cough. Larry found the dog on the floor and patted him. "Dangit, you're history now! Pa's gonna bury you in the barn, the way you smell."

Then he saw the three skunks heading for the stairway. "Come back!" he shouted.

Upstairs, Mom tried to smile at Hambone, but finally stopped the service. "Somethin' stinks 'round here, Reverend," she said, scrunching her nose. Hambone nodded.

Sarah stood holding a perfumed handkerchief to her face. "There's a bad wind coming into the house."

"Willy did it!" Terry laughed.

Willy fumed. "I did not!"

"Maurice, would you close the windows please?" Rev. Youngun said. "Must be something outside."

Told that boy to get rid of them skunks, Maurice thought. *I knew this would happen one day.*

"Wonder what smells out there?" Rev. Youngun asked, clearly embarrassed by the turn of events.

Maurice mumbled, "Ain't outside. It's inside."

Eulla Mae held her nose and played the piano with one hand, thinking, *Smells like someone tipped the outhouse over.*

Rev. Youngun sniffed again. "Sherry, run and get some of your ma's old perfume and sprinkle it around the room. It will help make whatever is coming in from the outside smell better."

"Maybe I can find out what's the matter," Sarah said, slipping off into the hall.

The skunks danced their way up the stairs. Dangit scrambled to his feet and took off after them. "Come back!" Larry screamed, but couldn't catch him. The skunks disappeared into the house.

At the top of the stairs, Larry ran into Sarah Bentley who was in full retreat screaming, "Skunks . . . skunks!"

"I'm in trouble now," he said, shaking his head.

Sarah ran into the living room. "You've got skunks in the house!"

"Sit down, Mrs. Bentley," Rev. Youngun said, motioning her toward the sofa. "I think you must have just seen Ratz the cat."

"No, I saw skunks," she said, falling onto the old sofa.

The sofa creaked, cracked, and then collapsed, sending her sprawling onto the floor.

"I told you that sofa needed repairs." Rev. Youngun smiled, helping her up and into his reading chair. "Now what was that about skunks?"

The disheveled Sarah could barely talk. "I saw three skunks . . . and they were trying to attack me."

Larry came into the room. "Has anyone seen my skunks?"

Terry shook his head. "Only skunk in here is Willy."

"I smell your skunks. They're 'round here someplace," Maurice nodded.

"Smell 'em?" Larry said. "I can't smell anythin'." He didn't realize that his nose was already blocked by the smell. He also didn't know that he stunk to high heaven.

Sarah Bentley took one sniff of him and pushed him back. "You've been skunked."

"No, Dangit was. I just grabbed him."

"Grabbed his stink too," Eulla Mae said, taking him by the arm. "You come on outside and get them clothes off."

She turned to her husband, who was now holding his nose. "Maurice, get that dog and bring him along," she said, pointing to Dangit, who'd dashed into the room looking for the skunks.

Eulla Mae pulled Larry out of the room. Maurice followed behind, holding Dangit by the scruff of his neck.

Rev. Youngun gulped and turned white. Mom looked at him. "You sick or something?"

Rev. Youngun shook his head as the three skunks approached. Terry stood frozen by his side, watching the skunks prance toward them with their tails held high.

Sherry came back into the room with the perfume and walked between the skunks as if nothing in the world was wrong. "Hi, Cain. Hi, Abel and Mabel," she said.

"Sherry . . . the perfume," Rev. Youngun whispered.

"Here it is, Pa," she smiled. Taking her sweet time, Sherry took the bottle out and began skipping around the room, dripping perfume wherever she chose.

When she stopped at the skunks and dropped some on their tails, her father moaned. "Splash it around where it stinks," he whispered.

"I am, Pa. The stink started here," she said, pointing to the skunks' raised tails.

As the room filled up with the aromas of skunk stink from the basement and the lilies of the field perfume Sherry was pouring, Mom looked at Hambone. "Ready?" Hambone nodded. "Just finish the 'I do' part," Mom said to Rev. Youngun.

Rev. Youngun looked at Hambone. "Do you take Mom to be your lawful wedded wife?"

Hambone just mumbled.

"I can't understand what you said," Rev. Youngun said, keeping his eyes on the skunks.

"He said, 'I do,'" Mom said.

"Let me hear it," Rev. Youngun said, keeping his eyes on the skunks.

Hambone cleared his throat and coughed.

"Say it," Mom said, nudging him.

"Do you take Mom to be your lawful wedded wife?"

Hambone nodded. "Do I."

"Say 'I do,' or there'll be no more free meals for you," she demanded.

Hambone blushed. "I do."

"And do you, Mom, take Hambone to be your lawful wedded husband?"

"I do, I do!" Mom shouted, reaching for the silver tray. "Now, give me the ring so I can keep my best cook forever!"

The moment she took the ring, Dangit came barking back into the room. He had slipped out of Maurice's grasp. The skunks bounced around on their tiptoes, ready to spray him again.

Though there wasn't any rice thrown, the skunks tossed enough stink juice around the room to last a lifetime. "My dress!" Mom screamed, as the skunks soaked her down.

Terry dropped the ring tray and ran screaming from the room, stubbing his toe. "Dangit, that hurts!" he shouted.

"Don't use his name wrong," Sherry warned.

But it was too late. Dangit perked up his ears at his name being misused and raced after Terry, pulling at the seat of his pants.

"Get off me, Dangit!" Terry screamed, hopping around the room, trying to keep his britches on.

But Dangit wouldn't let up and with a sharp twist of his head, pulled Terry's underpants clean off! Terry ran from the house holding his backside.

Willy wanted to laugh, but the skunks were heading for him. He stood frozen against the wall. "No . . . don't juice me." Mabel sniffed his leg and gave him a shot of skunk juice that covered him from head to toe.

Mom couldn't believe what had happened on her big day. Hambone said, "We gotta go, Rev. Youngun. Thanks for marryin' us." He tried to hand Rev. Youngun a five-dollar bill, but Mom snatched it away.

"You should be payin' me," she glared, then she reached for Hambone. "Hambone, hold me. I feel faint."

He reached his arms out, then caught a whiff and backed away, letting her fall. "Don't get near me."

"But we're married . . . honey," she said, trying to hold back the tears as she got off the floor.

"Now I know what for better or worse means," Hambone moaned, holding his nose.

"But I'm your sweetie . . . ain't I?" she asked, reaching for him.

"You stink," Hambone mumbled.

Rev. Youngun backed slowly out of the room, fearful that Mom would want to cry on his shoulder. Then he thought of the money. *For five bucks, I might just let her do it.*

13

Skunked Out

Behind the barn, Eulla Mae stripped Larry down to his underwear and scrubbed him as fast as she could with a wet rag. Inside the barn, Crab Apple the mule, Lightnin' the horse, and T.R. the turkey, made a racket over the smell that was drifting their way from the house.

Little Bessie the pig squealed and hid under the hay in the back of the barn. Only Bashful the fainting goat was quiet; at the first whiff, the goat had fainted dead away. The smell in the air was so bad that Crab Apple the mule kicked his stall door open to get outside for some fresh air.

Sarah Bentley ran into the yard, dousing her face with perfume. "Where's William?" she cried. Larry hid behind Eulla Mae, holding her cleaning rag in front of him.

"Here I am," Willy cried out, running up and hugging her.

"William . . . you . . . you . . . " his mother stammered.

"You stink, boy." Maurice nodded, holding his nose.

"Just wait till the church board hears about this!" Sarah huffed, grabbing Willy's hand and storming off toward her car. She cranked the engine, put Willy in the back, and drove off at high speed.

"That woman's mad as a wet hornet," Maurice said, shaking his head.

Eulla Mae shook her head too. "Ain't no good will come from all this."

Maurice shrugged and put his hands over his ears to block out all the animal sounds and smiled. "Those animals don't like the stink either."

Eulla Mae took the rag from Larry's hand and kept scrubbing. "Maurice, go get me a big pail of warm water, a box of laundry soap, a bar of lye soap, and all the canned tomatoes you can find."

"What you gonna do with them tomatoes?" Maurice asked, holding his nose at Larry's smell.

"They'll help take the stink outta his hair . . . now get on goin'," she ordered.

Maurice ran off holding his nose, mumbling, "Shouldn't have got outta bed today. Should have just laid there and read my Dracula story. Knew this was goin' to be a bad one when we was outta coffee."

Terry ran out of the house, followed by Dangit. He'd held it as long as he could, and now he had to get to the outhouse. From inside, the whole world could hear Mom bellowing at the top of her lungs.

"What happened?" Larry asked his brother.

"Mom got skunked by all three of your skunks, and Hambone don't want to hold her," Terry replied quickly. He ran into the privy and slammed the door.

Sherry came running around the corner. She took one look at her blushing brother and covered her eyes.

"Get outta here!" Larry screamed.

"I saw your undies," Sherry laughed, skipping off.

Eulla Mae chuckled. "Ain't no use in bein' bashful, now that you done stunk up the place." She laughed. "I was raised with five brothers."

Maurice brought out the items his wife wanted and by the time Eulla Mae had finished, the lye soap and scrubbing had left Larry pink from head to toe. But he did smell better.

"Now you don't stink." Maurice grinned. "You just smell bad."

Larry gratefully took the old sheet that Eulla Mae handed him and wrapped himself up like a newborn. He turned to see his father standing at the side of the barn, with Sherry behind him.

"Sarah Bentley said there'd be no money to fix the roof until the skunks are gone and you kids are punished," he said slowly.

Sherry clung to her father's legs. Terry looked down, and Larry closed his eyes. "What you gonna do, Pa?" Larry asked quietly.

"The skunks must go," he said, "and you kids have to scrub the smell out of the house."

"Where are the skunks now, Pa?" Terry asked.

"They went back into the basement and got into their cage," Rev. Youngun said. "I closed it up."

"But it wasn't their fault, Pa," Larry pleaded.

"I told you what would happen if they ever scented up the house. Now they've ruined a wedding and delayed our roof being fixed. If we don't get rid of them, Mrs. Bentley might try to get the board to hold back my next check."

"She's a wart," Terry mumbled.

"But she donates the money that pays my check. So the skunks have to go."

"Rev. Youngun . . . I need help," came a voice from the front yard.

14

Bottle Brother

Sammy Lester stood shaking in the front yard when Rev. Youngun came around from the side of the barn. "What's wrong?" he asked, knowing from Sammy's appearance what the answer was.

Still shaken by the bats and feeling the craving for alcohol send shuddering jolts through his body, Sammy got down on his knees. "You gotta help me. Drinkin's gonna kill me."

Rev. Youngun nodded. "You're the one killing yourself."

Larry stood with Terry and Sherry. He whispered to them both, "It's another bottle brother comin' to see Pa."

Maurice and Eulla Mae came and stood with the children by the side of the barn. "He's just a stumble bum," Eulla Mae said. "Just one of them no-goods from the saloon."

"That man needs help," Maurice said.

"That man needs to help *himself*," Eulla Mae said, shaking her head.

Rev. Youngun looked at Sammy and wondered, *How many more good men are going to lose their families, their homes, their way in life by continuing to indulge in this terrible habit?*

Sammy shuddered as he said, "Rev. Youngun . . . I've seen bats . . . bats flyin' everywhere. Wish I were back with Pa and Ma on the prairie."

Thinking that the man was delirious from the effects of alcohol, Rev. Youngun patted his head. "Liquor makes you see things that don't exist." Rev. Youngun turned to Eulla Mae. "Would you start some black coffee while I talk to this brother?"

"And Maurice," he said, turning to his friend, "will you go see if I have any old clothes in the house? Sammy here needs to take off his dirty clothes and put on some clean ones." He put his arm around Sammy. "Come, brother, let's go talk about this."

Eulla Mae started toward the kitchen. "You kids get more rags and buckets. We gotta clean out your house." Walking along, she called out orders over her shoulder. "Maurice, you open all the windows. Sherry, you go get any cologne your daddy's got and spread it around. Terry, you scrub down the livin' room floor. And Larry, you carry them skunks in the cage out behind the barn."

Rev. Youngun sat with Sammy on the bench beneath the white oak tree in the yard. Sammy looked at the cherry and maple trees around the house. The setting sun tinged the underside of the leaves a soft gold. Sammy drifted back to a happy time in his mind.

Long used to the strange ways of alcoholics, Rev. Youngun just sat silently, wondering what was going on in Sammy's mind.

In his mind, Sammy was standing with his mother in the attic, checking on the hams, pumpkins, onions, squashes, and dried peppers they'd put up for the winter. "You're a good boy, Sammy," his mother was telling him. "One day you'll grow up to be a fine man who'll do some good in this world."

"That's what I want to do, Ma," Sammy answered aloud.

Ma? What's he talking about? Rev. Youngun wondered.

Sammy didn't notice the puzzled look on the minister's face. He was just so happy to see his mother again.

"You're like an angel from heaven for us," he heard her say. "You know the doctor said I'd never be able to have children. But here you are, Samuel Lester." She smiled and pinched his cheeks. "A livin', walkin' miracle."

"I'm your little angel," Sammy mumbled.

"Sammy, are you talking to me?" Rev. Youngun asked.

Sammy snapped back. "Sorry, Reverend. I was just thinkin' 'bout my ma." A wave of shuddering came over him. "You gotta help me. I heard your tent speech on the evils of drink and—"

Rev. Youngun took his hands. "And you can lick this craving that's got hold of you, but you must ask for help from Him," he said, looking toward heaven.

"I'll ask for help from anyone. I just want to stop drinkin' before I die," Sammy lamented. His bloodshot gaze dropped in shame.

Rev. Youngun nodded. "If that's what you want, then get down on your knees and pray as if your life depends on it . . . because it does."

"Will prayer make me stop drinkin'?"

Rev. Youngun shook his head. "Just as you walked through the saloon door, you can walk out. It takes strength . . . and that's where prayer can help you."

"Help me," Sammy blubbered. "I'm ashamed of what I am." *Momma, I'm sorry . . . so sorry,* he cried in his mind.

"God won't force Himself on your life. You have to ask Him in." Rev. Youngun put his hands firmly on Sammy's shoulders. "Ask . . . and I'm sure He'll be listening."

"I wish my pa were here; he'd know what to do."

"Your pa would say the same thing," Rev. Youngun replied quietly. "He'd tell you to ask your Maker for help."

Sammy got down on his knees. Rev. Youngun noticed the pint bottle of whiskey in his back pocket and pulled it out. Before Sammy could protest, Rev. Youngun touched him on the back. "And I know you want me to smash this bottle as a sign of your wanting to end your craving."

Sammy's eyes followed the bottle as Rev. Youngun turned toward the house. Sammy didn't look sure about anything.

"Terry," Rev. Youngun called out, "come take this and smash it."

"Yes, Pa," Terry answered, happy to be pulled away from his cleaning chores.

Eulla Mae brought out a steaming cup of black coffee. "This is what you need to drink now."

"And after that, we'll give you a bath, some clean clothes, and send you out on the path to salvation." He looked up at Eulla Mae. "Cleanliness is next to godliness, isn't that right?"

Eulla Mae shook her head, looking at Sammy's mud-stained clothes. "You're askin' a lot from God," she mumbled, walking away.

Terry skipped up the ridge with the bottle in hand. He liked smashing the bottles for his pa. Stopping halfway up the slope, he opened the bottle and sniffed the cork. "Smells like cleanin' soap," he said, spitting in disgust.

On the top of the ridge, Terry looked at the bottle-shaped rock. He opened the whiskey bottle and sniffed again. *Whiskey stinks like old burned wood,* he thought, closing the bottle back up. *Wonder what it tastes like?*

He opened the bottle again, started to stick his finger in, then stopped. *Pa said it only takes one drink.* He sniffed it again. *Why would anyone want to drink this terrible stuff?*

Raising his arm, he smashed the bottle into a thousand pieces, then held his nose as the wind blew the whiskey smell around him. *Vodka doesn't smell like anything and gin smells like old pine needles. Beer stinks like sour socks and wine like rotten grapes. Why can't they all eat candy and drink sodas?*

Across the ravine, Mr. Palugee the pack rat shivered, watching Terry from behind the rocks. *Why'd he break that good bottle? I could have used it for somethin'.* He squinted his eyes. *That's the Youngun boy who burned that bag on my steps. That's the boy William Bentley, Jr., warned me about.*

Picking up his burlap sack filled with things he'd found on his treasure search, Mr. Palugee continued on his mission, looking for discarded things. *I'll have to keep my eye out for him sneakin' 'round my house. He probably knows 'bout my string. That red hair won't be hard to spot. I'll call the sheriff if I see him sneakin' round again.*

Rev. Youngun got on his knees with Sammy to pray for help. Sammy put his hands together. "Lord, please help me when my spirits are all used up."

Rev. Youngun looked at Sammy, then patted his pockets. "Best get rid of it all," he said, pulling another pint bottle from Sammy's coat pocket.

"I forgot about that one." Sammy blushed.

Rev. Youngun eyed the whiskey bottle. "Larry, come here and take this bottle away."

"Yes, Pa," Larry said. He took the bottle around to the back of the house.

Maurice came out and stood under the tree. "Eulla Mae's got a hot tub of water out behind the barn."

"For what?" Sammy asked.

"For you, brother." Maurice laughed. "Said you were too dirty to bathe in the house so she turned the trough into a bathtub for you."

"I took a bath last week," Sammy protested.

"And you look like you combed your hair with a beer bottle this morning," Maurice said, shaking his head.

Eulla Mae came out frowning. "Shiny Wilson just called from the marriage license bureau and . . . " she hesitated.

"What'd he say?" asked Rev. Youngun, preparing himself for the bad news.

"Said that couple you was countin' on comin' tomorrow canceled. Somethin' about the bridegroom gettin' cold feet."

Rev. Youngun's mood sagged like a deflating balloon. It took him a moment to get back on track. "God works in mysterious ways," he managed to say.

"It'll all work out," Eulla Mae said, resting a soothing hand on his shoulder.

15

Redbone's Misery

Ned Hutson knelt by his faithful Irish setter, trying to calm him down. "Redbone, quit pacin' back and forth. You gotta sleep sometime."

The dog looked exhausted. His eyes were bloodshot. One side of his mouth drooped. His breathing was labored, but he kept pacing back and forth in the dog run next to the barn.

"You want to go walk in the woods? You want to hunt squirrels or somethin'?" Ned asked.

All dogs have a routine, and Redbone had kept one up for years. He was hungry at the same time every day, wanted to walk at the same time every day, and had a regular sleeping place he went to at the same time every day.

Now he did none of that. He didn't even wag his tail. He just kept pacing. Then he stopped.

"Lay down, rest, boy," Ned said, rubbing the dog's back.

Redbone cocked his head up, snapped at the air, then raised his ears.

"You hear somethin'?"

The dog's hair bristled. Ned couldn't hear anything unusual, but opened the cage to let the dog out. Then he heard it. A dog barking from across the ravine over in the next hollow.

Redbone took off barking, howling like he was going to fight the world one last time.

Ned chased behind. "Redbone, come back! Come back, boy!"

There had been strange dogs in and out of the county for the past several months, and Ned was worried that Redbone was going to get chewed up trying to fight the pack of them. Some were big, rough-coated hounds and others were mixed breeds beyond identification.

Them dogs will kill Redbone, Ned worried, his heart racing as he tried to catch up with his sick dog.

Up ahead it sounded like a dozen dogs were barking. "Redbone, come back, boy!" Ned shouted.

Redbone faced the pack of dogs, hair bristling, teeth exposed, daring them to come any farther. He was determined to protect his home territory. The pack of dogs barked and growled, darting back and forth at Redbone.

The biggest was a hound with a collar that read "Gordo." Snarling, Gordo challenged Redbone to come on.

While the two dogs snapped and growled, the other dogs circled behind Redbone like wolves getting ready for the kill. Redbone spun in a circle wanting to protect his territory, but his instincts were dulled by the sickness that had set in to his body.

Before he could react, six dogs were upon him. Gordo dug his teeth into Redbone's neck and then ripped off his ear.

Ned came over the rise and instinctively grabbed the first thick branch he found and charged into the howling pack. "Get off him!" he screamed out, whacking the dogs with the branch.

Gordo charged forward, but Ned kicked him away. The dog charged again and almost bit Ned's leg, but his vicious teeth only ripped Ned's pants.

Redbone fought his best, but his best wasn't good enough against the savage pack. Two big hounds had him down, worrying his flesh, tearing his long, red coat.

Ned swung the stick and knocked the dogs off Redbone. Two more dogs came at Ned from behind, but he managed to turn and knock them away.

Gordo jumped at Ned again. He dropped to the ground to avoid the dog's flying leap, then got to his knees and brought the branch down on the dog's head. But Gordo didn't even flinch.

As quickly as the fight started, the dog pack melted away into the forest. Ned held the branch in front of him, ready for anything. Gordo was the last to disappear, barking out a challenge—almost seeming to declare that he'd be back.

When Ned's heart had stopped pounding and his breathing slowed, he looked down at Redbone, who was lying in the dust. "You're quite a mess, boy," he whispered, kneeling down. Dark red blood matted and mixed with the setter's coat.

Redbone was streaked with dust and blood. He yelped in pain as he tried to stand, but his left front leg wouldn't support his weight. His ears and neck were wet with fresh blood, and there was a deep, dark gash along his shoulder.

"You took a heck of a beatin'," he said, examining his dog's wounds.

"Got to get you home and clean you up," Ned said softly, picking up his longtime faithful companion. He took off the chain and rope collar and walked in silence back to his house. Redbone left a trail of blood behind them.

16

Dracula?

The Younguns and the Springers gave Sammy Lester a bath, filled him with hot coffee, and sent him on his way in a clean shirt and pants. Then Eulla Mae fixed a simple supper for them all. After they ate, Rev. Youngun said good night to Maurice and Eulla Mae.

"Thanks for helping . . . though I've said it a hundred times, I can never repay you for all you've done." Sherry hung on his leg, clutching her blankey.

Maurice grinned. "No need. We're neighbors. That's all that matters." Then he shook his head. "Can't understand why you keep givin' all your clothes away to those bottle brothers. You ain't got but two pair of pants left."

"Can only wear one at a time." Rev. Youngun smiled.

"And they're both about wore out," Eulla Mae said. "You best bring 'em over to my house so I can sew up the seams that are comin' apart."

"I will."

She smiled and sighed. "Get these kids to sleep," she said as she hugged Sherry. "They've had too much excitement for one day."

"Good night, you two." Rev. Youngun struck a match to his boot and handed them a lantern. "Take this with you and walk carefully. There's night dew on the rocks."

"Let's get home 'fore the bats come out," Maurice said, looking around a little suspiciously. "I hate them things."

"Come on, scaredy cat," Eulla Mae laughed, taking his arm.

"You keep your windows closed," Maurice said in a serious tone to

Rev. Youngun. "I heard the boys down at the feed store talkin' 'bout someone seein' a big bat bitin' on a steer."

Rev. Youngun looked down at Sherry's wide eyes; she was hanging onto every word, along with her blankey. As soon as he looked back at Maurice, she stuck her thumb back into her mouth.

Maurice continued, "Fella claimed it had wings 'bout five feet across and only backed off when he tossed garlic at it." Maurice leaned forward and whispered, "Said it was a vampire bat."

"Maurice, you've been readin' that *Dracula* book again," Eulla Mae scolded.

"No, I haven't. Only read Bram Stoker's book once . . . not twice," he teased. He looked at Rev. Youngun. "I know this ain't Transylvania, but just keep your windows closed tonight . . . I don't think that big bat they seen is just talk."

Sherry whimpered, "Are monster bats gonna eat me, Pa?"

"No, Sherry," Rev. Youngun said, signaling with his eyes to Maurice to stop the monster talk. Eulla Mae elbowed her husband, and Maurice got the message.

"Ain't nothin' to worry 'bout," Maurice said, trying to reassure Sherry. "Ol' Maurice was just funnin'."

"You go on up to sleep," Rev. Youngun said, kissing Sherry's cheek. "I'll be right up to tuck you in."

She scampered up the stairs, sticking her thumb in her mouth the moment she was out of her father's sight.

Maurice said in a softer tone, "I'm tellin' you, keep your windows closed."

"We got screens on them all, so don't you worry," Rev. Youngun answered.

"Screens won't keep out a vampire bat . . . trust me on that one."

"Come on, Maurice, 'fore you scare yourself and make us fall on the way home," Eulla Mae said, taking his arm.

Rev. Youngun patted Maurice on the back, sending him on his way. "You want a couple of ash wood stakes to carry along with you in case you meet a vampire?"

"You read Stoker's book too?"

"Let's just say that even this Methodist preacher has read more than just the Bible."

"Read this," Maurice said, handing him the magazine he'd kept rolled up in his back pocket.

Rev. Youngun looked at the story that Maurice had it opened to: "Dracula of the Ozarks." "Is this what you've been reading all day?"

"It's the *Magazine of the Ozarks*. You read this story. I bet somethin' like this could happen 'round here," Maurice said, dead seriously.

"You've been reading too many wild stories." Rev. Youngun chuckled. "Good night, folks," he said and closed the screen door.

Rev. Youngun watched the Springers walk off to their farm next door. *Dracula, vampires, bats, and skunks . . . what else do I need?* He opened up the savings box and sighed. *What I do need is money. No money from Mom and Hambone, and the couple canceled their marriage tomorrow.*

He picked up the magazine that Maurice had left with him and opened it to the article he'd marked with the folded page. A lurid, blood-dripping, pen-and-ink drawing stared back at him. The Ozark Dracula was drinking the blood of another Missouri victim.

I can't imagine why he likes to read these things.

Though momentarily tempted, Rev. Youngun put the magazine down and closed it. *Shouldn't be reading this. I should be reading Scripture or working on my Sunday sermon.*

Not really believing what Maurice had told him, but wanting to be on the safe side, he went through the house, closing the windows. *Better safe than sorry,* he told himself, trying not to think about the Ozark Dracula story he'd almost read.

After checking all the windows, Rev. Youngun couldn't stop himself from looking in the money box again. *No food. Sherry needs shoes . . . I guess I should have become a businessman like Gramps wanted me to be.*

Sherry came and stood by his desk, rubbing her blankey between her thumb and forefinger. "Pa, when can I get a pair of store-bought shoes? I want the red ones down at Mr. Bedal's store."

Rev. Youngun closed the box and put Sherry on his knee. "Some things just take time."

"But I've waited all my life for new shoes," she said, rubbing her sleepy eyes.

"Trust in the Lord . . . it will all come to pass."

Sherry squeezed his hand. "I do . . . but I know that *you* buy everythin' for us."

He picked her up and carried her up the stairs to her room. He said softly, "I'll get you those red shoes one day. I promise you."

"When?" she whispered. "I been dreamin' about 'em. Those shiny red shoes with the silver buckles and red heart design on the toe."

"They're very pretty shoes," he said, laying her on the bed. He checked her window.

"I really want them. Please, will you get them for me?"

"Say your prayers, and I'll do the best I can. And don't open your window."

"You can't keep angels out, Pa."

"It's not angels I'm worried about getting in," he said, trying to get Maurice's talk about Dracula out of his mind.

Sherry clasped her hands together, looking up at her father. "Is it okay if I ask Little Wings to help me? Maybe she can get them for me."

I'll take any help I can get, her father thought.

Rev. Youngun blinked and looked down at his earnest little daughter. "Angels have the ear of God . . . and all prayers help. Good night, sweet kitten," he said, kissing her forehead.

Sherry asked softly, "Do *you* have a guardian angel, Pa?"

"We all have someone watching over us." He smiled, gently pulling the door shut behind him.

Downstairs, Rev. Youngun opened his Bible. Before him was Psalm 148:2: "Praise Him, all His angels; praise Him, all His hosts!"

Sarah Bentley would call this just a coincidence, he sighed, staring at the page.

Vampire Bat

From the mouth of the cave, a wave of thousands of bats poured forth into the darkness as one black mass. Then another wave. Then another. It was time to feed, and they were very, very hungry.

Eating mosquitoes and other night-flying insects as fast as they could, the bats spread out over the dark hills of the Ozarks.

After all the other bats, except for the nests of baby bats in pockets around the cave had left, the big vampire bat lumbered out. It slowly took flight, gliding out over the hills, stiffly flapping its wings.

It looked for cattle, pigs, dogs, anything. It just wanted blood.

Sherry closed her eyes, wanting to see Little Wings, but when she opened them, her angel was nowhere to be seen. She was very disappointed.

"Little Wings, please help Pa buy the shoes I want. Just the red shoes. Not a dress or a dolly. Just the red shoes. Store-bought shoes . . . like the other girls have."

Sherry heard the scraping of wings on her windowsill and sat up excitedly. "That must be you, Little Wings," she said, jumping out of bed to open the window.

But it wasn't Little Wings lurking in the dark. It was the sick vampire bat, ready to drink again.

"Where are you, Little Wings?" Sherry called out to the black night.

The bat turned its head, not understanding but not afraid.

"Please, Little Wings, come into the room."

The vampire bat fluttered its wings and flicked its tongue in and out.

It looked at Sherry's neck, at the top of her nightgown. Sherry's neck looked good.

Downstairs, Rev. Youngun checked his secret desk money drawer. *One dollar and two cents. That's the sum total of the money left to feed the kids for the next week.*

He thought about his grandfather lecturing him during his visits: "Watch the pennies, and the dollars will take care of themselves."

Rev. Youngun picked up the two pennies. *What would Gramps say now?* he wondered.

He closed his eyes and saw the bear of an old man, standing before him at the fireplace. *Young Thomas, it's not what you earn, but what you save that keeps you out of the poorhouse.*

His grandfather had been quick with advice. Rev. Youngun smiled. *I guess Gramps would say I've learned the lesson of easy come, easy go. But while I guess it's nice to be rich, I've always found that a dollar weighs heavy in my pocket when I see someone hungry.*

"Little Wings . . . I knew you'd come," Sherry whispered, lifting up the curtains. The bat clung to the top of the window, watching. Sherry heard the flutter of wings again. She looked out, seeing nothing.

"I know you're hiding out there." She giggled, throwing up the window. "Come out, come out wherever you are," she said, pushing harder against the screen. She gasped as the screen fell out, landing on the lawn below.

Pa's gonna be mad, she thought. Her heart pounded.

She heard the flap of wings and looked out the window. "Where are you, Little Wings?"

Not seeing anything, she went back to bed. She left the window open. The bat peeked its head into the dark room and watched her slip into the bed, clutching her blankey.

"I just wanted to ask you for those shoes I saw, but if you're just gonna play hide-'n-seek, then I won't," Sherry said grumpily from under the covers. She snuggled her head down into the pillow. "Gonna find me another guardian angel who doesn't play games," she said, sucking hard on her thumb.

Wiggling in anticipation, the bat edged around the top of the windowsill, holding onto the wooden frame with its claws. It moved slowly, looking around, eyeing warily the strange contents of the room.

Sherry heard a rustling of wings and kept her eyes closed. "I don't care if you're here. I don't want to see you anyway."

Then she felt the movement on the bed. It seemed like two little feet were walking toward her. *Maybe Little Wings wants to snuggle in bed with me.* She smiled at the thought, making a loud slurping sound on her thumb.

The bat stopped, turning its head to the noise.

When the feet moved up her chest, she giggled. "Go away, Little Wings. I'm mad at you."

The bat stopped and stared. Cocking its head, it sniffed the air. It needed to drink to cool itself down. It flipped its tongue out toward Sherry's neck.

Sherry felt the little feet move slowly up her stomach. "You can't make me look." Sherry smiled, thinking she was playing a game with her guardian angel.

The bat stopped, then inched forward. With tongue darting and eyes wide, the vampire bat stuck out its fangs and bent down to drink.

"Ouch!" Sherry cried out when she felt the quick pricks at her neck. She opened her eyes. Facing her was the scariest, ugliest thing she'd ever seen!

"Pa, help!" she screamed, trying to push the vampire bat away.

The bat spread its large, thin black wings and moved its claws up and down. Normally, it would have fled, but the rabies had altered its senses. It started back toward Sherry, but she kicked it away.

"Pa, help me, help me!" she screamed.

The bat ran up onto her chest again, but Sherry ducked under the covers. Frustrated and needing to eat, the bat flew out the open window, into the night.

"Sherry, Sherry, what's wrong?" Rev. Youngun shouted, bursting into the room. Behind him stood the two boys, rubbing the sleep from their eyes.

"Are you okay?" Larry asked.

Sherry peeked out from the covers, then began to cry. "Pa, Pa," she blubbered, "a monster tried to kill me."

"Oh, jeesh," groaned Terry. "First it was angels, now it's monsters."

"She had a nightmare," Larry said in her defense.

"Quiet, you two!" Rev. Youngun said. "Go back to your room."

"It *was* a monster!" Sherry whimpered.

Rev. Youngun smoothed her hair. "Sherry, you just had a bad dream . . . that's all." He cuddled her in his arms, ignoring the thumb in her mouth.

"No, Pa. I thought I heard Little Wings comin', but instead it was a monster," Sherry said. She looked up at her father with pleading, frightened eyes.

Rev. Youngun looked at the open window. "I told you not to open the window, didn't I?"

"But I heard Little Wings wantin' to come in and . . . "

Rev. Youngun walked over and looked out. He saw the screen on the lawn below. Closing the window in disgust, he came back to the bed. "Young lady, I told you not to open the window and you disobeyed me."

"But Pa . . . I saw a monster . . . I did."

"What did it look like?" he asked.

"It had claws and long teeth and arms and black wings at least five feet long."

Terry stuck his head around the doorway and snickered. "And he probably had a cape and calls himself Count Dracula. Don't need no cuckoo clock with you around here."

His father shot him a piercing glare. "Get back to your room!" He turned to Sherry. "I'm sure you think you saw that. But you were dreaming. That's all."

"But Pa . . . I saw it . . . for real . . . I did."

Rev. Youngun sighed and stood up. "Go back to sleep, kitten. And even if your angel comes to the window with a brass band, don't open it . . . you understand?"

"Yes, Pa," she said sheepishly, wishing that someone would believe her.

"Good night, sweetheart." Rev. Youngun tiptoed out of the room and shut the door behind him.

As she drifted off to sleep, Sherry felt the spot on her neck where the bat had bitten her. "No one believes me . . . no one," she whimpered.

18

Night Moves

❖

Maurice sat on his front porch. He wanted to read "Dracula of the Ozarks" again, but he'd given the story to Rev. Youngun. He knew vampires weren't real, but he enjoyed the goose pimples he got when he read the stories at night.

Suddenly, Maurice heard a swooping sound and looked up. The biggest bat he'd ever seen in his life dove down through the air, then circled around.

Picking up a broom, Maurice stood at the steps, prepared to swat the bat if it came close. "Don't come near me," he yelled.

Eulla Mae called out from the bedroom. "Who you talkin' to, Maurice?"

"It's a big ol' bat!" he shouted swinging at the bat.

"If I didn't know no better, I'd swear you'd been drinkin'." She trudged toward the front door, wondering what was going on.

The bat swooped down at Maurice again, but dodged the swing of the broom. It circled around over the porch, then flew away as quickly as it had come.

Eulla Mae opened the front door. "Who in the world are you talkin' to?"

"A huge bat," he said, putting the broom down.

"I think you ought to quit readin' those articles. You're scarin' yourself half to death."

"It was a big bat, that's all."

"Neighbors hear you and they'll think *you're* batty."

"You should have seen it," Maurice said.

Eulla Mae shook her head. "You come on up to bed. You look tired."
"I'll be up in a minute," he said, kissing her cheek.

When she had gone back upstairs, Maurice looked out over the dark hills. "Guess I should just close the windows. Might get cold," he said, thinking only about the bat.

Back in Mansfield, in the dingy room he rented atop the barn of the boarding house, Sammy Lester kicked at the booze bottles in the room. His head burned and his body ached as if he had the flu.

He looked at the mess around him and closed his eyes. A bit of drool rolled down his chin. He was thirsty, but the thought of drinking anything, even water, made him gag.

"Pa . . . is that you, Pa?" he called out. But only the silent dust answered him.

Got to get control of myself. Got to quit hearin' and seein' things.

But before he could stop himself, he was back again. Back as a little boy on the prairie, when life was simpler. When his life was better.

"Sammy, you just sit there and watch the bake-oven. Tell me when the cornmeal cakes start steamin'," his mother called out.

Little Sammy watched the iron bake-oven sit on the coals. His mother stood at the table, mixing more cornmeal and salt with water, gently patting it into little cakes.

She greased the bake-oven with porkrind. His father took the iron bar and stirred the coals, careful not to get ashes into the dripping pan on the side.

I used to love to sneak bread crusts and dip them into the dippin' pan. Sammy smiled. *And I loved to help pour the milk from Betty the cow into the pans and watch it settle. And when that cream would rise to the top, Ma would let me spoon off some onto my cornmeal cakes and . . .*

"I ain't gonna think 'bout that no more," Sammy said to no one in particular as he slapped his hand on the table. But he recoiled at the pain, looking at the cuts and scrapes on his palms. *That darn Redbone shouldn'ta licked me . . . he was probably sick or somethin'.*

He felt his neck. *Musta gotten bitten by a skeeter. Gotta take care of myself.*

He felt a rush of fever. *Where's my fish shocker?* he wondered. He didn't see it anywhere in his room.

Then he remembered he'd left it down under the Willow Creek Bridge. The bridge meant water . . . which Sammy didn't want to think about.

He licked his lips wishing that the sick feeling would all go away. *It's harder to quit drinkin' than I ever realized.*

Inside his body, the rabies virus attacked his nerve cells and affected his brain. His body, weakened by years of alcohol abuse, was not able to fight back.

For a moment he couldn't remember his own name. *What'd Pa call me?* He tried to think, but the fever was too much. His back hurt. And so did his throat.

Maybe I've got the flu . . . yes, that's it . . . I've got the flu.

More drool came out of his mouth. He brought a cup of water to his lips, but smashed it against the wall, gagging at the thought.

Wish I had some ginger water . . . that's what Pa gave me when I was sick. Ma made up a batch of ginger water and sweetened it with sugar.

Like all children of the prairie, Sammy could remember the sweet-bitter taste of ginger water, which was a treat that made ordinary days into special days. But it was also the tonic his mother used whenever he was sick.

Sammy closed his eyes and suddenly he was back at Plum Creek. His father was holding him, trying to get him to drink. "You've got the flu, Sammy, but don't drink too much."

Sammy floated above his memory, watching the little boy he once was drink from the cup his father was holding. *I remember the cool wetness going down my throat. Ma told me that cold, plain well water would make me sick. That I needed ginger water, the special way she made it with sugar, vinegar, and ginger, warmed over the stove and drunk slowly. Said it would help cure the flu.*

He remembered the men behind the haying barn, getting him to drink ginger beer. Bodie, the big one with the drinker's face, kept urging him to drink the strong brew. "It's just like ginger water, 'cept it's got a kick," the old farmhand had told him.

Sammy saw himself trying the alcoholic beverage. He tried to scream, "Don't drink it! Don't start it!" But no words came from his mouth. All he could do was watch the fermented, bubbly drink go down the throat of the young boy he once was.

The memory vanished, and Sammy was left burning hot, wanting to drink but not wanting a drink. His throat muscles contracted, and his body seemed to bake him alive. He ran to the window and threw it open, praying that the cool night air would relieve him.

"What's wrong with me?" he bellowed. But the only answer was his own echo.

19

Cornbread and Honey

Rise and shine," Edgar Allan Crow called out, landing on the roof overhang outside Larry and Terry's bedroom.

"We're already up." Larry laughed. "You're too late."

"That crow's gonna get himself shot one of these days," Terry grumbled.

Larry inspected his rock collection on the wall shelves his father had put up. Larry liked to collect "things," but Terry liked to collect "treasures."

The items on Larry's shelves seemed to have purpose and were organized by groups. But Terry's shelves were a mess: a broken watch, three cow bones he claimed were from dinosaurs, and some "magic" sticks and lucky stones to use as the mood struck him.

From downstairs, Rev. Youngun's voice rang out: "Children. Breakfast. Eulla Mae brought over some cornbread and honey."

Larry hurried to slip into his pants. "Cornbread and honey." He smiled, rubbing his tummy. "I was worried we were gonna have to eat some of Pa's rubbery biscuits again."

"I'd starve 'fore I ate another one of those," Terry grumbled, messing around with his knickknacks.

"Come on, Terry. Pa's gonna be upset if you don't come down."

"He's already upset on account of that wart fibbin' on me 'bout the burnin' bag at Mr. Palugee's. Boy, I'd like to get even."

"Shouldn't talk 'bout gettin' even. That ain't the Methodist way," Larry cautioned.

"Might not be the Methodist way." Terry shrugged. "But it's the

Bible way. I heard Pa sermonize 'bout eye for an eye. I know what he was talkin' 'bout." He looked up at his brother, "Heck, I ain't even talkin' 'bout takin' Willy's eye. I just want to learn him a lesson."

"Children, come to breakfast," Rev. Youngun called from the kitchen again.

"You better hurry," Larry said.

"*You* hurry. I'll be down when I feel like it."

"Terry, come down right this instant!" Rev. Youngun shouted.

"Comin', Pa."

Rev. Youngun sniffed the cornbread cakes that were flavored with bacon fat. With the pantry empty and no money coming in, he had accepted Eulla Mae's neighborly gesture gratefully.

Larry sat down at the table and looked at the steaming, golden triangles of cornbread. Sherry sat across from him, rubbing her neck. "Wish this was cracklin' cornbread," Sherry grumbled. She hadn't slept well.

"Beggars can't be choosers," Terry said, skipping into the kitchen.

"We're not beggars, are we, Pa?" Sherry exclaimed.

Rev. Youngun shook his head. "No, we're not. Sherry, say the morning prayer."

"Make it short," Terry whispered.

She stuck out her tongue and began. They all closed their eyes. "Come, Lord, be our guest," she said.

Terry, opened one eye, saw that his father's were closed, and reached out for a nibble.

Sherry continued, "Bless this food that Terry is grabbin'."

Rev. Youngun opened his eyes. "Terry, put that down!"

Terry dropped the wedge of cornbread and bowed his head. Sherry smiled, then continued, "And thank You for the food, blessed by Thee."

Terry interrupted because he couldn't wait any longer, "And Lord, please pass the honey!" he chimed, reaching for the biggest piece.

Sherry sat quietly and waited her turn while everyone else dug in. "Sherry," her father asked, "are you feeling all right?"

Sherry's lower lip curled. "You don't believe me 'bout the monster bitin' me. But it's true. I swear."

"Don't swear," he said gently, passing her the plate of cornbread.

"But it was real."

"Maybe it was, Pa," Larry said, sticking up for his sister.

Terry's mouth was filled with cornbread, but he couldn't wait to get in his two cents worth. "Andmaybeshe'scrazy," he mumbled, dropping bits of soggy cornbread on his lap.

"Don't talk with your mouth full," his father admonished. "Swallow first, then tell me what you said."

Terry gulped, then smiled. "I said, 'And maybe she's crazy.'"

"I'm not crazy!" Sherry screamed.

"That's enough," Rev. Youngun said. He looked at his oldest son. "Larry, after breakfast I want you to take those skunks and let them go."

"But, Pa—"

"No buts about it. Those skunks are wild animals and shouldn't be kept in the house."

"They're livin' stink bombs." Terry snickered.

Rev. Youngun looked at Sherry, wondering what was wrong. She was too still. "Are you all right?"

"Just don't feel good. The monster hurt me."

"What'd it look like?" Larry asked.

"Like a monster . . . like a monster bat," she exclaimed.

"Bat, shmat," Terry mimicked. "The only bats 'round here are in your head."

Before Rev. Youngun could stop him, Terry jumped up and dashed around the table, flapping his arms. "Watch out for the bat . . . watch out for the bat!"

Rev. Youngun exclaimed, "You upset me to where I can't see straight!" He grabbed Terry by the belt. "Enough is enough!"

"Sorry, Pa," Terry whispered.

Larry tried to suppress a grin. Rev. Youngun looked at him. "I'm at the end of my rope with you children!"

"I didn't do nothin', Pa," Larry said, sticking up for himself.

"Don't use that tone of voice with me," Rev. Youngun said, then closed his eyes. *Calm down. Get a hold of yourself.*

He opened his eyes and looked at Terry. "Young man, maybe Mrs. Bentley's right. I've let you get away with murder."

"Didn't kill nobody, Pa," Terry said quietly.

"I was using a figure of speech. Now, you've made your bed, so you have to lie in it."

"He didn't make his bed, Pa," Sherry interrupted.

"It's just an expression," Rev. Youngun said, slapping his hand on his forehead.

"Could you speak American?" Sherry said.

Now I know why children should be seen and not heard, Rev. Youngun thought, looking at his three children. He looked at Terry, who made a face at Sherry.

"Wipe that silly grin off your face and go to your room, Terry." He turned to Larry. "And you, you go take those skunks into the woods and let them go."

"Can I go with him, Pa?" Terry asked.

"Please, Pa," Larry said. "I can't carry all three by myself."

"He *needs* my help," Terry added.

"The less you say, the better off you'll be," Rev. Youngun said, remembering something his father used to say to his brother and him: "Children should be locked in a closet until they're old enough to read Greek."

"Can I go, Pa?"

"Don't let him," Sherry said. "Until he says he's sorry for teasin' me."

"Sorry," Terry said.

Rev. Youngun shook his head. "Okay. You boys first go feed the barn animals, then get rid of the skunks. Sherry will help me with the dishes." Terry and Larry took off.

"Why am *I* bein' punished?" Sherry said, her eyes welling up.

"You're not being punished. I need help with the dishes." Rev. Youngun picked her up and hugged her. "And you're elected."

Sherry looked into his eyes. "I wasn't fibbin' about the monster bat comin' into my room."

"I'm sure you thought you saw it."

"It scared me . . . it did, Pa."

Rev. Youngun picked her up. "I'm here to protect you. You've got nothing to worry about."

As she snuggled against him, Rev. Youngun didn't notice the thumb in her mouth . . . or the two small red marks on her neck.

Cody

John Wolf enjoyed feeding time each morning. His animals, who gave him so much affection, seemed to live for that hour after dawn.

First, for his own breakfast, John munched on some leftover pork cracklings, licking his fingers as he pulled off the pieces that were still left on the cheesecloth trap. After two cups of black coffee, John was ready to begin the day.

He stood looking into the cooking fire, pushing his thinning hair off his forehead. Waves of heat changed the look of things on the other side of the fire. In profile, his face was ageless. The lines seemed to lead and mislead when people tried to guess his age.

But it was in the eyes. If you looked into his deep blue-green eyes long enough, they seemed to draw you in. Old eyes. John Wolf's eyes seemed very old indeed, with lines that seemed to hook together the deep pains he kept hidden.

Life was not easy for this man, but he made the best of it. He didn't use his last name and felt that calling himself John the Trapper said it all. It was all he said people needed to know about him.

John lived the pioneer life, dressing and cooking his own game, plucking the chickens, and preparing his own meals. Every day he carried water from the well to wash his dishes. The cooking pots had to be scoured with sand. It would have been easier if he'd had a wife, but not that much easier.

A robin landed on the windowsill, jealous of his own reflection in the glass. His angry beak-tapping seemed a message to John, as if calling him back from the terrible memories that haunted him. He laughed and tapped on the glass at the bird, wondering how in the world people could keep birds caged in their homes.

Wild birds are God's messengers, he thought, looking out toward his animal friends waiting to be fed. *Folks would think I'm crazy if they knew I talked to birds.* He smiled.

But that was what the carvings in the trees were all about. John would get a feeling, as if words were being carved into his brain. So he answered back through the trees, leaving carved messages for others to follow.

John stepped outside, breathing deeply the clean, invigorating brisk morning air. He loved the hills. *It's the hills that gave me life back again.*

He drank in the vista that greeted him every morning. Amidst the misty hills and wind flying through the trees, John saw the ever-changing artwork of the God he believed reigned supreme.

This ol' earth is like a ball of clay on a potter's wheel. Slowly movin'. Always changin'. What took millions of years to come to be can be dashed to pieces with the stroke of one of His ragin' storms.

With a feeling of awe, John nodded in appreciation to all that lay before him.

What had originally attracted him to Mansfield was that it was far enough south to have mild winters, high enough in the hills to have a constant breeze, and though encased by forest filled with game, there was plenty of good lowland for crops and grazing.

Game in the woods, fish in the rivers, birds in the air, and good springwater wherever you dig. Can't think of a better place to live.

John patted his faithful dog, Cody, on the head. "Well, boy, since you're from the Show-Me State, you show me which one to feed first."

The big Labrador raced ahead barking. John watched the dog jump and prance with the joy of being alive. *Treat animals right and they'll treat you right,* he mused.

Cody was the kind of dog who would do tricks only for John, shaking hands when no one else was looking. He had the run of the hills and loved his owner.

"Good morning, Sam," John said to the wet-nosed deer waiting to be fed. "How'd you sleep?" he asked, pulling on his earless lobe.

The deer nuzzled against his side, then pulled a piece of paper from

John's pocket and tried to eat it. "Hold on there! That's my carving for the day."

John, who faithfully read the Bible at dawn each morning, had found the passage he wanted to carve that day. He had learned to read at his mother's knee from the family Bible in the Kansas Territory. Now nearly every tree surrounding his homestead had a verse carved into it. He grabbed the piece of paper and put it back in his pocket.

He fed his pesky raccoon, Snowball. "Here you go, you little bandit," he said to his masked friend. Snowball took the food to the horse trough and washed it. John loved the smart, comical-looking creature and the way he used his hands like a human.

Cody barked, pointing to Ben the mule. "Hold on, you'll get yours," he said, taking a bucket of feed to the grateful mule.

John wiped his brow, admiring his handiwork on the black oak, maple, cherry, ash, elm, and sycamore trees around his cabin. "If you animals could only read," he said, shaking his head. "Why, I bet I've darn near carved half the Bible into the trees 'round here."

A friendly growl came from behind him. John turned to see Beulah the bear. Cody barked a welcome. "Thought you'd gone down the road to town for a sit-down breakfast." John laughed.

Beulah growled again and swiped in the air with her paw.

"I'm comin', I'm comin'," he said, taking over the two fish he'd caught in the creek trap. He watched the bear pull out the fish and devour them.

"Guess I'm spoilin' you." Beulah burped and shook her head, trying to wrestle the head off the fish. "Yes, I am. Why, I bet you've become too prissy to even go fish for yourself."

Shaking his head, John wiped his hands on his patched pants, tucked his wool shirt in, and adjusted his suspenders. "Don't know why I've been chosen to feed all you animals. Came up here to live by myself, but can't never seem to be left alone with all you critters comin' 'round."

Cody started to growl and was answered back by a growl. "What's wrong, boy?" John asked, looking around.

Then he saw it. A mangy raccoon was growling like a bear.

"Oh no," he whispered. Cody started forward, but John pulled him back by his tail. "Stay back, boy. Somethin's wrong with that thing."

Snowball crept forward, looked at the sick raccoon, and scampered back under the porch. John picked up his pitchfork and poked it toward the growling creature.

"Get on outta here!" he said loudly, trying to scare it away.

The diseased raccoon charged, but Cody sprang in front of John to protect him. "No, Cody, no!" John shouted, trying to kick the raccoon off his dog's back. But the animal growled louder than the dog, ripping at Cody's ears.

Unable to use the pitchfork, John took a pole and swatted at the raccoon. "Cody . . . get away . . . Cody . . . oh, Lord," he moaned, as the creature ripped off half the Lab's right ear.

Cody bellowed in pain and shook the creature off his back. The raccoon rolled on the ground, then charged toward John, but Cody jumped between them. Again the raccoon attacked him.

John knocked the raccoon off the Lab's back and took up the pitchfork to ward off the raccoon's next charge. But the raccoon appeared to back off.

He turned to look at Cody, who stood by his side, prepared to ward off another attack. "You saved me, boy," John said, reaching down to pat the dog's head. But the dog cried out in pain. "Sorry, Cody," John said, wincing at the sight of the dog's torn ear.

Then he heard the raccoon growl again. "What in the—" was all he could get out. Cody caught the raccoon by the hind leg, but the mangy creature clawed loose and came at John.

With a quick swipe of the pitchfork, John caught the raccoon and killed him quickly, putting it out of its misery. Cody jumped up, wanting to bite the raccoon again.

"Down, boy . . . he's dead."

John waited before he set the pitchfork down. He looked at the creature, scrunched his nose at the mange and smell, and examined the raccoon's face without touching it.

John recognized what was wrong immediately. He'd seen it before. He turned to Cody with a sinking feeling in his stomach. "This animal has rabies. I'll bet my life on it."

He put the raccoon into a burlap bag still without touching it, then scrubbed his face, hands, and arms with stinging lye soap. Even though the raccoon hadn't bitten him, he was worried that some of the spit had gotten on him in the fight. He even changed his clothes.

"Darn skunk winter," he said to himself. The winter temperatures had been so mild in the Ozarks that nature wasn't able to work its course. The freezing cold that usually killed off the sick animals hadn't come this year.

John looked at the burlap bag and then toward the porch under which Snowball was hiding. "If there's one sick raccoon, there's probably a bunch of 'em out there."

Though he lacked a formal education, John knew the ways of nature. And he knew that rabies was one of mankind's oldest and most-feared plagues.

He got his gloves from the woodshed and carefully examined Cody's cuts.

"You saved my life, boy," he said, as he washed the Labrador's ear and poured Dr. Flint's Bitters on it until the dog yelped in pain. Then he took one of the stove irons from the cooking fire. He held the dog down and cauterized the wound, hoping to burn out the poison.

"It's for your own good," John said, holding the dog tightly while the hot iron seared his flesh.

He knew that what he was trying was a last-ditch effort, but it had saved his life back in Kansas during the winter of 1888, so he knew it was worth a try. He blotted out the memory of what had happened to his family that fateful winter and concentrated on Cody.

John loved the dog and didn't want to shoot it, but any animal that got the disease had to be shot. *Please, God, let this burn out the sickness.*

Cody didn't understand why his master was hurting him. After several moments of sharp yelping, he went limp with pain and didn't protest when John locked him in the birch trapping cage. He crawled into the corner and moaned.

"Hate to do it, boy, but you got to stay in there till I get back. I'm goin' to go see Granddoc. Gotta find out if this 'coon's got the sickness."

With the mangy raccoon in the burlap bag over his shoulder, John picked up his rifle and headed to town. He had to confirm what he already knew.

Along the way he thought about the terrible Kansas winter with the crazy wolves coming at him. He tugged on his earlobe as he walked along, trying to forget the fear of dying and the smell of the hot iron burning his own flesh.

He looked at the Ozark skyscape, which was as changeable as the weather. He sniffed rain in the air, breathed in the cool winds, and sought calm. It was all he could do to keep the memories of his lost family from overpowering him.

Down by the creek, a seven-inch bullfrog let out a thundering croak. It seemed to remind John of the balance of life . . . that life goes on and is for the living.

21

In Sarah's Kitchen

Sarah Bentley admired herself in the hall mirror. Then she sat down primly on a parlor chair to enjoy the stack of magazines that lay on the table beside her.

Her husband, William Bentley, came down the stairs.

"Sarah, you're using an awful lot of perfume, aren't you?" he asked, picking up a copy of *Harper's Bazaar* to fan himself.

Sarah had worried that some of the skunk smell still clung to her, so she'd heavily doused herself with several different perfumes. "Just want to smell like spring flowers," she said, taking the magazine from his hand and laying it on top of the latest copy of the *Ladies' Home Journal.*

Bentley wiggled his nose and picked up the magazine to fan himself again. "Put on any more and I won't be able to breathe." He handed her the magazine and kissed her. "Got to go to town. See you around dinnertime."

William, Jr., followed close behind. "'Bye, Mother. I'm goin' to the store."

"Did Martha bury your clothes?"

"I think she burned 'em . . . and my bedclothes too," he said.

"Good," she said, taking a small bottle of perfume from her pocket and sniffing it. Willy slammed the door shut.

A few minutes later, Sarah's Siamese cat came dashing into the parlor. "Cuddles . . . what's wrong?" She heard a growl from the kitchen. "What in heaven's name is going on?" she said, cautiously walking down the hall.

Slowly turning the knob, Sarah peered around the kitchen door. On the counter were the imported luxuries she'd ordered: caviar, chocolates, and assorted personal items. The kerosene stove gleamed in the sun. She noticed a slight puddle under the icebox where the drip pan should have been. But she didn't see anything that could have made the sound.

Maybe I just imagined it, she thought. She opened the door and took a couple of steps into the kitchen, humming the song she'd heard was the rage of the Chicago trolley car parties.

Suddenly, a growling raccoon charged at her from behind the kitchen water pump. "Good heavens!" she screamed, barely managing to close the door in time.

The raccoon crashed against it, scratching in fury, trying to get through. Sarah looked through the glass panel and saw that the back door was ajar.

"So that's how you got in," she mused, looking at the creature. "What happened to your hair?" she asked out loud. The raccoon was nearly bald and had bite marks all over it. It answered Sarah with a vicious growl.

Sarah took a deep breath and went to the basement to get a hammer. "I can't have animals keeping me out of my own kitchen."

Marching up the stairs, she looked through the glass, saw the raccoon in the corner near the back door, and barged in, hammer swinging in front of her.

"Get out of this house . . . right now!" she screamed.

The raccoon charged forward, catching Sarah off guard. She managed a lucky swing and brought the two-pound hammer crashing down onto the raccoon's skull.

Sarah stared at the dead animal in shock. She didn't know how long she stood there before she heard the front door open and her husband call out, "Sarah, where are you?"

"I . . . I'm in the kitchen . . . come see this."

"I want you to read this article and . . . " Bentley came in and stopped dead in his tracks. "What in the world happened? Did it bite you?"

Sarah shook her head. "I've never seen anything like it. It just growled and attacked." She turned to her husband. "It must be hungry. I've heard raccoons are pesky, but this is ridiculous."

Bentley looked down at the foam crusted around the raccoon's mouth and the matted clumps of remaining hair. "I came to show you the article that Emily Grant wrote for this morning's paper." He held up the headline: "Rabid Raccoons Found in the Ozarks."

Sarah gasped and looked at the raccoon on the floor. "Do you think . . ."

Bentley shrugged. "There's supposedly an outbreak of rabies in the Ozarks, and some of the raccoons around here might be infected." He looked up at his wife. "I think this is one of them."

"Rabies . . . why . . . " Sarah fainted into her husband's arms.

By the time she came around, Bentley had gotten their housemaid to tend to Sarah, clean the kitchen, and close off the cat door. Then he took the dead animal over to Granddoc's to show the vet what had attacked Sarah in the kitchen.

Hope we don't have to quarantine the town, Bentley thought, taking the corner too fast in his automobile.

22

Sheriff Peterson

❖

Sheriff Peterson put his feet up on the desk. He was tired of arguing with J.J. about whether pigs were smarter than horses.

J.J. McAlister, the town's new dogcatcher, came from Hartville. He had accepted the Mansfield offer to do the same job for a five-dollar a week raise. "I'm tellin' you, it's easier to teach a pig anythin' than it is to teach a horse."

"J.J., pigs could all go to Harvard, and I still wouldn't want to train somethin' I like to eat. And besides," the sheriff chuckled, "who'd want to saddle up a pig? They're too squat and ugly to be good for anythin' but eatin'."

"Did I tell you that I think Sammy Lester's been shocking fish again?" J.J. asked, changing the subject.

"Where?"

"Down along Willow Creek. This morning I saw a bunch of fish along the bank."

Sheriff Peterson looked perplexed. "If he shocked 'em, why didn't he take 'em?"

J. J. shook his head. "You know what a drunk cooter that no-good is. Probably just passed out and forgot to get the fish."

"Least he ain't gamblin'." J.J. shifted his weight in the wooden chair and changed the subject yet again. "Remember what I told you 'bout right- and left-handed dice?"

Sheriff Peterson was trying very hard to like J.J., but he didn't like the trivia that the man always spouted off. "You can tell me till you're blue in the face that there's left-handed and right-handed dice. It just doesn't matter."

J.J. went on anyway. "And top and bottom dice too. I read where there's four correct and legal ways to put spots on dice and—"

Sheriff Peterson held up his hand. "And I don't care." Straightening the papers on his desk, he took a deep breath. "Did you come 'round here to jawbone, or you got somethin' on your mind?"

J.J. hadn't come to talk about smart pigs, drunks, shocked fish, or left-handed dice. He had come to talk about the rumors he'd heard about raccoons attacking people south of town, but he didn't know how to broach the subject.

J.J. took a deep breath of his own. "Sheriff, I think you need to be ready for the 'coon attack."

"J.J., what are you talkin' 'bout? 'Coon attack? There's nothin' like that happenin' 'round here. I'm more worried 'bout the roads gettin' washed out from all the rain we've had this spring."

J.J. shook his head. "I told you what happened over in St. Louis when I was workin' for the city and—"

"That was St. Louis. Big cities are full of diseases. Heck, just breathin' city air can make you sick. But the Ozarks, why this is God's country. Nothin' but clean air and good livin'."

Cubby George, the doctor's son, opened the door. The bell tinkled cheerfully. "Here's your paper, Sheriff," he said, tossing it over to him.

"Thanks, Cubby." Putting the paper down on his desk, the sheriff looked at J.J. "Where you hearin' these rumors of man-eatin' raccoons?" he asked derisively.

"Ain't rumors, Sheriff. I got it firsthand from Freckles over at the . . . "

"Freckles? Who's that?" the sheriff asked, scratching his head.

"You know—Slick Clinton's brother. The one who looks like a big freckle."

"You mean Jimmy? Yeah, I know him."

"Well, he was down in Branson, deliverin' a load of pipe when he heard 'bout a man who got attacked by a growlin' 'coon.

The sheriff shook his head. "I'll believe that when I read about it."

J.J. looked down at the newspaper on the desk and paused.

"Well, just read this," he said, pointing to the boxed story on the front page.

SPECIAL FOR THE MANSFIELD MONITOR
Rabid Raccoons Found in the Ozarks
by Emily Grant

Rabid raccoons have reportedly attacked several people throughout the Ozarks. Some of these friendly, cute, furry creatures that so many people adore may now carry the bite of death.

Attacks in Mountain Grove, Hollister, Walnut Shade, and as near as Dogwood and Norwood, show that these raccoons may be getting closer to Mansfield.

Though raccoons are curious, playful creatures, those with this horrid disease are something to worry about. Rabies is a virus that attacks the nervous system and leads to an agonizing death. Only if you receive the vaccination shots soon after you're bitten will you stand a chance of surviving.

No one knows how the raccoons got the disease, but everyone should be on guard. Once animals get the disease, they lose all fear of humans and are known to attack people even in buggies and on horseback.

People must beware of raccoons in general. We should all pray that next winter will bring an early, blistering freeze, which is the only way we can hope to eliminate this epidemic from our beautiful Ozarks.

"That proof enough?" J.J. asked.

Sheriff Peterson whistled. "Tell you what. If any of them 'coons get into this town, we'll have ourselves a problem. Heck, half the old ladies around here leave hard-boiled eggs on their porches to feed the critters."

J.J. stood up and put his thumbs under his suspenders. "I think you ought to call a town meetin' now. Warn everybody 'bout this."

"And scare everyone half to death? I think you're jumpin' the gun."

J.J. frowned, eyeing the sheriff through one eye. "If them sick critters are in Mountain Grove, they'll be here soon. You know it and I know it."

"Think so?"

"If they ain't already here, I'll be surprised."

Sheriff Peterson shook his head. "Just 'cause they've seen one up 'round Mountain Grove don't mean that we got to go to panickin'."

"Forewarned is forearmed," J.J. said like a politician.

"You sound like a ninny! It's like worryin' so much 'bout gettin' struck by lightnin' that you go around hidin' from the clouds."

"Ain't the same," J.J. said, and walked over to the gun rack on the wall. "You best get ready to organize some of the boys to go 'coon huntin'. Offer a bounty."

"Oh heck, J.J., if I offer a 'coon bounty, why, I'll have farm boys for fifty miles around shootin' every one they see."

"Better to shoot a few extra than have them things out runnin' 'round, bitin' and killin' the good huntin' dogs 'round here," J.J. said. "And I *am* the county dogcatcher, sworn to uphold the health laws of Missouri."

"If we have to go to shootin' dogs, I'll never get reelected, and that'll be bad for *my* health," Peterson said.

"Look, I'm just sayin' that rabid raccoons will bite anythin'—dogs, people, kids. You better just get thinkin' 'bout what you're gonna do when you get the first call."

"Call 'bout what?" Sheriff Peterson asked.

"About who got bit."

The phone rang and the sheriff's eyes went wide. He took the receiver off the wall phone. "Sheriff's office."

"This is Bentley."

"Mr. Bentley, what can I do for you?"

There was a pause, then Bentley said, "A raccoon with rabies attacked my wife."

"Attacked your wife? Where?" Sheriff Peterson said with alarm. J.J. crossed himself, saying a prayer.

"Right in the kitchen. But it didn't bite her."

"I'm comin' right over," Peterson said.

"Don't bother comin' here," Bentley said. "I took the raccoon over to Granddoc's."

"She tell you it had rabies?"

"Yes. Sheriff," Bentley said firmly, "I read the article in the paper, and I saw the raccoon. We've got ourselves a problem."

"You're tellin' me!" Peterson exclaimed.

"No. I want *you* to tell me what you're gonna do about it."

"As a matter of fact," Sheriff Peterson said, winking at J.J., "I've been sittin' here with J.J. McAlister the new dogcatcher, workin' out plans to rid the county of these varmints."

23

Granddoc Crawley

Granddoc Crawley was alone in her basement lab, studying the brain of the raccoon that Bentley had left her. She rubbed her old eyes, taking off her bifocal glasses to look again.

A thousand wrinkles marred Granddoc's complexion. Though she didn't have all that much use for man as a species, she felt a responsibility for the creatures of the earth.

Everyone called her Granddoc, though her name was Violet and she was unmarried and didn't have any children. Though not originally from the area, Granddoc was considered an old settler.

Like most of the old-timers in Mansfield, Violet Crawley's parents were prairie homesteaders. Her family had a penchant for moving through the tall prairie grass and amber fields that grew from the fertile plains. Granddoc's earliest prairie memory was of the prickly pear cactus in bloom along the trails.

Born in Minnesota and raised in Wisconsin, she'd traveled with her parents by wagon into the prairie, skirting the edges of Indian country in their continual quest to find a better place to live. She could remember the endless herds of buffalo they had seen. They were magnificent animals, coats ragged with shedding. And she remembered fondly the little calves with the beginning of horns protruding from their foreheads.

Her family had come to Missouri more than forty years before. They arrived in an old wagon drawn by two borrowed horses, carrying all their household goods and a tent to sleep in.

Following behind the family's wagon was Violet. And following behind Violet was her ten-month-old colt, a six-month-old calf, ten geese, thirty chickens, three goats, five shoats, six dogs, two cats, and a pig named Honker.

In an age when most girls were trained to be mothers, Violet's mother wanted her to be a teacher and used all her egg money to buy Violet books. Violet's eager, bright mind and love of animals caught the attention of a traveling veterinarian from Springfield, who encouraged her to be the first woman vet in Missouri.

So with the life savings of her parents in hand and a letter from her mentor, Violet applied to Cornell University and was accepted. It wasn't easy being the only woman in the class, but she persevered. Her class of 1883 diploma in veterinary medicine now hung on the wall over her desk. This had been her parents' last homestead, and their graves were on the knoll above the house where Granddoc now lived alone.

Though it had been too many years to count since she last rode in a wagon with her folks, that prairie feeling of freedom had never left her. She found herself thinking about it more and more as she got older.

Granddoc was a spry sixty-two and had seen almost everything that could happen to animals. But what she saw through her microscope now alarmed her.

She looked at the mangy carcass of the raccoon and shivered. *Just as dangerous dead as alive. Some things have no place on this earth,* she thought. The disease gave her goose bumps.

Though Granddoc was sure the animal was rabid, she wanted to double-check. Slicing the brain into thin sections, she made tiny slides for the microscope. She compared it to the pictures in her medical book. Carefully moving the sample with her gloved hands, she saw her worst fears confirmed. The pictures were identical.

"Rabies," she whispered.

She looked again and for a moment admired the awesome image of death before her eyes. Living death. She felt compelled to look again at the bitter slide before her.

Combined with what she'd read in the paper, she knew she had the proof that rabies had come to Mansfield. *No telling how many animals are sick with it,* she worried. *I'm just glad Sarah wasn't bitten.*

She called the Bentleys and gave them strict instructions to scrub down the entire kitchen and get rid of anything that the raccoon might have touched. Then she called Sheriff Peterson to tell him what she'd found.

"Bentley already called, and I read what Emily wrote in the paper this mornin'," he said.

"What are you going to do?" she asked.

"What can I do? Can't quarantine the town, and I can't send people off on a wild rampage, killin' every raccoon in sight."

"No," she agreed, "you can't do that."

"What do you suggest, Granddoc? You're the vet."

Granddoc paused. "You must warn everyone to be on guard. And no leaving eggs and scraps around to feed them and . . ."

"Guess that means Mom won't be able to feed that pack of 'em that comes 'round her restaurant each night." The Sheriff laughed.

"Heavens no! You'd best have someone there to shoot any of the mangy looking ones who straggle up."

"What 'bout traps? Should we have someone set them 'round town?"

"As long as they're capture traps and not those steel jaws that slice their legs off. You don't want to have half the dog population of Mansfield hobbling around on three legs."

The sheriff paused, then asked, "Think they're a lot of 'em around?"

Granddoc shook her head. "One is too many and where there's one, there's always more."

"Let me know if you see any more of them sick 'coons," he said.

"I'll call you. Don't worry," she said, putting the receiver back on the wall phone.

"Granddoc, are you down there?" came a voice from the top of the basement stairs. "It's me, John. Got somethin' to show you."

"Come on down. I've got something to show you," she replied.

John stepped carefully down the stairs, steadying himself with his hand on the wall, holding the burlap sack in front of him. He saw the carcass on the table and took a deep breath. "Guess you already know 'bout it then."

"What have you got there?"

Opening the bag, he showed her the mangy raccoon in his bag. "It came at Cody and me. If it hadn't been for Cody, the thing would've bit me."

Granddoc put on her gloves again and took the raccoon to her table and prepared to examine its brain tissues. "Don't think I need to check it but I will."

"I know what you're gonna find," he said quietly, pulling at his earlobe, "but I'm prayin' you won't find it."

"I know, John," she said.

"He was bit bad, Granddoc. All 'round his face. Nearly chewed his ear off," John said, self-consciously trying to cover his own missing ear.

"Cody's a good dog . . . a good dog," she said.

"He's the best. Cody's the only family I got left."

"Just sit down, John, and let me do my work."

They both knew that any animal bitten by a rabid animal had to be destroyed. There was no way to quarantine animals in the Ozarks, and with livestock and wild animals all around, it was the only way to protect the animals and the public.

After she looked at the brain sample, Granddoc took off her glasses and turned to John. "I'm sorry. I truly am."

John shut his eyes tightly, trying to hold back the tears. One managed to slide slowly down his left cheek. "I better be gettin' back to do what I gotta do," he said, pulling his cap down over his missing ear. "I don't want to do it . . . I don't wanna shoot my dog."

"You're doing the right thing, John."

John wiped the tear from his cheek. "Don't make it no easier," he said, pulling at his lobe. "I raised that dog from a pup. And now I got to kill Cody after he saved my life? That don't seem right."

Before he was off the porch, Granddoc picked up the telephone. "Sheriff, this is Granddoc. We've got another one."

24

Walk in the Woods

❖

Larry carried Cain and Abel, walking ahead through the woods. "Why do I got to carry Mabel?" Terry asked, licking the chocolate off his lips. He was secretly eating a Tootsie Roll and didn't want to share it with Larry. "I don't think she likes me," he said, warily looking at the sleek, black skunk.

"Mabel's a him," Larry said, wondering if he saw chocolate on Terry's lips. He sniffed the air but couldn't tell.

"Don't see why you named a boy a girl's name," Terry said, turning to sneak another piece of candy into his mouth.

I bet he's eatin' candy, Larry thought, eyeing his brother. But it was hard to tell since Terry was doing a good job of hiding his mouth.

"What are you eatin'?" Larry finally stopped and asked.

Terry just shrugged. His mouth was too full of chocolate to say anything.

"Are you eatin' some candy?" Larry asked.

Terry nodded. "Just a Tootsie Roll," he said, swallowing the mouthful in one gulp.

"Why didn't you give me some?"

"You didn't ask," Terry said.

"I didn't ask 'cause I didn't know you had any."

"It's too late now. It's in my tummy," Terry said, shrugging it off. He tossed the skunk up and down. "Let's just drop them right here."

"Don't upset him," Larry cautioned.

Mabel raised his tail and Terry held his breath, then said in a sweet voice, "I won't drop you here, you cute little stinkin' varmint. Just lower your tail . . . please." He breathed a sigh of relief when the skunk slowly lowered it.

"Come on," Larry said, stepping over a bull snake in his path.

Watching them from the woods was a pack of wild dogs.

Gordo and the others, some of which were now sick too, trotted along in silence, then went to raid the trash dump outside of town. But the boys, oblivious to the danger that had just passed them by, walked happily through the woods, surrounded by the rolling hills of the Ozarks. Scattered sinkholes pocketed the ravines, surrounded by a forest of pine, oak, and hickory.

They were in the highest part of the state, south of the Missouri River. Below them flowed the creeks and streams, making their way to the Missouri and Mississippi rivers. These woods and hills were the Younguns' playground. They had seen bears and even a panther behind their house, where they played Davy Crockett and Daniel Boone.

Their running paths were the same trails that the Osage, Delaware, Shawnee, and Pinkashaw Indians had used more than a hundred years before. Larry had even found several stone arrowheads, a club head, and flint chips in the caves and ravines where they played hide-and-seek.

He had learned some Osage words and legends from an aging Indian who lived near Mountain Grove. The word that stuck in his mind was *tzi-sho,* Osage for "sky people." The legend about the sky warrior had become Larry's secret fantasy.

In his mind, he could picture an Osage sky warrior, hunched over a chunk of flint, carefully flaking off the chips, working to make a perfect dart point. It was his secret warrior that he saw in the mists and reflections throughout the forest.

Terry saw things differently. He would just pick up any sharp rock smaller than a baseball and declare it the lost arrowhead of Chief Pinchafanny, which was the name of the made-up warrior whom he claimed took over his body when he chased Sherry around the room.

Still, there was something magic about their woods that Larry and Terry both felt. They saw it in the sinkhole ponds, in the shallow caves, in the dense forest, and in the tangled thickets that ringed their play area. Sometimes, in the mist of the morning, when they were out in the woods instead of doing their chores, they likened the foggy shapes that formed over the hills to Indian chiefs and great warriors.

Larry looked around as they walked, grinning proudly at the line he'd come up with to describe the Ozarks. *Green mysteries of life, growing in secret places, waiting to be found . . . waiting for the sky warrior to show the way.*

He looked around, hoping to see a reflection or image that could be his imaginary Osage, when he felt it. "Ouch!" he shouted, jumping into the air.

Terry laughed. "Old Chief Pinchafanny took over my body again Couldn't help myself."

"I ought to leave you here," Larry threatened in jest. "You'd nevei be able to find your way out of these woods."

"You think you know a lot 'bout the woods, don't you?" Terry asked, struggling to climb over a fallen tree.

"That's 'cause I read a lot."

"Well, tell me this, smarty pants," Terry said. "How can a bear hibernate for six months without doin' you know what?"

"What?" Larry asked.

"You know . . . droppin' a hot potato in the woods."

Larry looked at his brother like he was crazy. "Why you always askin' such squirrelly things?"

"Just somethin' I was curious 'bout."

Larry thought for a moment. "Some bears wake up and wander out to do their business, and some don't and sleep just fine for six months."

Terry spit against a tree. "I think you're makin' that up. How can anythin' sleep fine, holdin' it in for six months? Ain't natural, normal, or believable."

"But it's true," Larry said. "Now let's keep goin'."

"Tell that to the bears," Terry mumbled.

When they had made it to the top of the ridge across the ravine, they heard a barking sound behind them. "It's Dangit!" Larry said, holding the skunks so they couldn't see the dog.

"Musta slipped loose from his rope," Terry said.

"Come on, we gotta get outta here 'fore he scares these skunks and they stink us up again."

"Why don't we just drop 'em right here?" Terry said. "This looks like good skunk country to me."

"What do you know about skunks?" Larry asked.

"Enough to know that we ought to drop 'em and run."

"I want to take 'em back near where I found 'em," Larry said as he continued walking quickly.

"Their momma's dead. Orphan skunks can stink anywhere. Don't matter to them." He held Mabel out with one hand. "I say we leave 'em 'fore they stink us!"

Dangit's barking echoed over the hills. Larry raced ahead shouting, "Don't let Dangit catch you with the skunk."

"Where you goin'?"

"Over near Devil's Ridge."

Terry began trotting after his brother, trying to keep ahead of the fast-approaching dog. "We'll never outrun Dangit."

"We gotta try," Larry shouted, increasing the distance between them.

Terry climbed up on a boulder, looked at Dangit who was already halfway down the ravine, then at Mabel. "If you skunk juice me, I'll cut your tail off and feed it to the ants."

Mabel raised his tail. "I was just kidding," Terry whispered. He hurried to catch up with his brother.

Dangit was only a hundred yards behind them by the time they reached Devil's Ridge. Larry put down the two skunks next to a maple tree. "Go on, boys. You'll like it better out here than bein' in a cage." He turned to Terry. "Put Mabel down."

"I'm tryin'," Terry whispered. "But he's holdin' on to my shirt with his claws."

Larry lifted Mabel gently up and placed him on the ground next to a jack-in-the-pulpit plant. But the skunk ran back and tried to climb up Terry's pant leg. "Guess he likes you," Larry said.

"If this thing juices me, I'm gonna rub it in your face."

Dangit was less than fifty yards away when Mabel walked away and hid behind a big white oak tree. "Good girl . . . er boy," Terry said.

"Come on," Larry shouted, "let's run south and lead Dangit away." He shooed the three skunks into the bushes and took off.

Terry didn't want to argue and followed closely behind, screaming, "Geronimo!"

Dangit stopped, sniffed in the direction of the skunks, then turned and followed the boys.

As they passed by a cave on the side of Devil's Ridge, Larry saw a big bat come flying out toward them. "Look out!" he shouted.

Terry stopped in his tracks and turned just in time to see it coming at him. He screamed, rolling into the bushes. The big bat hovered above. "Larry, help!"

Larry watched the bat fly figure eights overhead. "That's the biggest bat I ever seen!"

25

Bat Attack

The bat flew around the trees then dropped straight toward Larry's head. Larry dove face first to the ground as the bat flew past.

"Hit him with a rock or somethin'!" Terry called out.

"Don't wet your pants over it," Larry said, wiping the dirt from his mouth.

"Do somethin'," Terry pleaded.

Larry stood up and grabbed a branch. He ran out waving it at the bat. "Go on, get outta here!" The bat flew at him, but Larry scared it off.

Dangit came charging through the bushes, barking loudly. The bat turned in circles, eyeing the dog, then swooped toward him. "No, Dangit, no!" Larry yelled.

Terry looked up from the bush he was hiding in and saw the bat trying to bite Dangit.

Gotta help, Terry decided. He picked up a rock, jumped to his feet, and threw it as hard as he could, hitting the bat's wing.

"Good shot!" Larry shouted, watching the bat fly awkwardly up into the air. "Come on! Let's get outta here!"

The two boys and the dog took off, not seeing the cave that the bat flew into. For the moment, death had passed up another chance.

A hundred yards away, they cut through a stand of pines, heading back toward the house. They stopped to catch their breath, letting Dangit run ahead and bark at birds.

"I bet that was the bat that Sherry was talkin' 'bout," Larry said, breathing deeply.

"That wasn't a bat . . . that was Dracula himself," Terry said.

"It was a bat . . . a big bat. Just like Sherry said," Larry said.

"Naw," said Terry, "she was just imaginin' her nightmare. That was Dracula."

They heard Dangit furiously barking and followed in the direction the sound seemed to be coming from. Larry saw pine bark fragments littered around the base of several trees. "Look," he pointed it out to Terry, "this means that there's a porcupine 'round here."

"What are you talkin' 'bout?" Terry asked, panting. "I don't see no porcupine 'round here."

"A porcupine scarred up these trees," Larry said. "Look at that one." He pointed to a pine with a big, white scar forty feet up its trunk.

Then Larry scratched his head. *This isn't right. Porcupines eat leaves and field plants in the summer and evergreen pieces in the fall. They don't begin eatin' on the inner bark of pine trees until winter.*

"Be careful," Larry said. "Somethin' ain't right 'round here."

"You're darn right 'bout that," Terry said. "First we carry stupid skunks into the woods to be near their dead momma, then we get attacked by Dracula, and now you want to talk 'bout porky-pines." He ran his fingers through his hair. "Jeesh. I ought to be home eatin' candy instead of traipsin' 'round in the woods with you."

Dangit came leaping over the log behind them and knocked Larry down, smothering him with his tongue. "Get off me . . . get off me!" he laughed, pushing the dog away.

"Let's go," Terry said.

"No, wait. I want to find this porcupine."

"For what? Go home and stick your hand on a pin cushion . . . same thing," Terry said.

Larry playfully shoved him. "You're just plain ignorant."

Suddenly, Dangit began yelping. "I think Dangit found him for you," Terry said.

Dangit came running back, pawing sharply at his muzzle. Larry ran toward the dog and saw that his face was covered with quills.

"Oh gosh! Dangit, come here, boy," Larry said, reaching to catch the dog's collar.

But Dangit was enraged with pain. He bellowed loudly, jumped away from Larry, and charged back toward the porcupine again.

"Come back!" Larry shouted, but Dangit was already lost in the bush.

Before Larry could drag him back, Dangit got another blast of quills onto his side and neck. Larry dragged him back.

"Hold him for a moment," Larry ordered his brother.

"What for?"

"'Cause I want to look at this porcupine."

Terry held onto the dog's collar and carefully pulled the quills from Dangit's face and neck. With each pull, the dog yelped painfully.

Larry circled the bush where he knew the porcupine was. He could hear it grunting and snapping its teeth. "Bet you're a biggun," he whispered.

Carefully parting the branches, he looked in and saw a huge porcupine. It stared back with its threatening, pig-like eyes. Larry froze in place as the porcupine arched its back. Every quill was fully erect, ready to be tossed.

"Oh jeesh," Terry said from behind him, "he's got quills stuck in his mouth."

But Larry didn't turn. He looked at the porcupine, wondering why it was snapping at the air. "Somethin's wrong with this one."

"Yeah," Terry said, pulling two quills from Dangit's gums, "he was born."

"Don't move," came a deep voice from behind Larry. He turned to see John Wolf standing there, cradling his shotgun.

Larry tried not to look at his odd, hanging earlobe but couldn't help it. "Mr. John," Larry said, "I was just lookin' at this strange porcupine and—"

"Step aside, boy," John ordered. He carefully parted the bushes, looked at the porcupine, and nodded. He reached for his missing ear, then shook his head.

"There's somethin' wrong with that animal," Larry said.

"I know it," John said. Then, without warning, he shot the porcupine.

"What'd you do that for?" Larry cried out, trying to get to the dead animal.

John held him back. "Had to, son. He had rabies."

"Rabies?" Larry whispered, looking at the porcupine, lying on its side. The quills had gone slack. It looked like a deflated balloon.

"How can you tell?" Larry asked.

"Porcupines don't normally growl and attack people. Look at his mouth . . . see that crust?"

Larry looked and nodded. "Can bats get it?" he asked.

"Sure. Why?" John asked.

"'Cause back on Devil's Ridge, a big bat attacked us."

Terry spit. "Weren't no bat. It was Dracula."

"How big?" John asked.

Larry described their encounter with the bat, then John looked him in the eye. "Did it bite either of you . . . or the dog?"

"No, sir," Larry said. "We fought him off."

"I saved the day," Terry beamed proudly while picking the quills off Dangit.

"Oh, you did?" John smiled.

"Yeah, I hit Dracula with a rock and scared him off." Dangit yelped as Terry pulled another quill. "Will somebody help me get these quills off Dangit?"

"Bring him over to me, son," John said. "I'll get 'em out."

Dangit instinctively trusted John and lay quietly on his side. Using his fingernails as tweezers, John carefully began removing the sharp quills, one by one.

Dangit made quiet noises of pain, drooling bloody saliva. Larry and Terry watched apprehensively.

"Think you're gonna need to take him to Granddoc. Just be glad that porcupine didn't bite your dog," John said as he pulled a small quill from the dog's gums.

"Why? What would have happened?" Larry asked.

John stopped and looked the boys in the eye. "You woulda had to shoot your dog."

"Shoot him?" gasped Larry.

Suddenly it dawned on both boys that they'd never seen John without his dog before. "Where's Cody, Mr. John?" Terry asked.

John paused, then said slowly, "Cody got bit defendin' me against a rabid 'coon. I had to shoot him this mornin'."

"You mean he's dead?" Larry asked, wide-eyed.

John nodded. "You gotta do that if an animal gets bit by one of these creatures with rabies."

"I'd *never* shoot Dangit," Larry said, putting his hands on the dog.

"Law wouldn't give you no choice," John said. "You best not be tellin' anyone 'cept your Pa and Granddoc 'bout what happened. If the dogcatcher finds out, he might just pull your dog in and shoot him to be on the safe side."

Terry watched John removing the quills. He couldn't take his eyes off the missing ear.

When he finished, John patted the dog. "You boys take him to Granddoc and let her have a look at him. Make sure I got all them quills out of his mouth and tongue."

"Thanks, Mr. John," Larry said.

"You say you boys saw that big bat up on Devil's Ridge?"

Larry nodded.

"You boys best stay away from there. That bat could have the sickness too," John said.

Terry had to ask. "Mr. John, what happened to your ear?"

John just shook his head. "That's a story for another time. You best be gettin' home, and stay out of these woods. And if you see any 'coons comin' at you, you run for your lives."

"Run?" Terry said. "Raccoons will just run away if you go at 'em."

"Not these," John said.

26

Dr. George

Sherry sat up in bed. She'd gone up to lie down right after helping with the dishes. She felt weak.

"Pa," she called, clutching her blankey. "I don't feel good."

Rev. Youngun put down his paper. He'd read the article on animals with rabies in the Ozarks and was worried about the boys being out in the woods.

"I'll be right up," he called out.

Taking off his reading glasses, he paused to look at the collapsed sofa. "That sofa's shot." He sighed, then looked out the window at the sky. *Hope it doesn't rain. I'm sure another big storm will spring more leaks in this roof.*

He walked up the stairs worrying about where the boys were.

"Hi, pumpkin," he said softly as he entered Sherry's room. He sat on the bed and put his hand on her forehead. "You do feel like you have a fever."

"I ache, Pa," she whispered, rubbing her blankey between her fingers and her nose.

"Where?"

"All over. And my neck hurts."

Rev. Youngun felt her throat, thinking she might have the mumps. "Doesn't feel swollen to me."

"Ouch!" she winced as his fingers touched where the bat had bitten her. "It hurts here," she whimpered, touching the spot. "Where the monster bat bit me."

Thinking about the article in the newspaper, Rev. Youngun

opened the window shade and closely examined her neck. He saw two small red marks. Oh, Lord. I didn't believe her. Something did bite her.

"Did a spider bite you?"

"No," Sherry said, shaking her head back and forth. "The bat bit me. The monster bat that came through the window."

He picked her up in his arms. "I better get you to Dr. George," he said, carrying her down the stairs. He left a note for the boys and carried Sherry to the horse buggy.

As they drove past the mailbox, he didn't notice her letter to Little Wings sticking out of the box. Sherry saw it and smiled as she snuggled against her father. *Little Wings will get me those red shoes . . . I just know she will.*

She remembered the angel's words. *If you believe, then it is true.* She looked up toward the sky. *I believe, Little Wings.*

Dr. George, the town's only doctor, had come to Mansfield by way of medical school in St. Louis. Mansfield needed a doctor and he needed a job. For the first time in Dr. George's life, it hadn't mattered that he was black. It was a simple exchange of needs.

That was years ago. Now he was a fixture of the town. By his own estimate, he'd birthed about half the current enrollment of the county school.

Sitting in his office, he thought about how his parents had raised him in a poor section of St. Louis, trying to live their lives in quiet dignity while the indignities of the world tried to push them down.

From St. Louis to the Ozarks, he sighed, rocking back on his desk chair. *Couldn't be farther apart.*

The Ozarks had overwhelmed him with its beauty. He spent his afternoons and weekends hiking in the hills, training himself to recognize the plants: blazing star, bluestem grass, and rattlesnake master. He even knew wild birds by sight, such as upland sandpipers, northern harriers, woodcocks, Swainson's hawks, and the other inhabitants of the forest. They never ceased to amaze him.

He'd grown to love Mansfield and its people. They always paid him, whether it was in money, vegetables, chickens, or helping out with chores. It was a good life in a good town with good people.

His practice was quiet and steady. The most serious emergency that had come his way this year was the food poisoning from the fried chicken sold at the traveling circus show.

But after reading the article on the outbreak of rabies, he was worried. With all the loose farm dogs, thousands of livestock, and enough wild animals to fill a hundred zoos, he knew what an epidemic of rabies could do in this part of the Ozarks.

So when Rev. Youngun brought Sherry in, Dr. George was very concerned. If one person had been bitten, there'd be others. He looked carefully at the bite mark, comparing the signs and her symptoms to his medical manual.

Rev. Youngun stood beside his sick daughter. "Maybe she just scratched herself while she was sleeping."

"Maybe," Dr. George said without looking up. "And maybe not."

"I told you, a monster bat bit me," Sherry whispered, wincing at the pain from the pressure on her neck.

"Maybe she got scratched by the cat," Rev. Youngun said, knowing he was reaching, but desperately wanting the bite to be from something else. "Ratz has some claws you wouldn't believe."

"Ratz didn't bite me," Sherry said firmly. "The bat did."

"You know how children are," Rev. Youngun said.

"Thomas," Dr. George said, "even if we weren't one hundred percent sure, I'd still have to treat this as a rabies bite."

"Why?"

"Read this," Dr. George said, handing Rev. Youngun some literature from his files. "This will explain what we're facing."

Rev. Youngun looked at the first page.

What Is Rabies?

Rabies is a deadly, acute virus that can affect every warm-blooded animal. It is sometimes called hydrophobia, which translates to "fear of water." The nickname is misleading, because the affected animals are not afraid of water; it's just that they have difficulty drinking due to paralysis of the tongue and jaw.

Rabies is usually transmitted by a bite, where the infected saliva enters the wound. It occurs most frequently in dogs, and humans are quite susceptible. While rabies can occur during any season, outbreaks usually appear in the spring and fall.

Rev. Youngun rubbed his eyes. *Please, God, save my little girl.
You've got to save Sherry.*

Dr. George sat back using a smile to hide his fears. He handed Sherry
a small lollipop, then motioned with his head for Rev. Youngun to
follow him.

"Sherry, your father and I need to speak for a moment. We'll be right
back." Sherry smiled, happy to have the candy.

In the living room of his house, which was where his office was, Dr.
George shook his head. "Without examining the bat that bit her, I can't
be one hundred percent certain."

"So she might not have rabies?" Rev. Youngun asked hopefully.

"She might not. But I can't take the risk of waiting to see." He put
his hand on Rev. Youngun's shoulder. "I've never heard of anyone
surviving after the symptoms have appeared."

"What can we do?"

"We have to get a telegraph message to the main hospital in
Springfield. See if they've got some of the rabies vaccine. That's all
we can do."

"And if we don't get the vaccine in time?"

Dr. George shook his head. "I don't want to talk about that. We've
got to get that vaccine. That's all there is to it."

Rev. Youngun thought about the terrible article he'd just read and
imagined Sherry foaming at the mouth. "Send the telegraph. Whatever
it takes, get that vaccine down here."

Dr. George knew that the Younguns didn't have much money. "It
won't be cheap."

Rev. Youngun took the doctor by the shoulders. "My daughter's
life's worth everything I have . . . even my own life!"

They locked eyes for a moment, then Dr. George went into the back
room and called down to the train station to have Stephen Scales send
the message. What he didn't tell Rev. Youngun was that he also called
the bank to wire a guarantee of funds from his own account to pay for
the vaccine.

*Rev. Youngun doesn't have any money, and I couldn't live with myself
if she died, knowing that she could have been saved if I hadn't hoarded
pieces of paper.* He shook his head. *Might not be a rich big city doctor,
but I'm gonna be one that sleeps well at night.*

Back in the examining room he told Rev. Youngun what to do.

"Remember, don't let anyone eat or drink from anything she's touched. Her spit can carry the sickness. You tell the boys that, you understand?"

Rev. Youngun nodded.

From the other room they heard Sherry say, "Little Wings . . . are you sure I'll like heaven?" There was a pause, then she said, "Well, if it's as wonderful as you say, I'll love it!"

"Who's she talking to?" Dr. George asked.

Rev. Youngun rubbed his eyes again. "Just an imaginary friend."

Sherry peeked in through the door. "Pa, Little Wings was here."

"She was?" Rev. Youngun said gently. "What did Little Wings tell you?"

Sherry beamed. "She told me all about heaven."

"Little Wings?" Dr. George whispered behind Rev. Youngun. "What's she talking about?"

Rev. Youngun whispered into the doctor's ear, "Sherry thinks she has a guardian angel."

"We can use all the help we can get," Dr. George said. He picked Sherry up and smiled at her. "You tell that angel of yours to stick around and watch over you."

"She is." Sherry grinned. "She's always with me."

Dr. George hugged her, then turned to her father. "Now take Sherry home and say some prayers."

"That's already been done," Rev. Youngun said.

"Say some more to be on the safe side. I'll be saying them too."

"I'm not scared anymore, Pa," Sherry smiled, "'cause I know that heaven's a good place . . . 'cause I believe. That's what Little Wings told me."

"Just get the vaccine. I'll pay whatever it costs," Rev. Youngun said to Dr. George quietly.

"We'll work something out." Dr. George smiled.

Rev. Youngun started to leave, then turned. "I pay my bills."

"I know you do. But maybe you've got a guardian angel you don't even know about." Dr. George smiled. "Now get that girl home and put her in bed."

Cubby, Dr. George's adopted son, came in from the backyard. "Is somethin' wrong, Pops?"

"Cubby," Dr. George sighed, "you let me know if you see anyone with little wings flying around here." He walked back to his study, leaving Cubby scratching his head.

27

The Red Shoes

On the way back to the house, Rev. Youngun stopped the buggy in front of Bedal's General Store. Sherry was asleep on the seat, hugging her blankey and sucking her thumb, so he took the time to look at the shoes she wanted.

Set amidst the display of thread, dishes, pots, pans, plows, and imported canned goods were the shoes. She'd look like an angel in those shoes, he sighed, thinking about the school play every fall.

Knocking the mud off his shoes, he went inside for a closer look. Carefully walking around the molasses barrels, sacks of tea from China, and coffee bean bags from South America, he made his way over to the display in the window.

He picked up the shoes and marveled at the craftsmanship.

"You thinkin' of buying them?" Lafayette Bedal, the owner of the store, called out in his French-Canadian accent.

"Just wanted to look, that's all."

"Cost five dollars." Bedal smiled. "But they'd sure make some little girl happy."

Five dollars! I can't afford them, Rev. Youngun thought glumly, *walking out of the store. He climbed back into the buggy and took one last look at the shoes, then looked down at his daughter.*

The shoes won't matter if that vaccine doesn't get here in time, he thought, clicking the buggy reins. *Wish I'd caught that bat . . . then we'd know for sure if Sherry's got the sickness,* he thought as the buggy pulled down the muddy street.

❖

At the hospital in Springfield, they looked at the telegraph message from Dr. George. "We're short on rabies vaccine already," Dr. Moore said.

"Can we get more from St. Louis?" his assistant, Mary Lou, asked. "This country doctor says he's wired a hundred dollars from his bank to cover the costs."

"He's taking for granted that we'll send what we have."

"Why wouldn't we?" Mary Lou asked.

Dr. Moore shook his head. "With that outbreak down in Branson and the one in Little Rock, we're going to have to ration our supply."

Mary Lou read the message again. "But this doctor has a sick little girl who'll die without it now."

"Everyone who gets bitten will die without it. Once we run out, that's it," Dr. Moore said, matter-of-factly. "It's all a matter of numbers."

"But this little girl's not just a number."

"Mary Lou, I told you, you can't get personal in this business. One life is like another."

"But we have some vaccine now," Mary Lou pressed. "So we should send enough to Mansfield to take care of her and maybe one or two others. His bank's guaranteed more than enough money to pay for it."

Dr. Moore shook his head. "I'll authorize you to send down one bottle by train. Enough for an injection per day for twenty-three days."

"But what if something happens? What happens if they spill some or break the bottle or—"

Dr. Moore held up his hands. "That's their problem. I can't be responsible."

Mary Lou shook her head. "No, it's not your problem, it's *her* problem. If something happens to the bottle of vaccine, then she'll die . . . and you know it."

Dr. Moore shrugged. "Pack it carefully then . . . and telegraph that country doctor that it's coming. Send it by train. I hear the roads going south are too muddy to travel on."

When Rev. Youngun got home, Dr. George called to tell him that the vaccine was on the way by train. He also told him about the rabid animals that Granddoc had examined.

"Might be painful what Sherry's gonna to have to go through, but this way, she'll most likely live."

Rev. Youngun closed his eyes. *Most likely . . .* "When will the vaccine get here?"

"By tomorrow morning, God willing," Dr. George said.

Rev. Youngun felt helpless. "Thanks for calling," he said.

"Just keep an eye on her in case her fever starts going up. That's one of the early signs."

As Rev. Youngun trudged up the stairs, he felt that a huge rock was sitting on his shoulders.

But the rock got even heavier. Sherry's fever went up.

Back in his office, Dr. George rubbed his temples, then put his hands together. *Dear Lord, please bring this medicine in time. If she doesn't get it within forty-eight hours, that little girl will die.* He stopped, then remembered something else. *And, Little Wings, wherever you are, stay with Sherry. She needs an angel on her shoulders to pull her through.*

28

Dangit

❖

Larry and Terry stood on the front porch of Granddoc's and knocked lightly. "Maybe she's not here," Terry said after a moment.

"Give her time," Larry said. "Mr. John said to get Dangit looked at."

Down in the basement, Granddoc put the two raccoon bodies into a bag to take behind the house and burn. She looked up when she heard the knocking.

"Hope it's not another one," she said, propping herself against the wall for a moment before she made her way slowly up the stairs.

She opened the door and smiled at the two Youngun boys. "What have you got there?" she said, looking at Dangit.

"Mr. John said we should bring Dangit to you," Larry said.

"Yeah," Terry piped up. "He got hit by a porcu-pincushion and—"

"A what?" Granddoc asked.

"He means a porcupine," Larry explained.

Granddoc didn't want to show her alarm. But after what she'd been looking at in the basement, she was worried. "Did you bring the porcupine?"

"Naw," Larry said, shaking his head. "Mr. John said that he'd bury it, but that we should bring Dangit to you to make sure that we got all the quills out of his mouth."

"Did the porcupine bite Dangit?"

Terry and Larry shook their heads. "No. Just quilled him," Larry said.

"Good." She sighed. "Bring him into the back room so I can take a look at him."

On the examining table, Dangit was tense and uncomfortable. "He doesn't like the cold table on his belly," Larry told her.

"I know, son," Granddoc said, "but that's my examining table, and that's where he's got to be."

Terry looked at the syringe in her hand. "What's that needle for?"

"It's just something to put Dangit to sleep."

"But he slept last night," Terry protested.

"I've got to look into his throat to make sure there aren't any quills stuck down there. You wouldn't want Dangit to choke to death, would you?"

As the needle went in, Dangit looked at his two masters as if he were wondering why they let her do this to him. As the shot took effect, Dangit slumped over fast asleep.

Granddoc worked quickly, removing little quills from his gums and throat with tweezers. After she finished, she looked at the boys. "I think I got them all out."

"How're we gonna get Dangit home?" Terry asked, looking at the sleeping dog. "He's out cold."

"Guess we can carry him or go home and get the wagon," Larry suggested. "But he's heavier than a sack of taters."

Granddoc smiled. "You boys just leave Dangit here. I'll let your father know that Dangit will be okay."

"But when can he come home?" Larry asked.

"You come back for him in the morning. I'll make a nice bed for him in one of my cages in the back."

Terry scratched his head, and Granddoc looked at him. "You check yourself for chiggers?"

Terry's mouth dropped. "Chiggers?"

"Or ticks?"

Terry suddenly felt itchy all over.

"How about parasites? You check for them?" she smiled. She was having fun with him.

"What do par-a-sighs look like?" Larry asked, now feeling itchy himself.

Granddoc laughed. "They're so small you can't see 'em."

She went on to explain. "Ticks, flies, chiggers, and mosquitoes are just like freeloading relatives. They drop by for a quick meal on your body, then take off. And your body's neighbors, like fleas, lice, and bedbugs, they're the worst sort. They just homestead in the house and eat the droppings from your body."

Terry made a face. "Droppin's? In the house?"

Granddoc laughed. "I'm talking about skin flakes that are always dropping off."

Terry held his arm up and looked. "Skin flakes like snowflakes?" he asked.

"No, son, you're always shedding but you just can't see it."

Don't believe her, Terry thought. "What 'bout those par-a-sighs?" Terry asked, scratching his scalp.

"Parasites. They're all over your body, but they're too small to see."

Terry looked inside his shirt, and Larry checked out his arm. "Don't see any," Larry mumbled.

Granddoc smiled. "You've got them sitting on your eyebrows and laying eggs in your underwear right now, and you don't even know it."

"Do not!" Terry said, scratching the seat of his pants, just to be on the safe side.

"Don't worry—they won't hurt you. Parasites are your friends. You need them to keep your body clean. Now, you boys run on home, and I'll take care of Dangit for you."

Larry and Terry hugged their dog good-bye, then headed back toward their house. Granddoc watched them go, then picked up the telephone and called Rev. Youngun, who told her about Sherry and the bat. Hanging up the receiver, she closed her eyes. *The Youngun girl might have rabies, he said. Looks like we've got ourselves an epidemic about to break loose.*

Larry and Terry hadn't gone more than a hundred yards, when Terry took his brother's arm and said, "I thought Sherry was crazy, seein' angels, but I think ol' Granddoc's a fruitcake."

"Why?"

"You believe you got par-a-bites layin' eggs in your clothes right this minute?" Terry asked, dead serious.

Larry thought for a moment, then said, "She said we couldn't see 'em."

Terry shook his head in disgust. "Tell you what. I could feel anythin' that was tryin' to lay eggs in my pants." He scratched his backside. "Ain't no invisible par-a-sigh chickens layin' eggs in my britches."

"You're just ignorant," Larry said, hitting Terry's arm.

Terry punched him back. "I'll say it again: Granddoc's a fruitcake."

"But she's a doctor," Larry protested.

"Don't matter. Doctors can be fruitcakes too," Terry said, wiggling around, feeling kind of itchy.

29

Mr. Palugee

Mr. Palugee waded through the junk in his backyard. Stepping carefully over two old axles, a broken butter churn, and a rusted gas lamp, he stopped to examine a branding iron that had slipped into the soggy ground.

"If I ever get a steer, this will come in handy," he mumbled, wiping it off on his pants.

He saved everything he bought and anything he found that might have some possible use. That was the way he wanted to live. But the mess scattered all over his property drove his neighbors crazy.

Lately, though, Mr. Palugee's quiet pack rat life had been disturbed. The bag of burning dog mess on his front porch still upset him. *Why'd that kid waste the good bag? I could have used the bag for somethin'.*

He sighed and shook his head. *Kids today don't know the value of things. They wasted those matches to light the bag. I could have started a good campfire with even one of them.*

Today he'd found the bag of trash scattered on his front steps. He hadn't noticed Willy Bentley snickering in the woods and never suspected that he had been the one who had rung the bell and then run away. After Mr. Palugee closed the door, Willy ran home and told his mother he'd seen the Younguns at it again. So Sarah Bentley called Mr. Palugee and told him it was the work of the Youngun boys because her son, William, Jr., had seen them.

"Your son's a good boy. You tell him that for me, y'hear?" Mr. Palugee shouted through the cracked mouthpiece on the phone. He was too cheap to get it fixed.

"I know he is." Sarah smiled. "I tell him that every day. You just call Rev. Youngun, and tell him what his little hooligans did. It wasn't nice to dump trash on your steps."

"Yeah," Mr. Palugee said, "throwin' good trash around ain't right."

Sarah hung up, not understanding what he meant.

Across town on Devil's Ridge, John found the place where the Youngun boys said they had been attacked by the bat. *There's got to be a cave of' em 'round here someplace.*

John was afraid. He turned quickly at a sound behind him. "Just the wind," he whispered.

Usually not one to be afraid, John slowed down his breathing to take back control of his body. Slowly the goose bumps went away.

He remembered what the old Sioux guide had taught him in Wisconsin: To hunt well, you have to show no fear. Be in control like the owl. He sits in the tree and hoots, scaring the rabbits, because they can't see him. When they panic and run to the owl, they become his meal for the night.

A shadow crossed in front of him. John looked up and saw the biggest bat he'd ever seen flying slowly through the woods.

He tried to get a clear shot, but the bat had no pattern to its flight. All John could do was follow its zigzagging trail. He lost sight of it within minutes.

Got to find that bat . . . and its cave, John thought, standing on the edge of the ravine. *Then I'll trap these sick 'coons and whatever else is bringin' death to my woods. I'll hunt 'em like the owl does.*

30

Vaccine

Mary Lou left Dr. Moore's office and took the precious vaccine to the Springfield train station. *We should send more,* she thought. *That doctor in Mansfield paid more than enough.*

She thought about Dr. Moore's penchant for profit and felt dirty. Charging so much for medicine to save someone's life didn't seem right to her. *Profiting from misery shouldn't be allowed.*

At the station, she watched the train master take the package. "Handle that carefully," she said. "That's gonna save a little girl's life."

"I'll treat it like a baby," he said. "Just hope the boys on the train do the same."

"Will you say something to them for me?" she asked. "Without it, there's no hope."

"What happened? Some girl sick or somethin'?"

"Somethin'," Mary Lou nodded. "Somethin' like rabies."

"Rabies! Where she live?" he asked, looking at the package. "Mansfield! They got rabies down in Mansfield?"

"Just this case is all that I know of."

The train master guffawed. "Heck, where there's one there'll be a pack of 'em."

"Just make sure this gets there safely, please," she pleaded.

"We'll do our best. I'm just glad you warned me 'bout the rabies down thataway. I don't want none of my boys out takin' a smoke and gettin' bitten by some crazed animal."

After Mary Lou had left, the train master took the box to the shipping room. "Nathan, you make sure this box gets on the afternoon train headin' east, you hear?"

Nathan nodded. "I'll put it right here," he said, indicating the area marked "Eastbound." "Heard 'bout the storms they've been havin' over thataway?"

The train master thought for a moment. "Read somethin' about an inch or so of rain fallin'."

"Roads are like a swamp the load haulers tell me."

"Trains run on rails. They always get through."

Back in Mansfield, Sammy Lester burned with fever.

He felt like tearing at his hands, pulling at his face. It was a feeling so powerful that it scared him.

He couldn't shake his headache. He groaned, feeling his forehead. His jaws ached, so he moved his teeth up and down to loosen the joints. Drool slithered down the corners of his mouth.

Maybe I need a drink. He reached into his pockets, but he couldn't find any money. After searching through his dirty room, he came up empty-handed.

Sammy sat on the bed. *What am I gonna do?*

Then he remembered his fish shocker. *Bet it's still down under the Willow Creek Bridge. I'll just get it and shock enough fish for one drink. Just one drink. That's all I need. Then I'll get me some dinner. Maybe a home-cooked meal at Mom's Cafe . . . that'll do me good.*

Putting on his hat sideways and not bothering to change the clothes he'd slept in, Sammy stumbled down from his room above the barn.

"Looks like Sammy's drunk again," Billy Watkins said. He owned the rooming house and had spent his life renting to the down-and-outers who passed through.

"Don't think he's drunk," his brother Jack said. "Looks sick to me."

"He's a boozer. You can see it in his eyes," Billy said. "They all look sick."

Sammy's eyes ached and his head pounded. His throat was parched, but now he didn't want to drink. He tried to lick his lips, but there wasn't enough spit to wet them, let alone lick off the crust that had caked on the corners.

He raced up the hill behind the barn, trying to outrun the pain. *O God, make me better! Make it go away!*

On the hill above town, Sammy couldn't stand the pain any longer and screamed out in agony. The sound echoed over the town, like animal howls, bouncing off buildings and across the ravine.

Not knowing where he was going, he stumbled through the woods, across the south fork field, and ended up in the county graveyard across from the Methodist church. He lay panting against a tombstone, trying to pull himself together.

"Rise and shine!" Edgar Allan Crow squawked, sitting on the tombstone next to him.

"Get outta here," Sammy said with a gravelly voice.

The crow flew away, leaving Sammy to his misery.

Sammy Lester was dying. And there was nothing he could do except die one painful inch at a time. The disease was taking control.

All he wished for was to be a little boy again with his parents. Back on the prairie. Back before his life became consumed by alcohol.

In his mind he wasn't lying in a graveyard. He was sitting in his mother's wildflower garden, waiting for a piece of pull candy.

31

Terry's Poem

❖

Rev. Youngun sat at his desk and worried about Sherry. Grand-doc had called, and he was relieved that Dangit was all right. But then Mr. Palugee had called, accusing the boys of dumping a sack of trash on his front steps.

Rev. Youngun tried to assure him that his boys hadn't done it, but Mr. Palugee had gotten it firsthand from Sarah Bentley that her son, William, had seen his boys do it.

Rev. Youngun thought about calling Sarah but decided it would be a waste of time. No matter what he said, she was going to believe her son.

I just hope my boys didn't do it. He sighed. *But I'll still have to send them over to Mr. Palugee's house to make their peace.*

He went upstairs to check on Sherry, glad that the vaccine was on its way from Springfield. She burned with fever. He knew that any delay in getting that vaccine would be fatal.

When Larry and Terry got home, Rev. Youngun stopped them at the door. "I'm glad Dangit's okay, but we've all got to pray for Sherry."

"What's wrong, Pa?" Larry asked.

He told them that Dr. George thought she might have rabies from what looked like a bat bite.

"We saw it, Pa!" Terry exclaimed.

"You saw what?"

"We saw the monster bat that bit Sherry. It looked like Dracula!" Terry said.

"Where?" he asked. If they could catch it, they'd know whether it was sick.

"Up on Devil's Ridge," Larry said. "It swooped down and tried to bite Terry and me."

"But I saved Larry when I hit it with the rock," Terry said proudly.

Rev. Youngun was quiet for a moment, then said, "If we had the bat, we'd know if it had rabies."

"Bet it did, Pa," Larry said without thinking. They told him about the porcupine attack, and how the bat didn't seem to have any fear of humans either.

"Is Sherry gonna be all right?" Terry asked.

"If she gets the vaccine in time, Dr. George says she'll probably make it."

"Is she gonna die, Pa?" Larry asked, tears suddenly welling up.

"God willing she won't, son."

Terry looked at his father. "How'd she catch the bees?"

"Rabies," Larry corrected.

"She was telling the truth when she said a bat bit her," Rev. Youngun admitted, feeling ashamed that he hadn't believed his own daughter.

Terry felt a bad feeling coming over him. Like he was going to suffocate. *I gotta tell her before she dies,* he whimpered to himself. He raced toward the stairs.

"Where you going?" his father asked.

But Terry didn't answer. He crept slowly into Sherry's room, his heart beating with the pain of a guilty conscience. "Sherry . . . you 'wake?"

Sherry turned halfway over in the bed. "What do you want?" she said weakly.

"Just wanted to tell you I'm sorry for sayin' you're crazy and makin' fun of your angel."

Sherry was taken aback. "Are you feelin' okay?"

Terry nodded in the darkened room. "Pa said you might die so I wanted to tell you 'fore it was too late."

"Do you really believe in my angel?" she whispered.

Terry looked at her drawn, pale face. "I do 'cause you do," he said quietly.

"Don't believe you." She smiled weakly. "You're just sayin' that 'cause Pa told you to."

"No . . . I just felt like sayin' it," Terry said. *She looks real sick,* he worried. He shivered with fear of what might happen.

"What's got into you?" she asked.

"Just things," he mumbled, then ran from the room. He pulled up the sheets of his bed and took out his candy stash. He ran back to Sherry's room and handed it to her.

"What's this?" she asked weakly. "It's your candy." She looked at him with a questioning look.

"It's for your trip."

"My trip?" she asked.

Terry shrugged. "Wouldn't want you to go flyin' up to heaven hungry . . . and I wouldn't want you sittin' up there with God, tellin' on me."

Sherry laughed so hard that the cloth fell off her forehead. "Hurts to laugh," she whispered, beginning to cough.

"And here's two cents," he said, pulling the pennies out of his pocket.

"What's that for?" she asked.

"To go toward your shoes." He smiled.

"Thought you didn't like me," she said.

"Never said that," Terry responded.

"Did so . . . in those mean poems you're always sayin' 'bout me."

"Made up a nice poem for you," he said.

"You did? Tell it to me."

"I'll tell it to you later," he said, not expecting her to want to hear it.

"No, tell me now," she whispered.

Terry was in a spot. He hadn't really made up a poem. "No, I'll come back."

"Please . . . tell it to me."

Terry thought for a moment. *Let's see. I need somethin' to rhyme with sky.*

Roses are red,
Blue is the sky,
Sherry's goin' to heaven,
'Cause she's gonna die.

Terry shook his head. *No, can't say that. Let's see, what rhymes with red? And he thought:*

Girls are dumb,
And roses are red,
Please forgive me,
Before you're dead.

"What are you thinkin' 'bout?" Sherry coughed. "Tell me the poem you made up for me. Is it a nice one?"

Terry nodded. "It's so nice that you won't believe it," he said, wishing he hadn't gotten himself into this mess.

"I don't believe you made one up anyway." She pouted.

"Did too," Terry said, then held up his hands.

"Little Wings, Little Wings,
Please guard this bed,
Put God's blessings,
On Sherry's head."

"That's pretty," she whispered, touched by his words.

Better leave while I'm ahead, he thought. "I worked on it all day. Sweated up my brain thinkin' 'bout you."

"I better sleep now," she said. Terry started to tiptoe out but stopped when Sherry asked, "Is Dangit here? I wanna pet him."

"He's at Granddoc's. Got quilled by a porky-pine and she's keepin' him till mornin'."

"Wish I could see him," she whispered, then turned toward the wall, sticking her thumb back in her mouth. It wasn't long before she dozed off.

Terry went back downstairs to the living room, straight into the accusations from Mr. Palugee. His father looked at him and said, "And Mr. Palugee said that Willy said—"

Terry shook his head. "We didn't do it, Pa."

"Yeah, you can see Mr. John and ask him," Larry said. "We were up in the woods lettin' the skunks go, just like you told us to."

Rev. Youngun put his hands on their shoulders. "I want you to go tell that to Mr. Palugee. Willy told him—"

Terry interrupted again. "I told you that wart's a fibber. I bet it was him that did it."

"He is a fibber, Pa, honest," Larry said.

"Why would he do that?" Rev. Youngun asked.

"To get us in trouble," Terry said. "He acts like a Goody Two-shoes, but he'd rather climb a tree full of bumblebees than tell the truth."

"Son," Rev. Youngun said, putting his hand on Terry's shoulder, "maybe you need to look into your heart and—"

"And then go punch him," Terry said, crossing his arms.

"There will be no fighting," Rev. Youngun counseled.

"We don't want to fight . . . but we didn't do it," Larry said.

"Our family name is involved," Rev. Youngun said.

"Pa," Larry said, "didn't you tell us that you got to stand up for things you believe in?"

"Yes," Rev. Youngun nodded, knowing his own words were about to be used against him—again.

"Well, if we don't stand and call him a fibber, then we won't be upholdin' the family name."

"Yeah, people will be callin' us the chicken family . . . or Rev. Fibber's kids and—"

"Maybe so," his father said. "But I want you both to go tell Mr. Palugee what you've told me."

"Don't you believe us, Pa?" Larry said, his eyes wide.

"Of course I do. It's just that the proper thing to do is to go tell him that you didn't do it."

"Why can't we call him?" Terry asked.

"Because I want you to go see him in person."

"Why can't we send him a letter? Or a telegraph message?" Terry pressed. "I hate goin' near his junkyard. It's got a jinx on me."

"Because," Rev. Youngun said with exasperation in his voice, "I want you to go tell him you didn't do it."

"Please, Pa. He hates kids," Terry pleaded.

Rev. Youngun shook his head. "He's an old man. Maybe there's something you can do around his house to help him."

"You mean like burn the place down," Terry said, scuffing his shoe against the floor.

"Terry, not another word like that out of you!" Rev. Youngun exclaimed. Larry turned his face to hide his smile. "And Larry, I want you to go do what I ask. Take Terry with you."

"Mr. Palugee's house is creepy, Pa," Larry said.

Terry jumped up and down. "Mr. Palugee's place is a mess, Pa. You can't even call it a rattrap 'cause rats wouldn't live there."

Rev. Youngun smiled. "Go on into town, and do what I've asked you to do. And mind your p's and q's when you're talking to him."

"P's and q's?" Terry huffed. "Those letters are probably lost somewhere in his junk pile."

Rev. Youngun pushed Terry toward the door. "You just go and be polite to Mr. Palugee. He'll probably call Mrs. Bentley and tell her everything you say."

"Good," Terry huffed, "'cause I'm gonna tell him to go see Willy the wart and put the blame on him."

"You'll do no such thing. Now go clean up and hang your wet towels on the bar," Rev. Youngun said, pointing toward the bathroom.

"Ain't never heard nothin' sillier," Terry pouted.

"What's that?" his father asked.

"Cleanin' up to go to a junkyard. Doesn't make sense to me."

Rev. Youngun took a deep breath. "You only get one chance to make a good first impression in life. Now go on, and wash the sweat out from behind your ears. This is just a slice of life you'll have to live with."

As Terry went up the stairs, he whispered to Larry, "It's a slice of baloney, if you ask me."

"What'd you say, young man?" his father called.

"I just asked Larry if he was hungry, Pa."

I'll bet, Rev. Youngun sighed, counting the years until Terry would turn eighteen.

32

J. J.

❖

Granddoc went in to check on Dangit who was starting to wake up. "How you feeling, boy?" she asked.

Dangit wagged his tail and moaned. "Hurts, doesn't it?" She smiled, checking on the quill wounds. "You got yourself a heap of scabs, you know it?"

Setting down bowls of water and food, she heard the phone ring upstairs and hurried to answer it without locking the cage. Dangit looked at the open cage door and stepped out. He looked around the basement, saw the opened window above the lab table, and jumped out.

J.J. McAlister, the dogcatcher, drove his wagon slowly along the muddy east roads near Granddoc's. There had been reports of wild dogs roaming the farm area, and the farmers were worried that they would kill their livestock.

At the crest of the hill, J.J. saw Gordo and three other wild dogs coming through the field to his left; he saw another dog running away from Granddoc's house. He brought the wagon to a halt on the side of the road, careful not to get it stuck in a mud rut. He got out, carrying his long net.

Hanging from his hip was a pistol. The sheriff had made fun of his pistol, but J.J. wanted protection. Now he was glad he had it.

Creeping along the edge of the underbrush where it wasn't so muddy, J.J. surprised the four wild dogs, netting one immediately. "Got you!" he shouted, holding the net over the snarling, wild animal.

Gordo charged at J.J., but the dogcatcher managed a lucky kick in the dog's belly. The other dogs circled around, waiting for the chance to attack. They were mangy, sick-looking animals, with wild eyes and foam-crusted lips.

J.J. took the pistol from his hip and shot the first one that came at him. Gordo charged again and for the first time, J.J. noticed a collar under the big hound's matted hair. The third wild dog sprang at him, but J.J. managed to wound it.

Standing over the wounded one, he looked down, knowing that the animal had the sickness. "I'm doin' you a favor," he said as he shot the animal. He did the same to the one in his net.

Gordo ran off into the woods, howling for revenge. J.J. watched it run off. *Someone's huntin' dog's gone crazy with rabies . . . not even house dogs are safe.*

As he put the dead animals on his truck to be burned, he saw Dangit peeking out from behind the bushes.

"Another one!" he shouted. "Come here, boy," J.J. said, moving carefully forward with the net in one hand and the pistol in the other.

This one looks like a house dog too. Kind of looks familiar, he thought, but he wasn't able to place where he'd seen the dog.

Dangit backed away. J.J. saw the scabs all over his body. *This one's got the sickness too,* he decided.

Dangit was still weak and confused from the medicine that Grand-doc had given him. Within a minute, he was locked into the back of the truck.

J.J. looked at him as he snapped the cage lock shut. "County law says I got to hold you for forty-eight hours. If nobody claims you, then you're dead. And if somebody claims you, they'll have to prove that you don't have rabies. Only Granddoc can do that."

He peered into the cage. "You look like one sick dog to me." Dangit just moaned as he was driven toward the animal disposal farm.

As J.J.'s wagon clumped through town, leaving mud clods behind it, Mom looked out and shivered. She knew what would probably happen to any animals it carried.

Hambone came up and watched the slow-moving wagon move

down Main Street. "A dog's life ain't all it's cracked up to be," he said solemnly. "Anybody want some rooster fries?" he called out.

"You're nuts," joked Stephen Scales, who'd stopped in to drink coffee.

"Not me, them." Hambone laughed, putting a plate down on the table.

He turned to Mom and continued their discussion. "I still think we oughta pay Rev. Youngun *somethin'* for marryin' us. Skunks weren't his fault."

"No. And don't you be slippin' him any money when I'm not lookin'."

Ain't right, Hambone thought. *We owe him for that weddin'.*

On the other side of town, Dangit saw Terry and Larry walking toward Mr. Palugee's house. From his cage in the wagon he wagged his tail and barked, trying to get their attention.

"Shut up!" J.J. snapped, hitting the cage with his stick.

Dangit moaned, but the boys didn't hear him.

33

Back to the Junkyard

❖

Mr. Palugee busied himself with his new bag of finds. The trash bag those Youngun boys had dumped on his front steps contained all kinds of goodies.

"Bet I can find a use for this," he beamed, holding up a bent fork. He dug around in the bag some more, then broke into a big smile. "Oh, happy day," he sang out, holding up the broken dentures. "This will save me if I need false teeth."

Humming while he poked through the trash, he blinked twice, then reached through a pile of mushy fruit rinds. "Look at this!" he gasped, holding up a piece of string. "This is what I really need!"

He took the string and knotted it onto the big ball he'd been saving for years. What had begun as a hobby had developed into an obsession. And every time he found a new piece, he thought of a new use.

"Let's see. I can use my string ball to . . . to . . . tie up fifty bags of stuff."

Collecting string had led to saving everything else. Cans, bottles, wire, signs . . . whatever he found and liked, he saved. And since he saved it all, everything was everywhere.

But he didn't want any visitors. Guests were about as welcome as dead fish, which was why he was so bothered by those town kids sneaking around his place.

Willy saw Larry and Terry walking toward Mr. Palugee's and followed them, hiding in the bushes. *I bet they're goin' to blame me for that bag of trash. But no one saw me do it.* He smiled. *And no one believes the Younguns. Everyone knows that preachers' kids are bad.*

He chuckled to himself over the burning bag of droppings he had left on the porch. *That was the funniest thing I've ever seen. Mr. Palugee came runnin' out when I rang the bell. When he saw the fire, he just began stompin' and stompin', makin' the biggest mess I've ever seen.*

Willy giggled in the bushes next to Mr. Palugee's property. *And when I put that bag of trash on his porch, I thought he was goin' to have a heart attack.*

While Willy spied on the Younguns, he tried to think of another way to get them in trouble. *Maybe I should tell Palugee they tried to steal his precious string ball.* Willy laughed to himself. *Silly old coot, he'll believe anythin' I tell him 'bout those Younguns.*

Terry looked around at the mess in Mr. Palugee's yard. "He must be waitin' for a flood."

"Why's that?" Larry asked.

"'Cause this old fool's been savin' for a rainy day all his life. Must think he's Noah Junior or somethin'."

"That ain't nice," Larry frowned, not liking any joking around with the Bible.

"And this place is a dump," Terry said, kicking a broken flowerpot off the stairs. "And what's he need a double-decker privy for anyhow?"

"I don't know." Larry shrugged.

"There's only one of him so he can't sit on more than one hole at a time. Don't make sense." Terry thought for a moment, then laughed. "Maybe one's for number one and one's for number two. What do you think?"

"I think you're a goof." Larry knocked on the door, lightly first, then a little harder. "Wonder where he is?"

Terry picked up a broken bird feeder. "Maybe he's out robbin' trash cans or stealin' broken bottles or somethin'."

"You better hope he doesn't hear you." Larry frowned.

"Who cares? He already doesn't like us. You think I care what this pack rat thinks?"

"But Pa said—"

"Pa said to tell him we didn't do it. So let's just tell it to the door and go home," Terry said.

Larry looked through the dirty window. He couldn't believe what he saw. "Look at this," he whispered.

Terry wiped a spot clean and peered in. "Oh, jeeoh," he said, "It looks like the underside of my bed."

It was worse. Piles of newspapers lay everywhere. Stacks of magazines sat on what appeared to be chairs. What was once the sofa held two old sinks and a mattress. On the stairs lay mounds of unmatched shoes.

"Looks like a junk jungle," Terry whispered, amazed at how anybody could live in such a mess. *Even I couldn't live like that.*

"Folks say he's strange," Larry said quite seriously.

"Strange?" Terry laughed. "He's lost his marbles! Matter of fact," he said, picking up another broken flowerpot, "he's about as cracked as this." He tossed it over his shoulder.

"Don't, he'll hear you!" Larry said sternly.

"He probably can't hear nothin' 'cause he's got broken ol' hearin' horns stuck in his ears."

"You're worse than ignorant," Larry said. "Maybe he's around back. Come on, let's get this over with," he said, heading for the side of the house.

Terry tagged along, mumbling, "He's playin' privy peekaboo."

"Ssshhh, he might hear you," Larry whispered.

They made their way past two broken iceboxes, an upturned plow, an old Conestoga wagon, and a broken gas lamp. The Younguns didn't see Willy creeping behind them.

They've really had it this time! Willy snickered under his breath.

Mr. Palugee sat on his homemade throne in the backyard, looking over his treasures. *A man's home is his castle,* he mused. *And what a castle I have. My father was right. One man's trash is another man's treasure.*

He truly loved all the junk he'd saved and was happiest when he could sit in the middle of it, thinking of all the things he could do with it if he ever got the time. But time was precious to Mr. Palugee, because when he wasn't tinkering with his junk, he was scouring the trash dump and back roads, looking for good things to bring home.

Terry was the first to see him through the back window. "There's king quack, sittin' on his throne." Larry nudged him to hush, but Terry only nudged back. "The only thing Mr. Palugee hasn't saved are his marbles, 'cause I got 'em," he winked, pulling two cat's-eye marbles from his pocket.

Palugee saw them whispering in the yard. "Get outta here!" he screamed. He jumped up from his seat and stomped to the door.

"Let's do what the man says," Terry whispered, spinning around.

Larry caught him by the waist of his pants and held him in place. "We came to talk to you," Larry said as the door swung open. "Tell you our side of the story."

"I don't want to talk to anyone. Just go away," Mr. Palugee said.

"Let's do what he says," Terry whispered. "He's a cuckoo bird."

"Can't. Pa said we have to tell him we didn't do it."

Terry turned toward Mr. Palugee and whispered, "We didn't do it." Then he turned back to Larry. "Okay, we did it. Now, let's get outta here."

"Mr. Palugee," Larry called out, stepping forward. "Our pa said we had to come tell you that we didn't put that trash on your front steps."

"That's not what William Bentley, Jr., said," Mr. Palugee shouted, looking around to see if there were any other children invading his domain.

"That wart's a fibber," Terry shouted out.

"What was that?" Mr. Palugee asked.

Larry clamped his hand over Terry's mouth. "What Willy said ain't the truth, Mr. Palugee. We were out in the woods with Mr. John and—"

Mr. Palugee shook his head in a condescending way. "Mrs. Bentley assured me that her son was tellin' the truth."

"And I assure you he's a liar," Terry said, putting his hands on his hips.

Palugee sighed. "*I* believe what he says."

"Believe that, and your house ain't a junkyard," Terry mumbled, looking at the water bugs swimming in the rainwater that had collected in the old washbasin.

"Did you say somethin', boy?" Mr. Palugee asked.

"That Willy must have seen someone else in your yard," Terry said without blinking.

Larry rolled his eyes, always amazed at his brother's quick thinking. "Anyway, we just come to tell you that we didn't do it."

"And I didn't put that burnin' bag of DDD on your porch," Terry added.

"DDD?" Palugee said, perplexed.

"Yeah, dog doo-doo," Terry said. "Willy did that, and I'll bet he put that trash on your steps too."

"Mrs. Bentley said you'd probably accuse her son of that," Mr. Palugee answered, shaking his head, grinning at their audacity.

Willy came running around the side of the house. "Mr. Palugee, Mr. Palugee!"

"What is it, William?"

"The Younguns opened your front door and tried to take your ball of string and—"

Mr. Palugee's face went livid. "My string! My precious string! You little devils stay away from my property!"

"We didn't do nothin'!" Terry shouted.

Larry just shook his head. "I don't believe this!"

Mr. Palugee ran around the house and found his ball of string stuck in the front doorway. Willy looked at the Younguns and smiled. "You're in trouble now."

"You're a fibber," Larry said, eyeing Willy.

"And you're a chicken," Willy mocked, sticking out his tongue.

Terry gave him the evil eye. "I think we ought to hang him by the ankles from the top privy hole and—"

Willy backed away. "I'm gonna tell my ma."

Terry jumped on Willy's back and pulled his hair. Willy howled in pain, sobbing, "Don't hurt me!"

"You tell Mr. Palugee the truth!" Terry screamed, shaking the boy's head.

"Mr. Palugee!" Willy wailed. "Help me!"

"Stop it, Terry," Larry said, trying to pull them apart. "He's just a crybaby."

Mr. Palugee came toward them. "You bullies! Two against one! I'm goin' to call your father right now!" he said loudly, then turned to go back inside to find the phone.

Larry closed his eyes, while Willy rubbed his head. "I hope your pa spanks the tar outta you," Willy sneered.

Terry held up a handful of Willy's hair. "And I hope you go bald, you wart."

"We didn't do nothin'," Larry said coldly. "You're just lyin' to get us in trouble."

"It's my word against yours." Willy laughed.

"And it'll be my fist against your face," Terry said, starting forward.

"No, Terry," Larry said. "Pa said we shouldn't fight."

"I ain't fightin'," Terry said, throwing air punches at Willy. "I just want to step on a cockroach."

"You boys better leave now," Mr. Palugee called from the house. "I told Sarah Bentley what you did."

"Why'd you call her?" Terry asked defensively, scoring a knock-out air punch in his mind.

"Because she knows what to do about you two hooligans," Mr. Palugee said, trying to stand between the boys and what he felt was an extremely valuable broken lantern.

"But we didn't *do* anything, Mr. Palugee," Larry said. "Willy's makin' it up."

"William? I don't think so," Mr. Palugee said, looking fondly toward the little deceiver. "Now, you boys leave and don't you take anythin'."

"Mr. Palugee," Larry said, looking around at all the junk in the yard. "You've got nothin' to worry about."

Terry started to leave, then turned. "Say, Mr. Palugee . . . ."

"Yes," the old man said cautiously.

"Why do you save all this stuff?"

Mr. Palugee thought for a moment, then said, "Some things are worth keeping."

Terry scratched his head. "Some things, yes, but everythin'?"

Palugee shook his head. "Not everythin'. But I save the things I like. You'll understand it one day."

"You like livin' this way?"

"It's the way I want to live my life," Palugee said. "Now go on, get outta here."

"Let's get home," Larry sighed.

"I was just askin'," Terry said defensively. As he passed by Willy, he whispered, "See you 'round, wart."

34

U.S. Angel Mail

❖

Teddy Walters, the postman, picked up the mail from the Younguns' postbox. As was his habit, he glanced at the letters to see where they were going.

"What's this?" he wondered, looking at Sherry's crudely written envelope:

LilTle WIngs
Hev-van
Frm Sherry

Teddy had seen all kinds of letters addressed to Santa, but this was the first one he was supposed to deliver to heaven. Getting back on his horse, he rode around the bend to the Springers' house.

He waved to Maurice, who was up on a ladder repairing a broken screen on the side of the house. "What you doin' up there?"

"Just keepin' the bugs out," Maurice said.

"You be careful on that ladder," Eulla Mae called out. "What's the news, Teddy?" She was churning butter from her rocker and thinking about life.

"Oh, a little of this, a little bit of that, and a whole lot of mud," Teddy said, kicking the mud off his shoes.

"Heard any good gossip?" She winked.

"Heard that Sally Berry is havin' another baby."

"That's six in six years." Eulla Mae whistled.

Teddy got down off his horse. "Say, let me show you somethin' cute," he said, pulling out Sherry's letter to Little Wings. He handed it to Eulla Mae.

A loud noise came from the back of the house. "Did you hear somethin'?" Teddy asked.

"Just Maurice. He's always makin' noise." Eulla Mae looked at the child's writing on the envelope and turned it over. "How you gonna deliver this?"

"On a wing and a prayer." He laughed.

"Really, don't you think you ought to open it? Might be she's got a problem that her daddy needs to know about."

"Can't. If I open it, I could get in trouble," Teddy said seriously.

Eulla Mae looked at the letter, dying to know what was inside. "What about if *I* open it?" she asked.

"Ain't supposed to let nobody but the addressee do that," Teddy said matter-of-factly.

"Well, unless you're the U.S. Angel Mail, this letter will just end up in a trash can down at the post office."

"Not necessarily. We save a lot of the cute ones to show people," Teddy said.

"Same thing. If this girl's got a problem, then no one will ever know." She started to open the letter, but Teddy reached out to stop her.

"You're not supposed to do that!"

"She's sendin' it to me."

"Your name's not Little Wings."

"It is now." She smiled, taking out the letter. "Now you go on about your route and leave me to my heavenly duties."

"Ain't you gonna tell me what it says?"

"Why should I? Letters are private." She gave him a smug grin.

Teddy mounted his horse and looked at Eulla Mae. "Next time I hear any gossip, I'm gonna keep it to myself."

"So will I," Eulla Mae said, "See you tomorrow, Teddy."

From behind the house, Maurice called out, "Honey, could you come 'round here?"

"All right, hold on," she said, setting the churn handle back down.

She found Maurice sitting on the roof, but the ladder had fallen to the ground. "What you doin' up there?"

Maurice frowned. "I'm lookin' for a cloud with a silver linin' . . . what you think I'm doin' up here?" he said, his face flustered.

"Maurice, you come down here. I want to show you somethin'."

"That's fine. Just put up the ladder, and I'll come right down . . . or do you want me to jump?"

After a half hour of trying to figure out what the pictures and symbols in the letter meant, Maurice grinned. "Rev. Youngun told me 'bout her believin' in an angel she calls Little Wings."

"But what does the letter *say?*" Eulla Mae asked in frustration. "I can't figure it out."

Maurice took the letter and put it in his pocket. "I'll just go ask her."

"But then she'll know you read the letter."

"No, I know how to find things out from those kids," he said, heading off toward the Younguns' house.

But as he crested the hill between their properties, he saw a huge black bat flying toward Devil's Ridge. "Bet that's the same one I saw before," he muttered. "Shouldn't be out durin' the day."

Suddenly, he felt a shiver go up his spine. "My daddy used to tell me, 'Beware when the night animals come out in the light of day.'"

The sky darkened over the hills. Maurice pulled up his collar and hurried to get to the Younguns' before the rain hit. Stormy weather was coming.

35

Under Siege

❖

Back at Mom's Cafe, the talk was solemn. The mood was one of a town under siege. Word had spread fast about Sherry and the raccoon and the dog attacks. Some whispered about John having to shoot Cody, and about a big bat that had been seen in broad daylight. The cafe patrons were nervous.

Mom and Hambone had started arguing again about paying Rev. Youngun a marrying fee, so things were tense between them as well. They continued to argue as Mom started a fresh pot of coffee behind the counter.

"Man's got kids. Just think 'bout it, honey," Hambone whispered, trying to calm her down.

Dr. George came in and ordered a cup of coffee. Mom set it down and walked away. Hambone shuffled over. "Heard 'bout that little Sherry. She gonna make it?"

Sipping the coffee, Dr. George closed his eyes for a moment, then said, "I've been praying all day. Praying that the vaccine gets here in time."

Hambone went to the back room and came back with a foul-looking mixture in a glass. He set it down in front of the doctor.

"What's that?" Dr. George asked.

"My health tonic. My grandfather drank this every New Year's Eve and lived to ninety-eight."

"What's in it?" Dr. George asked uneasily, seeing something staring at him from inside the glass.

Hambone laughed. "Drink a pig's eyeball and castor oil, and it'll cure all your ills," Hambone drank it down, while Dr. George gagged. "Don't let him bother you none, Doc," Mom laughed,

Dr. George tried to smile. "I wish curing rabies was that easy."

At the Younguns', Sherry rolled over in bed, burning with fever. "Dangit . . . I want to pet Dangit."

Her father stood at the doorway, trying to decide whether he should call Granddoc and go get the dog. He decided against it for the moment and changed the cloth on Sherry's head.

At the county animal disposal farm, J.J. put the body of another dog that had been sick into a burlap feed bag and started out to the burning pit. Passing by a squat, brown dog that was moaning, J.J. said, "Nobody's gonna claim you. You're too old." He kept walking.

In the next cage, Dangit lay in the corner and watched the man walk by and waited. Why didn't the kids come to take him home? The fat brown dog put its paw through the cage onto Dangit's head, and they began moaning together.

The phone rang in Granddoc's kitchen. It was Rev. Youngun. She assured him that it would be best to come get Dangit in the morning, after the dog had slept through the night.

Granddoc went to the top of the basement stairs. "Howl if you need something," she called out to Dangit.

But nobody heard her.

36

Fish Shocker

Sammy Lester gulped, hardly able to swallow. The woods and the hills seemed different. Nothing was the same. Mud was everywhere. His hands and neck burned, and he could hardly stand up straight. He felt as if he had been beaten up while he was drunk and then caught the flu.

He couldn't remember why he'd left his room in the first place. All he could remember was that it had something to do with water.

But it seemed as if he'd roamed for hours. *What's wrong with me?*

Sammy stood on the rise of the small hill, just north of the Willow Creek Bridge, and looked at the traces of sunlight sneaking through the clouds. For a moment he was back on the great fenceless prairies, back before he became addicted to alcohol, back when he was a young boy traveling with his parents.

He closed his eyes, wiping the sweat from his forehead. *Pa used to stand me on the fence posts around our claim, and we'd watch the wind race across the summer grasses.*

I remember how pretty the monarch butterflies were, jumping around like little pixies. Tall grasses all around me, prairie flowers everywhere, the whole world like a colorful pioneer quilt.

I used to pick Ma bouquets of sweet williams. Big bunches of the wild blossoms. They looked like little purple flags. The creek bottoms were covered with 'em. Found 'em as we walked to church and . . .

Sammy began crying. Big, heaving sobs. *I'm crying like a baby*, he thought. *A grown man, crying like a baby . . . over flowers.*

He didn't know why he was sick. All he knew was that he hurt all over, was confused, and wished he had a drink of whiskey to dull the pain. A wave of dizziness overtook him, and he was back standing on that fence post beside his father.

"Little Sammy, look out there."

"Yes, Pa," the boy said, looking out over the sea of endless land. A prairie chicken flew by.

"Look out and tell me what you see."

"Flat land," the boy said.

His father laughed. "Looks flat, but there's a fine roll to the land that's like the big ocean back east. It's always got some motion to it."

Sammy looked. "All the grass seems to be runnin', Pa."

"That's right. The prairie never rests. It's always tellin' you to get on with your business."

His father pointed out scenery around them. "Look over there by that prairie pothole. There's blazing star, black Samsons, and over there's some pasqueflower, and up yonder is some butterfly milkweed and compass plant."

"How do you know all that?"

"Son, what you're lookin' at is the lawn of God. With the way the homesteaders are breakin' it up, it ain't gonna be here one day."

"Pa, there's 'nough here for everyone on earth to have a piece."

His father laughed. "Boy, one day you'll understand what land-hungry and money-hungry people will do to everythin' beautiful if you let 'em. It's human nature and I don't know why God put it in us humans to be like that."

His father put his arm around the little boy and said, "Sammy, it's just too bad that Mother Nature's good things can't last forever. But you remember what I'm tellin' you. When the prairie is all gone and the buffalo are only memories, it'll take another heaven and earth 'fore it'll all come back. God spent seven days puttin' it together; it's a shame we can't spend seven days plannin' how to save it all."

Sammy shaded his eyes from the sun and looked out over the subtle roll in the land. "Can we save anythin', Pa?"

"Sometimes we get so all fired up in doin' what we're doin' that we can't even save ourselves."

Sammy looked at his father, then all of a sudden the young boy caught a glimpse of a broken-down drunk who could barely stand on his own two feet—the broken-down man he would become.

Frightened, Sammy Lester ran screaming through the woods, until he had outrun the memories, then he collapsed against a pine tree, panting.

Got to stop thinkin' 'bout the past. Got to remember why I came up around here. Then he remembered. *My fish shocker. That's what I came out to get. Must have had a blackout again,* he thought, rubbing his temples.

Down below on the muddy road Sammy saw the Youngun brothers walking back on the grassy edge from Mr. Palugee's. Without knowing why, he followed them, staying out of sight.

Then a paranoid thought struck him. *Bet they're goin' to steal my fish shocker!* Suddenly he raced ahead through the brush. *Bet they're gonna trade my fish for drinks.*

"Stay away!" he screamed, running toward them and waving his arms wildly.

Larry and Terry looked up, eyes wide. "What was that?" Terry whispered.

Larry saw the flash of a man's arm up on the hill. "Someone's runnin' through the bushes."

"Don't come any farther!" Sammy shouted.

"Look . . . he's up there," Larry said, pointing to the top of the hill.

Sammy paced back and forth, throwing his arms up and down. "It's that Lester man," Terry said.

"Who?"

"That bottle brother Pa cleaned up."

"Looks like he's drunk again," Larry said.

Sammy suddenly stopped and forgot what he was worried about. He looked at the boys, then ran off screaming, back toward town.

Larry shivered. "Somethin's wrong with that guy. I hope someone helps him."

"Drinkin' must do somethin' terrible to you," Terry said.

"Let's get outta here," Larry said, running off down the path.

At the Willow Creek Bridge, they stopped to skip rocks. Terry was the first to see it. "What's this?" he asked, picking up the crank and batteries from the old wall phone.

"Looks like a broken phone to me," Larry said.

While Terry fiddled with it, Larry took off his shoes and waded into the water to pick up some more skipping rocks. He stopped and stood on top of the copper wires that connected to the phone.

Terry sat on the bank, tinkering with the broken phone. He didn't know it was Sammy's fish shocker. "Wonder what you do with this thing?" Terry mumbled, cranking the handle.

Suddenly, Larry cried out, "Woo-wow-ow-ohh!"

Terry stopped turning the handle. "What's wrong?" he asked. He was going to say something else, but stopped when he saw his brother's hair standing on end.

"Somethin' shocked me," Larry said, too scared to move.

"Maybe somethin's in your undies bitin' you." Terry shrugged.

He cranked the handle once and again, Larry yelped. "Feels like somethin's nippin' or shockin' me."

"Maybe you stepped on an electric eel." Terry laughed, cranking the handle again, trying to make it turn faster.

"Stop! Oh-wow-oww-no-oh-oh!" Larry screamed, jumping up and down like a dancing chicken.

Terry stopped cranking. "Somethin' wrong with you?"

"Quit doin' what you're doin'," Larry said breathlessly, stepping out of the water.

"I was just crankin' this and . . . " Terry stopped. Fish began floating to the surface in front of them.

"What in tarnation?" Larry gasped.

"I think this thing's a magic fishin' pole or somethin'," Terry said, looking at it with renewed respect. "Bet we could make a million dollars with this thing!"

Larry looked at it. "Let me try it," he said, cranking the handle.

More fish floated to the surface. "Pick up those wires for me," he told his brother. "Let's see what they're connected to."

Terry began pulling in the wires while Larry tried turning the crank again. "Holy moly, ouch, stop, you're killin' me!" Terry screamed.

Larry stopped. "I was just turnin' the crank and . . . " He paused, looking at the crank which went to the batteries which connected to the wires. "When I crank it, it must send a shock through the wires."

"Let's take this over to Willy's and—"

"Stop talkin' like that. That ain't the Bible way."

"Bible don't say nothin' 'bout wirin' up a wart's toes and shockin' the minnows out of him." Terry kicked the sand and thought, *I wish Willy were here. I'd like to wire up his clothes.*

"What should we do with it?" Larry asked.

"Keep it."

"But it doesn't belong to us," Larry said.

"Finders keepers, losers weepers," Terry said, picking up the crank and batteries. "We should take this over to Mr. Palugee's and wire up the bottom seat on Ol' Watch Out Below. Bet we could jolt Mr. Palugee up to the second floor," Terry giggled.

Larry couldn't help but laugh. "I ain't gonna listen to no more of your crazy talk." He tried to sound stern. Larry paused, then said, "Wait a minute. Let's take home some of these fish."

"For what?" Terry said.

"For food," said Larry.

"Good idea." Terry nodded. "No sense in wastin' 'em. Pa can cook it real nice with cornmeal, and we can have a good meal for once."

Larry frowned. "What will we tell Pa? How do we say we got the fish?"

Terry shrugged. "The truth. We were down here and the things just popped to the surface."

Larry shook his head. "He'll never believe that. He'll think we're up to something."

"Nope," said Terry, "he'll see that we're gonna eat real food for a couple of days. Come on, let's get these fish loaded."

Larry and Terry pulled in the slippery fish and managed to wrap them up securely enough in their jackets. Then they looked at the fish shocker.

"You carry the wires," Terry said to his brother, putting the crank and batteries under his arm.

"Sure," Larry laughed, "so you can shock me again."

Thunder cracked overhead, followed by bolts of lightning crackling over the hills. "We better get home," Larry shouted.

Terry grinned as they ran. *Wonder how Willy'd like it if I wired up his nose and cranked this thing up?*

At the edge of Willow Creek, Sammy Lester gave up looking for his fish shocker. He felt the drops of rain and writhed in agony, wishing he were back on the prairie with his father. "Take me back, God, please!" he shouted.

No one answered except thunder in the distance. *I'm alone at the edge of my life,* he thought, feeling the tears well up in him again. *I'd be better off dead.*

But he wasn't alone in his discomfort. The rabid animals of the hills felt the rain in the air and cringed. The disease had spread, and none of the infected animals liked the rain.

Up on Devil's Ridge, John felt the signs coming at him from all directions, but he kept focused, watching for the bat through the rain. *Raccoons actin' crazy. Wild dogs roamin' the hills. Sick bat bitin' a little girl. Somethin' don't feel right.*

He wiped the rain from his eyes, then blinked. *There it is.* He watched the vampire bat slowly make its way up the hill. *Gonna follow this big bat. Find its cave and burn it out,* John thought, trying to keep the bat in sight. *I knew it would come flying back up to Devil's Ridge. It was only a matter of time.*

Then he saw the cave behind the big boulder that acted as a sort of door. The big bat flew back into the darkness, shaking the water off its wings.

The rain let up a little, so John looked around and found the tree he wanted. Taking out his knife, he began carving from the inspiration he felt.

As the darkened sky broke loose again, John put down his knife. He smoothed away the traces of bark from the message he'd carved from Romans in the blackjack tree near the cave's entrance: "For he who has died has been freed from sin."

He read it over and over until the driving rain blinded his vision. It was too wet to do any cave burning that evening.

37

Rocking Chair Wisdom

Maurice managed to beat the storm and arrived at the Youn-guns' house as the first raindrops fell. He took off his muddy boots and found Rev. Youngun trying to get supper ready.

Without even a word of greeting, Rev. Youngun told Maurice about Sherry's illness and about the vaccine that was on the way.

"Pray it gets here in time," Rev. Youngun said to his friend.

Maurice hugged his shoulders. "Eulla Mae and I'll both be prayin' day and night for that little thing. Just be glad it's comin' by train. I hear the road to Springfield's all but washed out."

"I don't know what I'll do if . . . if . . . it doesn't—"

Maurice shook his head. "Ain't nothin' gonna happen to that sweet little angel. God will take care of her."

Maurice could tell that Rev. Youngun was on the verge of crying, so he excused himself and went up to sit with Sherry in her room.

Sherry lay quietly in her bed, a cool washcloth over her forehead. Maurice opened the door slowly. He didn't want to wake her if she was asleep.

"Hi, Mr. Springer," she said weakly, looking up from under the covers.

"How's my sweet girl?" he asked, trying to be cheerful. *Oh, Lord, she looks sick.*

"Not so good," she said, wincing as if it hurt to talk. "What's bees?"

"Bees? Why, you know what they are."

"I heard Pa tell the boys I might have bees and—"

Maurice didn't smile at the irony. "If you got bees, then you're still my honey. Now you're sick . . . but you're gonna get better."

"Little Wings says I'll like heaven."

Taken aback, Maurice tried not to show his concern. "Heaven's a wonderful place, but there's no need to be thinkin' 'bout goin' there yet. You're gonna be Maurice's little angel here on Earth for years and years to come. Why," he smiled, "I'm gonna even be godfather to your kids when you have 'em."

Sherry giggled and snuggled her little hand into his big one. "And I'll give Pa a hundred-dollar weddin' fee when I get married." She smiled.

"You been wantin' somethin', somethin' special?" Maurice asked, thinking of the letter.

Sherry shrugged, looking out from under the wet cloth on her forehead. "Might."

"And you'd tell ol' Maurice if there was somethin' you wanted special, wouldn't you?"

"Might," Sherry nodded, pushing the damp cloth back up from her left eye.

"And you're about to tell me, ain't you?"

"Might." She smiled.

Maurice sat back, waiting for her to go on, but she didn't say a word. "Well, might you better tell me now, 'cause I've got to send a few prayers up to heaven. Thought you might want me to include a few for you."

Sherry shook her head. "Little Wings already knows what I want."

"How does she know that?"

Sherry smiled. "I sent her a letter to heaven. Told her all 'bout the red shoes in Bedal's store that I want."

"Red shoes," Maurice smiled. "What you want red shoes for?"

The corners of Sherry's mouth dropped. "I ain't never had store-bought shoes before. Only church hand-me-downs. Shoes that other girls wore before me."

"I see," Maurice said, sitting back. "And these shoes is somethin' you've been prayin' for?"

Sherry nodded. "That's why I sent Little Wings the letter. To get me them red shoes."

"But why didn't you ask your pa?"

"I did," Sherry exclaimed, "but Pa don't have any money to even fix the roof. He'd buy 'em if he could . . . I know that. . . . He'd buy 'em if he could." One by one, tears began to slide down her cheeks.

Maurice reached over and hugged her, ignoring Rev. Youngun's warning about not letting her saliva get on him. "There, there," he said, kissing her cheek. "I'm sure that Little Wings will do somethin' for you . . . I'm sure that you'll get them shoes you want."

"Are you sure?" she whispered, squeezing his hand.

"Cross my heart and hope to . . . " he stopped, not wanting to say the last word.

She was too sleepy to care that he didn't finish. The storm pounded on the tin roof over her bedroom. He rocked her to sleep in his arms, thinking about when he could get down to Bedal's.

Got that money hidden back in the barn. I was savin' it for a new shotgun. But this is important. No one's got to know if I help the angels out just a little bit.

Downstairs he heard Rev. Youngun shout for help. "Maurice, please come down here! There's a flood comin' in!"

When Maurice reached the bottom of the stairs, Rev. Youngun was dashing around, trying to catch the leaks. "Get some more pots, quick!" he shouted to Maurice.

Maurice grabbed all that he could find in the kitchen, even pouring the beans out of the pot on the stove. "This ain't right!" Maurice said, holding a coffee cup to catch a fast-dripping leak until Rev. Youngun brought out another pot. "The church ought to fix your roof!"

"Nothing I can do about it," Rev. Youngun said grimly, coming back with a big jar. "Sarah Bentley controls the purse strings at the church."

Maurice took the cup to a new leak that had started near the porch window. "Why don't you and me fix it?"

Rev. Youngun shrugged. "I don't have the money for materials," he replied, a little embarrassed.

"Heck, Reverend, you got enough good will in this town to get anythin' you want on credit."

Rev. Youngun shook his head. "I don't want to go into debt. My father taught me to pay cash for everything."

"But he never expected you to have to swim in your own house," Maurice countered. Another leak began in the corner. "You're gonna need more pots or we might as well just plant a garden in here."

Rev. Youngun looked around at the leaks dripping in all directions and broke out laughing. "This is ridiculous," he said, marching off toward the kitchen.

"Where you goin'?"

"I'm going to call Sarah Bentley up and give her a piece of my mind."

"Watch out, woman! Thomas Youngun's comin' to speak his mind," Maurice hooted.

He saw another leak beginning and threw up his hands. *He's hot with frustration. Roof's leakin' like a sieve . . . Sherry's sick as she can be. . . and he's been havin' trouble with the boys.*

Rev. Youngun cranked up the phone and called Sarah. But before he could begin complaining about the leaks, she started in on Mr. Palugee's latest accusation.

Maurice listened from the edge of the door, holding a cup in his hand to catch another leak. *Those boys are in trouble now,* he thought. *They been at Palugee's again.*

"Hey, Mr. Springer, what you doin'?" Larry asked, standing at the front door dripping wet.

"You better take your boots off. They're full of mud."

Terry put the fish shocker out of sight on the porch. He looked at the way Maurice had his head turned toward the kitchen, and asked, "You listenin' to somethin'?"

"I'm listenin' to your pa catch heck from Sarah Bentley over somethin' you two done over at Palugee's."

"We didn't do anythin'! That Willy's a liar," Terry said, wiping the water from his eyes.

"Might be and might not be," Maurice said. "But you boys best get ready to 'fess up, 'cause your pa's in no mind for monkey business."

Their father came back into the living room from the kitchen. "Boys, I'm so disappointed in you that I don't know what to say."

"I do," Terry spoke up. "We didn't do it."

"You're always innocent, aren't you, Terry? You never do anything wrong, to hear you tell it." Rev. Youngun sighed, shaking his head.

"This time it's true, Pa," Larry said. "That Willy Bentley told a fib to Mr. Palugee."

"And why is everybody ganging up on you?" Rev. Youngun asked, thinking his kids were trying to wiggle out of trouble. "Why do you always say everyone else is fibbing?" He threw his hands up in the air. "This will be the talk of the church supper tomorrow night."

"Because we're preacher's kids," Terry said. "Everybody blames preacher's kids for everything."

Maurice spoke up. "Some truth to that, Reverend."

"And what's that?" Rev. Youngun asked.

"Just that it's natural for some folks to look for all bad in kids who are children of men who are all good. Kind of like gettin' back at your teacher, I guess."

"We ain't all bad," Larry said.

Terry thought he was being helpful and added, "We might be half bad, but not all bad."

"That was dumb," Larry whispered to his brother.

"Sit down here and tell me what happened," Rev. Youngun said.

The brothers proceeded to tell everything, without fudging. The only thing they left out was seeing Sammy Lester, which they just forgot.

At the end of it, Maurice said, "I believe 'em and so should you."

"I guess I'll have to confront this head-on at the church supper. Most everyone will be there and, knowing Sarah, she'll have told all the ladies her version of what happened."

"By the time Willy gets through, people will think we're bandits or somethin'," Terry moaned.

Larry shook his head. "Ain't right that we got to defend ourselves for what we didn't do."

"Mrs. Bentley's word carries a lot of weight in this town." Rev. Youngun sighed.

Maurice shook his head. "Just 'cause the Bentleys got money don't mean you got to believe what they say."

"Why does she pick on us?" Larry asked. "We've never done anything to her."

Rev. Youngun paused. He had tried to teach his children right from wrong; to see the good in people. That the law was the law.

But what was happening defied the nice little box he wanted to keep life in.

Maurice saw that he was struggling with what to say and stepped in. "Why don't you go see how Sherry is and let me talk to these boys a minute. You got enough to worry about."

"But I want to—"

Maurice shook his head. "There's some things a father can say, and there's some things a good friend can say. Just the way the world is. Okay?"

Terry suddenly remembered about Sammy Lester and said, "And, Pa, you remember that bottle brother—"

Maurice cut him off. "One thing at a time."

Larry whispered into his brother's ear, "Better not mention that now . . . and don't talk 'bout that fish-shockin' thing."

Maurice turned to Rev. Youngun. "You go upstairs and check on Sherry. I'll take care of things down here."

Rev. Youngun slowly climbed the stairs to Sherry's bedroom, feeling as if he had the weight of the world on his shoulders. *Sherry might die . . . we're out of money . . . roof leaks . . . Dangit's hurt . . . kids are in trouble . . . Lord, give me strength.*

Maurice looked at the boys, then took them each by the hand over to the big rocker in the corner. "You two stand here and listen to me."

Sitting down with a creak of the rocker and his bones, he began, "You boys are gonna learn that greed can make people do bad things. Like tryin' to get everythin' for yourself and tryin' to control people's lives."

"I don't understand," Larry said, looking quizzically at their neighbor.

"Well, boys, take Mrs. Bentley. She's got the money, and you got the roof that leaks." The two boys looked around at the pots all over the room. "So to make your pa do things she wants him to do, she holds back the money for the fixin'."

"But it's the church's money," Terry said.

"But she's the one who gives the money to the church," Maurice said.

"That oughta be against the law," Larry mumbled.

"Sometimes the law can be mean and greedy too," Maurice explained.

He rocked for a moment, then leaned forward toward them both.

"Boys, you make do with what God gives you. Do the best you can in this life, and remember that you're really no better than anyone else walkin' beside you."

"We're not better than Mr. Lester?" Terry asked.

Maurice shook his head. "We're all on this earth just a little while. If we go to thinkin' we're better than the down-and-out, soon we'll all find ourselves out-and-out unless we give each other a helpin' hand."

Larry nodded. "People are people."

"But why are some people so mean?" Terry asked.

Maurice shrugged. "How many millions of folks you think seen an apple fall from the tree? But it took ol' Isaac Newton to ask why. Why's that?" Neither boy spoke. Maurice patted Larry on the back. "Just takes good folks to start askin' why 'bout the meanness, and when that happens, the only ones left worryin' will be the mean folks."

He continued. "The hardest thing to learn to have in life is a sense of humor, and the greatest thing to have in life is a sense of humor. Some people never find it at all."

"You mean like Mrs. Bentley?" Larry asked.

"Maybe that's her problem," Maurice said thoughtfully.

"I love you, Mr. Springer," Larry whispered.

"Me too," Terry said.

"I love you boys too," he said quietly, rocking back and forth. "Just remember, we're only on this earth for a short time, and the Lord measures your life in what you done for others, not in what you done for yourself."

He looked down at Terry who had his hands folded and was mumbling. "What you doin'?"

"Prayin'," Terry whispered.

"'Bout what?"

"Sherry."

"Take me home," Maurice said, not quite believing what he'd heard.

"I want God to help her," Terry said, looking into Maurice's eyes.

"Me too," Larry said. "I don't want her to die." He and Terry both snuggled close to Maurice.

"Amen," said Maurice. He pulled the boys onto his lap. "Let's all say a prayer for that angel upstairs."

He hugged the boys against him and rocked slowly, letting their silent prayers float up to the heavens. The creaks of the rocker were answered by the dripping of water into the pots, jars, and cups around the room.

Keeping Score

❖

Sheriff Peterson stood by the map on his wall in the office, looking at the circled areas where raccoons had been spotted. The crackling lightning and pounding thunder shook the wood-frame building, but he paid it no mind.

He turned to John the Trapper. "You've killed a sick raccoon and a porcupine?"

"And my dog," John said, pulling on his earlobe.

"And Cody," Sheriff Peterson acknowledged. "You also caught three 'coons in your traps?"

"Let one go, and had to kill the other two. They had the sickness."

The sheriff continued, looking at the homely man. "Bentley killed that 'coon that got into his kitchen. Hambone killed one behind the cafe. Ned Hutson said his dog Redbone most likely died of the sickness. Said he got bit by a crazy raccoon that was attacking him."

"Anybody know who that big wild dog in the pack that's roamin' the hills belongs to?"

"No, J.J. saw it. Said it almost bit him." The sheriff paused to sip his coffee. "And Shultz, up in the north county, right about here," he said, pointing to the map, "called in to say he killed two 'coons and two wild dogs from that pack."

"Were they sick with it?" John asked.

Sheriff Peterson nodded. "Granddoc says that someone should go shoot the rest of them dogs. Says that if they're sick and runnin' in a pack, that they just as easily can hunt down children as attack other animals."

"What's J.J. doin' about it?" John asked.

"He's out roundin' up stray dogs. Granddoc's been gettin' on him to not just take in any dog he finds, but he says county law's on his side."

"And if the dogs look sick?"

"Then he catches 'em and takes 'em back for disposal, or shoots 'em on the spot." The sheriff shrugged.

"You put out a warnin' for folks to keep their dogs off the streets?" John asked.

"Strays or house dogs, it don't matter," the sheriff said. "We can't let this disease keep spreadin'."

John traced the pattern of attacks on the map. "Only thing that will stop it is a good freeze."

"Winter's a long way off."

"Then you best keep this map here to keep score with."

The sheriff paused, adding new circles to the map. "Score ain't lookin' too good, John," he said, wiping his face on his sleeve.

"More like a battle report."

"We're in a war with nature herself. Nature gone mad. If we don't stop it, it'll stop a lot of us," the sheriff said, staring at the map.

"You think that Youngun girl's the only one who might have the disease?" John asked.

"No tellin' how many folks might end up gettin' it. I've been askin' the newspaper to run more stories, warnin' folks." He stopped and asked in a confidential tone, "Have you heard anyone or anythin' howlin' in the hills?"

"Howlin'?"

"Or screamin' or somethin' like that. I've been gettin' calls 'bout someone or somethin' up in the hills, scarin' folks."

John sighed. "Lots of bad things in the dark." He didn't elaborate.

The sheriff looked at John through new eyes. "Have you seen or heard a howlin'?"

John changed the subject. "I tracked that big bat up to a cave on Devil's Ridge."

"You did?"

John nodded. "Might be the same one that bit the Youngun girl, and it might not."

"Bats hang together," the sheriff said, circling Devil's Ridge on the map. "Let's you and me go up there and burn 'em all out."

"Burn all of 'em?"

"Can't take the risk of a couple thousand sick bats flyin' 'round. They'd pass the disease from here to kingdom come."

John picked up his hat and rifle.

"Where you goin'?" the sheriff asked.

"Rain's let up. I'm gonna try to make it back to my cabin before it begins again. Come on up at dawn, and we'll go burn out them bats."

"I'll see if I can make it through the mud." As John opened the door, the sheriff joked, "Watch out for the bats and the howler in the woods."

"I got my protection," John said, pointing above. "He's always with me."

"Well," Sheriff Peterson smiled, "just keep that rifle loaded in case He's doin' somethin' else when that howler comes at you."

Rev. Youngun came downstairs and stepped out onto the porch just as the rain was ending. He took one look around and then stomped into the house. "Boys!"

Larry and Terry came running. Rev. Youngun's voice was stern. "What are all those fish doing on the porch?"

Terry spoke up. "Pa, they just appeared. It was like a miracle."

Rev. Youngun looked at his son. "What do you mean?"

"Me and Larry were down at Willow Creek like we said, and these fish, why, they started poppin' right out of the water," said Terry. "So we hauled 'em in, thinkin' we could have 'em for supper."

Rev. Youngun looked very tired. "Fish don't just pop out of the water, son."

"I've heard about 'em, Pa," said Terry. "You know, flyin' fish? Uncle Cletus said that sailors see 'em all the time."

They all were silent for a moment. Then Larry said quietly, "We don't have to eat 'em, Pa. We just thought you'd like it and there was no sense wasting 'em."

Rev. Youngun looked at his sons. *How can they look so innocent?*

They certainly do try. But where on earth did they get these? It surely would taste good, though, with some pepper and cornmeal . . .

"Well, boys," he started slowly, "I don't understand, and I don't like it one bit. But it's food, that's for certain. So I thank God for it. You boys clean them and I'll fry them up." Then he went into the kitchen.

Terry looked at Larry. "I shocked 'em, so you clean 'em."

"We both shocked 'em," Larry said. "Come on." They scrambled outside to clean the fish. Before long the fish were frying, and the Youngun house smelled like a good supper for the first time in a long, long time.

On the other side of town, Maurice scurried home under the rain, carrying the lantern that Rev. Youngun had loaned him. He strode quickly along the familiar but soggy path that now looked ominous in the dark.

As the moon came out, shimmering off the rain-soaked hills, a scream of pain echoed in the air for a brief moment. It sounded like a howling in the hills.

Maurice stopped and spun around. Goose bumps and shivers ran wild up his spine. He heard the howling again, only this time it was answered by the pack of dogs from the other ravine. In the moonlight he thought he saw a massive hound, standing on the hill, baying toward the sky.

Then he saw something else. "What the heck is that?" he asked in the dark, holding the lantern in front of him. His boots were heavy with mud. *Somethin's out there . . . somethin' bad.*

Lightning cracked, and for a moment he thought he saw a man on one hill and a dog on another. *Sweet Jesus, protect me,* he prayed, trying to unstick his boots from the mud.

But in the ensuing darkness, he shook it off to his imagination. "Weren't nothin' but me seein' things . . . been readin' too many of them Dracula stories," he said to himself, trying to pull his boots out of the mud hole he'd stepped in.

But it wasn't his imagination. It was Sammy Lester on one side and Gordo on the other. The rabies had taken over both of their minds.

Maurice started running as fast as he could, mumbling, "Yea, though I run through the valley of death, I shall fear no evil, but I do want to get home fast, Lord."

39

Going Insane

Moments after John left the sheriff, Emily Grant the newspaper reporter called. "Sheriff, this is Emily. Could you give me any information you have on the rumors about something bizarre running through the woods?"

"Why? You writin' a story?"

"I already did, but I think I've got some information for you."

"Well, all I've gotten are calls about someone screamin' or shoutin' in the woods."

"Or howling?" she asked.

"I didn't want to describe it like that, but some of them have said he ... or it ... has been howlin' in the woods north of town."

"I think you'd better come out here," she said slowly, "because your howler's up near the Willow Creek Bridge."

"What do you mean?"

"I just came back from that direction, and I believe I saw the person who's been doin' it."

"Did you get a good look?"

"Sort of. It looked like Sammy Lester . . . only he was all muddy and acting crazy. Running in the dark like a wild animal."

Sheriff Peterson laughed. "Lester? Well, heck, that explains it. He's probably just off howlin' drunk again."

"He looked sick, Sheriff."

"Drunks always look sick 'cause they don't eat right," the sheriff said. "That Lester," he chuckled. "Boys down at the saloon are goin' to have a good one over this."

"I hope you're right," Emily said, "because acting crazy is what happens to folks with rabies." She paused. "With all due respect, sir, if I were you, I'd check it out."

"I'll come up and take a look." He sighed, getting up from his desk.

"The roads are bad. Please let me know what you find," Emily said.

The sheriff nodded to the phone. "I'll do that, young lady."

Rabbi Wechter, the circuit-riding rabbi who serviced the small Ozark Jewish community on horseback, pulled up his collar to the approaching rain. He'd ridden along the muddy roads for miles, making very slow time. "Hope we can get to Mansfield before we get soaked," he said, patting his horse, Shalom.

Shalom whinnied a response, then tried to turn away from the road ahead. Someone, or something ran across their path, screaming in the darkness.

"What was that?" Rabbi Wechter said, trying to hold the horse in place. The hair on the back of his neck bristled with fear.

But just as quickly as it came, it was gone. The only proof that something was in the vicinity was the echoing scream-like sound that hung in Wechter's ears.

His mind danced with images of ghosts and dybbuks that, according to Jewish folklore, were spirits of the dead that invade the body of a living person and possess it.

Maybe I'm seeing things, he said to himself. *I don't need to be thinking about dybbuks. All I need is a warm bath and a good night's sleep. I didn't see anything at all,* he thought, trying to convince himself.

But fifty yards farther, the horse stopped. A set of thick, muddy footprints crossed the road. Rabbi Wechter slapped the flanks of Shalom and took off toward the safety of the town, splashing through the mud.

Sammy Lester ground his teeth, watching the rabbi ride away.

Sheriff Peterson dismounted at the Willow Creek Bridge, and made his way through the thick mud down to the water's edge. He swung a lantern to each side, trying to see through the dark and rain. But before he could look around, he heard a horse galloping down the muddy road and went back up the bank to see who was in such a hurry.

The sheriff turned up his lantern and stood in the middle of the road, waving it around. "Slow down, slow down . . . looks like you're in a race with the devil himself!"

Rabbi Wechter brought his horse to a pounding stop. "I . . . I thought I saw something cross the road, and then I heard it following me."

"What exactly did you hear?" the Sheriff asked.

But before the rabbi could answer, they heard a screaming sound coming toward them down the dark road. Rabbi Wechter's horse reared up and galloped away toward town. There was nothing the rabbi could do but hold on.

Sheriff Peterson stood his ground, not knowing what was coming down the road at him. All thoughts of Sammy Lester just being on a happy drunk evaporated quickly.

As the screams got closer, the sheriff unstrapped his holster. Holding the lantern in front of him, he shouted out, "Stop right there!" But the screams just came closer.

"I said, stop right there!"

Sammy Lester recognized the sheriff's voice, and something in his clouded mind told him to stop. He halted at the edge of the light, rubbing his face and moving his jaws up and down. A line of drool had crusted down his chin. He moved his mud-crusted shoes up and down, making a sucking sound as he lifted them from the ooze.

Sheriff Peterson stared, speechless. Sammy was covered with mud, stickers, and briars. His hair was matted with sweat and rain and mud. *He looks like a crazy man . . . like an escaped lunatic,* he thought.

"Sammy . . . is that you, Sammy?" the sheriff sputtered.

Sammy began pacing back and forth in the mud, drooling from the corners of his mouth.

"Are you drunk or somethin'?" said the sheriff.

Sammy began laughing hysterically, then stopped when his throat tightened up. "Hot . . . so hot . . . " Sammy flung himself into the mud, screaming, "Sweet corn! Gimme some sweet corn, Momma . . . I'm a good boy."

Lord in heaven, he's gone insane, the sheriff thought as he watched Sammy roll around in the mud. His hand slowly crept to the butt of his pistol.

"Sammy, why don't you just come on back and sleep it off in the jail. After a good night's sleep, we'll talk about it in the mornin'... all right?"

Sammy jumped to his feet and looked frantically from side to side. He seemed to see things in the bushes at the side of the road. "Sweet corn's at its peak. I can eat me ten ears of it, Pa. I can, Pa! I can!"

Sheriff Peterson gripped the butt of his pistol, not knowing what Sammy was thinking, but knowing what would happen if Sammy jumped on him. *Got to keep him in my sights... can't let him bite me.*

But Sammy didn't care if the sheriff couldn't see the beautiful prairie sights that were all around him in his mind. Before him were rows of big-eared yellow Seneca Chief corn and the long, thin, elegant, white ones called Silver Queen. It was summer inside Sammy's head, and the hot noon sun was at its peak.

"Can't we cook 'em now, Pa? Bet Ma could make up some butter and—"

Dogs howled in the distance, from the ravines near town. Sammy snapped back to where he was and felt the burning rage come over him again. He took a step toward the sheriff and stopped, moving his jaws up and down as if they were sore.

"Hold it right there," the sheriff said. "I think you've got rabies, Sammy... I think you do... heaven help you." Sammy just snarled and moaned. "Have you been bitten by an animal? Talk to me, Sammy," the sheriff pleaded, truly afraid.

Sammy rolled his eyes without reason, then whispered in a ragged voice, "A bat... and Redbone... bat and Redbone... bat and Redbone."

"Can't understand you," the sheriff said, trying to pull his left foot from a mud hole. "What you mean about a bat and Redbone? Redbone's dead... he died from the..." the sheriff's hand began shaking. "Did Redbone bite you? Did the bat bite you? Answer me, Sammy!"

The dog pack sounded closer. Sammy looked around and screamed out a dog sound into the air. All around them, thunder and lightning cracked and another deluge of rain poured down, putting out the lantern.

"Stay right where you are," the sheriff said to the darkness, feeling as if he was sinking in quicksand. Sammy just laughed in the inky blackness, then began moaning.

Got to tie him up. Gotta lock him up 'fore he kills someone. Fumbling with his lantern, the sheriff turned in circles, trying to see where Sammy was. *Wish this mud weren't so thick.*

By the time he lit the lantern again, Sammy had disappeared. From the hills dogs howled again, and something that sounded like Sammy answered them. *He's crazy . . . he might just kill someone.*

Sheriff Peterson followed as best he could through the mud but couldn't find a trail in the rain. So he headed over to John's cabin, to wait for the dawn so they could burn out the bats on Devil's Ridge. The ooze of the mud seemed not to want to let him go.

After supper, their stomachs full, Larry and Terry heard the howling sound. They crept down to their father in their nightclothes and saw their father leaning back in his chair with his eyes closed.

"That's what Mr. Lester sounded like, Pa," Larry said, standing by his father's desk.

Rev. Youngun had fallen asleep and awoke with a start. "What . . . what?"

"The howlin'," Terry said, tugging at his sleeve. "That sounded like the man we saw in the woods today."

"What howling?"

"Didn't you hear it?" Larry asked. "It woke us up."

Rev. Youngun rubbed the sleep from his eyes and listened, but heard nothing. "What were you saying about Sammy Lester?"

Larry told him about their encounter with the bottle brother. "You boys go back to sleep. I guess Mr. Lester's gone back to drinking again."

Then he stopped. They all heard the screaming. Terry ran to the window and looked out. "That's him!"

But when the rain began pounding on the roof again, they couldn't hear anything else. Rev. Youngun opened the front door. Terry and Larry stood behind him, peeking around his legs.

At first they saw nothing, but then, when the lightning crackled overhead, they saw him. Sammy Lester was ripping at his face, screaming things that sounded like words, but words that meant nothing.

"Sammy, what's wrong?" Rev. Youngun shouted out into the storm.

But he couldn't understand what Sammy was saying. It sounded like something about a bat.

"He looks sick, Pa," Larry whispered.

"Looks like he's been rollin' in the mud," Terry mumbled.

Wish the boys didn't have to see this . . . it's not good for them. "Stay back, boys," Rev. Youngun said, stepping out onto the porch.

Sammy shouted. "Help me . . . help me, Pa! I'll be good," he screamed, wiping the mud off his face.

Terry and Larry looked at each other. "Who's he talkin' to?" Terry whispered.

Larry shrugged.

Wind and rain whipped across the porch. Rev. Youngun shielded his eyes. Lightning flashed the front yard ablaze, cracking the tree behind Sammy in half. The look of agony on Sammy's face sent chills down Rev. Youngun's back.

He's got rabies, Rev. Youngun thought.

"Sammy, get under the cover of the shed! I'll call the doctor and—" the crack of lightning and the boom of thunder cut him off. Then they were plunged into darkness.

They could hear Sammy scream out in the blackness of night, "Pa . . . we need to fix the fences, Pa . . . I'm not too little to help . . . I can swat the blackbirds from the yellow corn." Sammy ran in circles, shooing imaginary blackbirds.

"What's he talkin' 'bout?" Terry whispered.

Rev. Youngun said a prayer to himself for Sammy's soul, then turned to his sons. "He's sick, son. Something's wrong with his mind."

"He's got rabies, don't he, Pa?" Larry asked.

Rev. Youngun could only nod yes. For several moments they could see nothing, then lightning cracked again. Sammy wasn't there.

Rev. Youngun closed the door. "Check all the windows, now!" he ordered.

When the house was secure, he called the sheriff. But Alice, the phone operator on duty, said the sheriff was out, chasing after rumors of someone making noises in the woods.

"Tell the sheriff that I saw the person. It's Sammy Lester."

"Was he drunk?" joked Alice.

"No. Tell the sheriff that he wasn't drinking. Tell the sheriff he's got rabies."

He put down the phone and covered his eyes. *Please, Lord . . . don't let this happen to Sherry. Bring her that vaccine in time!*

Upstairs, Sherry didn't hear Sammy's screams. All she could hear were the scraping sounds in her dream. Something was scraping at her window.

Frozen with fear in the bed, she saw the vampire bat trying to get through the screen. All she could see were the big, black claws reaching out to get her.

"Help, Pa! Help!" she screamed.

Then she awoke from the nightmare, bathed in sweat.

Sherry closed her eyes and put her hands together. "Now I lay me down to sleep," she whispered quietly over her folded hands. "I pray the Lord my soul to keep."

The rain pounded on the roof above, but she kept on praying, "And if I die before I wake, I pray the Lord my soul to take."

She thought she saw a light appearing in the corner of her room. She looked at her angel that only she could see and asked, "Tell me more about heaven, Little Wings."

Across the state, the train carrying the vaccine slowed down to clear the trees that had fallen in the storm. The conductor looked out into the driving rain and whistled.

He turned to his assistant. "Must be twenty trees down in front of us."

"Maybe we should wire Springfield and have 'em send down a wagonload of tree cutters."

The conductor shook his head. "Roads are so muddy, take at least two days for 'em to get here. No, we'll be here a day or two, chopping these trees off ourselves."

At the animal disposal farm, Dangit lay in the corner of the cage, not liking the smell of fear on the animals around him. He had kept his eyes open all evening, waiting to jump up the minute he might see one of his masters coming to get him.

Inside the office, J.J. hadn't slept well, thinking about the big wild dog with the collar that had attacked him. *I gotta get that one 'fore he hurts someone,* he decided, rubbing his eyes.

40

Burn Them Out

❖

Up in the hills, John stoked up the cooking fire to make coffee for the sheriff. The smell of smoke, coals, the burning coffee, the red embers all brought a rush of memories back to John.

He remembered his two sons in the predawn hours, tugging on their boots. Their horses were picketed nearby, waiting to greet the dawn, the stars above telling them that day was not too far off. His wife making them a carry lunch. *She was a jewel among women.*

"Get your canteens and hunting knives, boys," he'd told them. "A mountain man can always survive if he's got those two things."

He saw his own features in the faces of his two sons, who looked up to him. *They would have made darn good hunters,* he thought, feeling the stabbing pains of sadness sweep back over him even after all these years.

"Got any white sugar?" the sheriff asked.

"Remember, I told you ain't got no sugar," John said, relieved to be saved from the past.

"I like it black anyway." Sheriff Peterson shrugged.

"Once we start the fire, we got to work fast."

"It ain't gonna be easy, but if we put enough brush and wood in the mouth of the cave, we can create enough smoke to kill them all," Sheriff Peterson said.

John nodded, setting out the tin coffee cups. "After we get the bats, then you and me gotta go dog huntin' to get the rest of that wild pack."

"Them wild dogs scare the devil out of me. 'Specially that big one with the collar."

John nodded and the sheriff continued; "Heard from some of the hill folks toward Mountain Grove who said he's been killin' their sheep."

"First the bats, then the dogs," John said, looking into the dancing fire flames.

At the first light of dawn, John the Trapper and Sheriff Peterson headed out to burn the bats in the cave. The trails in the woods were hard to travel on. Everything seemed to ooze with mud. The heavy mist around Devil's Ridge seemed to play tricks on their eyes, but nothing was going to stop them from their mission.

"There he is," John whispered, pointing out the big vampire bat swooping down through the woods toward the cave.

"It don't look real," the sheriff whispered.

They watched the bat fly into the cave along with a group of smaller bats, rushing to avoid the dawn. The two men gathered dead limbs and brush. They broke the branches off a cracked tree that had been protected from the rain by the arch of the cliff.

With one match, flames crackled through the pile of brush and wood they'd built in the mouth of the cave. The high-pitched screams of bats assaulted their ears.

"Get back!" John shouted.

Thousands of bats flew into the blazing fire, trying to escape the heat and choking fumes. John stood ready with his rifle.

Inside the cave, the big vampire bat unwrapped its wings and flew slowly toward the flames. The floor of the cave was covered with other bats that had already died.

Flapping its wings, the enormous bat burst through the flames, going out into the dawn with half of its left wing burned off. It was an eerie sight, watching the bat struggle for life, trying to escape.

"This is his last flight," John said quietly. He cocked his rifle, took careful aim, and shot the bat down.

The two men watched as the burning bat dropped slowly over the edge of the ravine, never to rise again. John said good-bye to the sheriff who made his way through the mud and deep puddles back toward town. The smoke in the cave would finish the job.

John walked to the white oak that hung over the ravine and carved a passage from First Corinthians, cutting deeply into the wood: O Death, where is your sting? O Hades, where is your victory?

41

Fever's Goin' Up

❖

After finishing with the bats, Sheriff Peterson went home to clean up. But not even a hot bath seemed to take away the feeling of gloom that had come over him.

At the office he got the message about Sammy from Rev. Youngun. Wanting time to think, he rode slowly through the hills.

When he got to the Younguns' house, he asked about Sherry, then got straight to business. He told Rev. Youngun about burning out the bats and his encounter with Sammy down by the Willow Creek Bridge. Then he listened to what the Younguns had seen after that.

"I'm gonna use your church supper tonight as a town meetin'," the sheriff said. "We need to get everyone workin' together to fight these raccoons and dogs."

"I don't see a problem with that," Rev. Youngun agreed.

The sheriff put on his hat. "You keep a lookout for Sammy," he said to Rev. Youngun on the front porch. "Tell them kids to keep a watch too."

"I will when they get back."

"Where are they?" the sheriff asked, concerned.

"They went to get their dog from Granddoc's. He tangled with a porcupine and got pretty scratched up."

"Well, when they get home, you warn them to stay near here. We've got sick raccoons, bats, dogs, and a crazy man runnin' 'round."

Rev. Youngun shook his head. "You have any idea where to look for Sammy?"

"We've got half the men in the county lookin' for him, but Granddoc says that rabies will make you act like an animal. So no tellin' where that poor soul is holed up."

"It's a terrible thing that's happened."

Sheriff Peterson nodded and looked Rev. Youngun in the eye. He had brought an extra pistol along and handed it to the minister.

"What's this for?" Rev. Youngun asked, looking at the gun.

"I know you don't like guns, but Sammy's not right in his mind and them rabid dogs need to be shot if they come 'round."

Rev. Youngun looked at the pistol. "I don't think I'll need it," he said, handing it back.

But the sheriff refused to take it. "Keep it high up on the shelf in the kitchen. Just in case."

After the sheriff left, Rev. Youngun prayed for Sammy Lester. *Please, Lord, give him peace. Take him to a better place where he won't be sick any longer.*

Feeling helpless and alone, wishing Norma was alive, he put the gun up on the shelf in the pantry, then went up to Sherry's room to sponge-bathe her.

He knelt beside Sherry's bed and gently rubbed her skin with cool water. She was sound asleep. Her body was so hot that her father began to cry softly. *What if she dies? I don't think I could live if that happened.*

Finally Sherry's voice broke into his thoughts as she woke up. "I don't feel so good, Pa. I hurt all over."

"I know you do, sweet kitten, but Dr. George says the vaccine will be here today. Then you'll be all better."

"When's Dangit comin' home?" she asked weakly.

"Soon. The boys went to get him."

"Anybody home?" came Eulla Mae's voice from downstairs.

"I'll be right back, sweetheart," Rev. Youngun whispered to Sherry. He kissed her on the forehead, tucked the blanket back around her shoulders, and closed her door behind him.

Rev. Youngun went down to the entrance hall. "Come on in, Eulla Mae."

The stout woman entered the kitchen, carrying a bag of food. "Brought some things for you and the kids to eat," she said, reaching into her bag.

"Thanks, Eulla Mae. I didn't even fix the boys breakfast," he said, staring at the floor for a moment.

Eulla Mae shook her head. "Why don't you go into town and get ready for the church supper. I'll fix food for the boys and go up and take care of Sherry. You did bathe her and fix up her hair, didn't you?"

"Not her hair," he said sheepishly.

"Land's sakes! Don't you know that sick girls need their hair done in the worst way? Now you go on outta here so I can do some girl things."

Rev. Youngun nodded and smiled ruefully. "I'm glad you came."

"I'm here to help now, but one day you're gonna need another momma to move in here and be with these kids."

The wall phone rang. Granddoc was calling to ask if Dangit was there. "Isn't he with you?" Rev. Youngun asked.

Granddoc sounded exasperated. "I was afraid of that. Think he got out of the cage last night. What a mess this is."

"What should we do?" Rev. Youngun asked.

"Keep an eye out. Dogs usually try to make it home. 'Cept if they're hurt or . . ."

"Or what?" Rev. Youngun asked.

"With those wild dogs running around, no telling what could happen if he tangles with them." She anticipated his worry and said with false cheerfulness, "I'm sure that Dangit will be on your porch any minute, looking for food."

After he hung up, Rev. Youngun didn't say anything to Eulla Mae. He just walked to his desk, got his coat and hat, and drove the buggy into town. *I want to be the one to tell the boys,* he thought.

Secret

At Mom's Cafe, Sammy Lester's name was on everyone's lips. Everyone had a theory and swore they'd heard the howling.

Maurice stopped by for coffee. He kicked the mud off his boots before entering, then nibbled on the rooster fries that Hambone was handing out as samples.

"Maurice, what you think 'bout Sammy?" he whispered.

"He ain't gonna live long."

"Where you think he's hidin'?"

Maurice made a face. "Don't want to speak ill of the dead or soon-to-be dead. You understand?"

"What you up to today?"

"Just goin' to the post office and the feed store. That's 'bout it," Maurice said.

Hambone looked around, then whispered, "Would you mail this for me?" He held out an envelope.

Maurice looked at the envelope. It was addressed to Rev. Thomas Youngun. "You forgot to put your return address on it . . . and a stamp."

Hambone took out two cents and handed it to Maurice. "Here's for the stamp."

"But what 'bout the return address?"

"It's a secret," he whispered. "Please don't tell anyone about this."

"Not even Mom?" Maurice said, raising his eyebrows.

"*Especially* not Mom," Hambone said.

"Okay, your secret's safe with me."

Maurice paid for the coffee and went to pick up supplies. At

Campbell's Feed Store he tried to stay out of the crazy-man talk, just wanting to do his business and go home. He knew what he'd heard last night and wanted to keep his ideas to himself.

While his wagon was being loaded, Maurice sauntered over to Bedal's General Store and knew immediately that the red shoes in the window were the ones Sherry wanted.

"Whewie, those are pretty shoes." he smiled, thinking how she'd look wearing them in the school play. *She'd look like a fairy princess come to life.*

Checking the money in his pocket, he went in and bought the shoes. He swore Mr. Bedal to secrecy.

Lafayette Bedal was confused. "But Rev. Youngun was in here lookin' and—"

"Either you swear to keep this a secret or you don't get a sale," Maurice said. A shrewd businessman, Bedal took the money.

Then Maurice went to the post office and tied up the shoe box.

The postmaster looked at the return address: Little Wings, Heaven. "Is this a joke or something?" he asked Maurice.

Maurice laughed and shook his head. "No sir, I got a little girl who's wishin' on an angel's wing and now she's sick. I'm hopin' this will make her feel better."

"Why don't you just take 'em out to her yourself?" he asked, looking at Sherry Youngun's name on the package.

"They're supposed to be comin' from heaven. How'd it look for me to come carryin' them in if an angel's supposed to be sendin' 'em?"

The postmaster looked over at Teddy, the mailman, then whispered to Maurice, "I don't think Teddy looks much like an angel, either."

Maurice shrugged. "Don't say nothin' to that blabbermouth or he'll let on."

"But what will I tell him if he asks?"

"He won't ask." Maurice winked and started to leave, then remembered Hambone's letter. "Oh yeah. Send this along too . . . and here's two cents for the stamp."

Rev. Youngun rode slowly across the Willow Creek Bridge, keeping out of the deep ruts, looking for Dangit and the boys. Once in Mansfield, he decided to stop at Bedal's store to look at the red shoes in the window, but they were gone. All Bedal would say is that someone bought them.

"But who?" Rev. Youngun asked, feeling very dejected.

"A man came in with a pocketful of money. Said he had a special little girl who'd love those red shoes."

"So do I," Rev. Youngun mumbled.

"What was that? Didn't hear you, Reverend?"

"Nothing . . . nothing at all."

Rev. Youngun left the store, more depressed than he'd felt in a long time. Then he ran into J.J.

"Think I got your dog," J.J. said.

"You do? That's great!" Rev. Youngun exclaimed.

"Cubby, Dr. George's son, recognized your dog this mornin'. I caught him with that pack of rabid dogs."

"But Dangit's not sick and—"

J.J. held up his hand. "Too much at risk. You ought to know that, with your girl sick and all."

"But he's a house dog, not a wild one."

J.J. coughed. "The big hound that's been attackin' folks has a collar on it. Someone says it has the name Gordo on it. That dog was someone's pet, but he's got the sickness."

Rev. Youngun felt the weight of sadness descend on him. "What will happen to Dangit?"

J.J. shrugged. "The law says I gotta keep the dogs forty-eight hours, then get rid of them if they look sick. Your dog looks sick, Reverend. He's all scabbed up and—"

"But he got hit by a porcupine—"

J.J. looked down, then into Rev. Youngun's eyes. "You can always get another dog for your boys, but you can't get your children back. Wait a week or so, and I'll bring a puppy 'round and they'll forget all 'bout this other dog."

Rev. Youngun watched J.J. drive the animal wagon off. *Sherry's sick. Shoes are sold. We're out of money. Dangit's going to be put to sleep. What am I going to tell the boys?*

On the other side of town, Larry and Terry held their breath as they passed the graveyard. Superstitions die hard, and though neither believed it, neither one wanted to be the next to die. So they held their breaths, trying to get to the other side without breathing.

But halfway across, Edgar Allan Crow buzzed overhead squawking, "Rise and shine . . . Rise and shine!"

Terry started to giggle and tried to tickle Larry into breathing. Before they knew it, they were wrestling on the cobblestone entranceway to the graveyard, breathing as if there was no tomorrow.

"Now you done it," Larry said.

"Couldn't help it," Terry shrugged. "Heard that stupid crow squawking—"

"Rise and shine," the crow screeched, dive-bombing toward something that lay on top of a grave.

"Boys, boys!" their father called out from behind them. He was relieved to find them. He pulled the buggy to a halt. "Come on, get in."

Larry shook his head. "But we ain't got Dangit yet and—"

"Rise and shine," squawked the crow.

Rev. Youngun looked over and recognized the muddy body of Sammy Lester, lying on top of a grave. "You boys stay here," Rev. Youngun said, climbing up onto the low wall to get a better look.

Life was passing quickly out of Sammy Lester's body. His mind was traveling into worlds beyond comprehension, flying him over the rolling mantle of the lush prairie lands he loved as a boy. Bison and elk and flocks of prairie chickens ambled around the wagon in his memory.

Though the man's body was ravaged by years of alcohol abuse and the rabies infection, his mind was at peace, saying good-bye to all he had loved. Then his thoughts stopped forever.

He's dead, Rev. Youngun thought, taking off his hat.

"Pa, what's wrong with that man?" Larry asked.

Rev. Youngun looked at his sons. He stepped away, saying a silent prayer for poor Sammy Lester. "Boys, you get in the buggy. I don't want you seeing this," he ordered.

They rode in silence listening to the ooze pull at the wagon wheels until they got to the sheriff's office. Rev. Youngun reported finding Sammy's body. Then as they crossed the Willow Creek Bridge, he told them about Dangit and about J.J.'s offer to bring them a new puppy.

Larry and Terry burst into tears. They didn't want a new puppy.

They didn't want another dog. They only wanted Dangit . . . or no dog at all . . . ever again.

Back at the house, Sherry's fever alarmed Eulla Mae.

"Drink this water," she told Sherry, cradling her in her arms. "Got to get this fever down."

"My head hurts," Sherry moaned.

"I'll go call the doctor," Eulla Mae said, gently putting the girl's head back down onto the pillow.

Wringing out another cloth, she placed it on Sherry's forehead and went to the kitchen and called Dr. George. But all he could tell her to do was keep a wet cloth on her head. "The vaccine's on its way," he added.

"But she's so hot, Doctor. Feels like she's cookin' herself to death."

"Eulla Mae, there's nothing I can do without the vaccine."

"Oh, Lord, when's that vaccine gonna get here?"

Dr. George paused. "It should have been here on the morning train, but the train hasn't arrived yet."

"Maybe somethin's happened to it," she said. "Sherry's callin' out. I best get on back upstairs."

"Keep wet cloths on her head and feed her liquids. I'll check on the train," he said before Eulla Mae hung up.

When Dr. George called the station to check on why the train was late, the train master told him about the trees that had fallen on the track up near Seymour. The engineer and his men were clearing trees off the tracks, but it was taking longer than expected.

Dr. George snapped. "But I've got a sick patient who needs her medicine that's on that train! Without it, she's going to die."

"Dr. George, I'm sorry. I'll call you if they telegraph any updates on the train."

"But can't you send someone in a car to go get the package off the train?"

"Doc, ain't no car gonna make it through these roads. Heck, my wagon got stuck comin' in to work. Don't you worry, I'm sure they'll get the tracks cleared by tomorrow."

By tomorrow! Dr. George thought, hanging up the phone. *Every hour that Sherry has to wait is an hour less chance she has to survive.*

That vaccine only works if she gets it in time. There has to be some way to get that vaccine here if the train doesn't come. But he looked at the map. *Seymour's too far to walk. God, please get those tracks cleared in time.*

He paused, rubbing his tired eyes. *If it doesn't get here tomorrow, Rev. Youngun will be burying Sherry next to her momma.*

Town Meeting

Even with the almost impassable roads, almost everyone in town showed up for the Methodist church supper to learn what they could about the outbreak of rabies. Father Walsh had organized caravans for his parish members, and Rabbi Wechter had brought out most of the county's small Jewish community.

Even Mr. Palugee came, but he seemed to spend most of his time picking up bits of string he found on the floor. Rev. Youngun did his best to make everyone comfortable, thankful that Eulla Mae had stayed home with Sherry.

Sheriff Peterson told the hushed crowd about Sammy's death, about the bats being burned out, and about J.J.'s estimate that there were less than half a dozen of the wild dogs left in the pack.

While a heated discussion went on about what could be done, Larry and Terry sat in the corner, worried about Dangit.

Granddoc came over and sat down beside them. "What's wrong, boys?"

"Ain't right that Dangit's gotta die," Larry said.

"He ain't got the sickness," Terry said.

"I'm sorry, boys. I'm sorry that he got out of my basement."

"But can't you talk to Mr. McAlister and get him to let Dangit go?" Larry asked.

No matter how she tried to explain the county laws, the danger of rabies, and how Dangit had been picked up running with the rabid dog pack, the boys wouldn't accept that Dangit had to die.

Granddoc tried to give them hope. "J.J. said he'll get you another puppy and—"

Tears came to Larry's eyes. "Don't want any dog but Dangit. We raised him from a puppy."

"Yeah," Terry said, eyes full. "We practically birthed him ourselves."

After Granddoc left, Willy, who had been watching from the corner, walked by with a smirk on his face. "That's what happens to boys who get caught at Mr. Palugee's."

Larry made a fist and said, "Get outta here."

Willy stuck out his tongue, not seeing Terry's foot in front of him. He tripped, knocking two chairs down.

"You tripped me!" Willy said, dusting himself off.

"Tell it to your mother," Terry said.

Willy looked around, then whispered, "Mr. Palugee loves his string ball, and he's gonna raise you-know-what when he finds it gone. You boys should really think twice 'fore you take it."

"We ain't gonna take it," Larry said.

"And who's gonna believe you when it happens?" Willy smiled and walked away.

It was decided by consensus that the citizens would form a patrol to hunt the dog pack and weed out the sick raccoons. But as Granddoc, Sheriff Peterson, and J.J. described what to look for, lightning and thunder cracked and thundered, making everyone uncomfortable.

Then two shots rang out from behind the church. "What's happenin'?" Sheriff Peterson shouted from the small stage.

The horses shrieked from the stable area as another shot rang out. By the time the townspeople had reached the back of the church, the shooting was over.

They found John Wolf holding his rifle, looking at three mangy, dead dogs on the ground. "Caught 'em sneakin' up on the horses," he said.

"They bite any?" the sheriff asked as rainwater dripped down his face.

"No. But the big one with the collar came close."

"Got away?" several people asked, looking around.

John nodded. "Looks like a nearly dead dog. He's a big hound with no hair on his head. Went that away," John said, pointing west.

"Gordo," the sheriff said. "He's got that name on his collar. We gotta get that dog. Let's track him down tonight."

"Can't it wait till morning?" Father Walsh asked. "You can hardly even walk in this mud in daylight."

"Father," John said, "if we don't kill this dog, then it could bite someone, and we'd have another Sammy Lester on our hands."

As the lightning cracked, the rain subsided. John looked at the people in front of him and tugged on his earlobe. "Just one bite can send a man into a frenzy worse than hell itself. And it can take away everything you care about."

No one moved as John told the story about the night the rabid wolves attacked him and his wife and young sons in the Nebraska Territory. How he thought he'd killed all the wolves, but one had managed to escape. And when he was out fixing the fences, the sick wolf had bitten his wife and two sons.

"I came running and fought him off. Bit off my ear in the fight, he did. I put a hot poker against my flesh and burned out the poison, but my wife and kids were beyond help."

John closed his eyes, trying to block out the memories that awaited him each night. "My wife and kids died like Sammy . . . screaming at me."

No one spoke for a moment. Then the sheriff organized volunteers to track the dog. The men left quietly, knowing it was their duty, but knowing they had every right and reason to be scared. With each step, the thick, pulling mud seemed to be trying to stop them.

Those who remained behind helped clean up. Stephen Scales came from the telegraph office and handed a copy of a message to Dr. George, who was putting away the chairs. He read the short message, then looked over at Rev. Youngun.

"Thomas, I've got some bad news for you," Dr. George said, handing him the telegraph message.

> Telegraph Message——Telegraph Message
> Springfield-to-Mansfield train delayed near Seymour STOP Waiting for crews to help clear trees from tracks STOP

Rev. Youngun dropped the message, haunted by the image of Sherry dying like John's family or Sammy. "She can't wait for that train!"

"I know it," Dr. George said. "Seymour's only just up the road. But with these muddy roads, it might as well be on the moon. She needs the vaccine by morning."

"Isn't there any other way?"

Dr. George shook his head. "Sheriff said that supply wagons can't even make it up here from Branson. We just have to hope they can clear those tracks in time."

As Rev. Youngun laid down the telegram in despair, Larry picked up the message and read it. He listened to his father and Dr. George talk. *I've been to Seymour before. It ain't but just a third of a day's ride.*

Then he knew what he had to do. It was all he thought about as they rode home in the thundering downpour that had begun again, making the bad roads worse.

When Larry saw how sick Sherry was, he was more resolved than ever. She moaned for Dangit and cried for someone to make her feel better.

Late that night, after Terry fell asleep, Larry left a note for his father and went into the kitchen looking for gloves. As he rummaged around, he found the pistol.

Rev. Youngun never let the boys handle guns. But Larry had seen enough nickel movies to know how the cowboys carried them. And since this was a life or death matter, Larry decided to take it along.

Sticking it into his belt, he went out to the barn and saddled up their horse, Lightnin', which was not easy since the horse stood fourteen hands tall. Giving it water and a carrot, Larry then mounted and rode off into the dark toward Seymour.

Rabid dogs and raccoons were not on Larry's mind. All he was thinking about was saving his sister. He knew she would die without the vaccine.

It's just ridin' distance . . . just down the road . . . I'll be back by mornin' . . . if nothin' stops me.

No one watched him ride off down the muddy roads . . . except for the big mangy hound with "Gordo" on its collar.

Swollen River

❖

While all but the night owls slept, Larry rode by the light of the moon, trying to remember the way. He knew where the North Star was, that the sun came up in the east and set in the west. But he'd only been to Seymour twice, and both times it was in the back of a wagon.

Wish I'd paid more attention, Larry thought, thinking of the silly things that Terry had done to his sister and him along the way. *Kept me from watchin' where I was goin'.*

No landmarks stood out in his mind. There were no distance markers. Each fork in the road gave him another chance to be wrong. But there was nothing he could do about it at that moment.

Lightnin's hooves squished along the wet roads. As Larry rode down the densely wooded roads, the night skies played tricks with his eyes. The cattails in the creeks that twinkled in the moonlight seemed to come alive. Patting the pistol under his belt, he wished he'd brought along something to eat.

The intermittent rain had soaked him, so he was cold. He wished he had put on his pa's heavy jacket. Lightnin' breathed heavily. "You're doin' good, boy," Larry said to comfort himself as much as to encourage the horse.

He thought about the Indian he'd always pictured chipping away at the arrowhead now in his collection. *Wonder how he'd find his way?* Then it came to him. *There's a road that forks up to a pond that's got wild hibiscus and buttonbushes around it, just this side of a creek. That's the fork that takes you to Seymour.*

The deep pine forests and the smell of the rich, peaty soil of the swamp opened his nostrils as he rode along the narrow road. Larry was careful to avoid the muddy bogs on the downhill parts of the road, but still Lightnin' stumbled and came close to throwing him a couple of times.

The smell of mineralized groundwater hung in the air. As the first rays of the morning sun blazed over the eastern hills behind him, Larry rode confidently, looking for his guidepost.

On the ridge above the road, he saw turkeys scratching for acorns in the early morning mist. Squirrels ran from Lightnin's pounding hooves. A pileated woodpecker swooped out of the trees and glided down into the forest that ran along the creek that had overflowed its banks from the heavy rains.

"You're doin' good, Lightnin'," Larry said, patting the flanks of his horse.

A deer jumped across the road, followed by two upland sandpipers. Crayfish frogs sang out as he approached the chert and granite rocks up ahead. There was another fork in the road.

Maybe I took the wrong fork back there, he worried, looking frantically around.

The sun glistened off the dewy cliffs. Larry imagined he saw his Osage Indian, his sky warrior, hunched over a flint nodule, carefully flaking off chips. The warrior seemed to wave, pointing for Larry to go right at the fork in the road ahead.

Larry blinked. It seemed so real. Then the morning mist shrouded over the cliff and the image was gone.

Trusting his senses, he took the right fork and came upon the pond with the wild hibiscus and buttonbushes. *Gotta hurry,* Larry thought, confident now that he was on the road to saving Sherry's life.

There should be a river just up ahead. Cross it and I'm almost there.

At the bottom of the hill, he came to the river, but it was dark and swollen, filled with broken branches. The dark water looked frightening. Lightnin' reared up, not wanting to cross.

"Whoa . . . hold on!" Larry shouted, trying to keep the horse from bolting.

The last time he'd crossed this river, he had been in the back of a wagon. The water had hardly touched the rims of the wheels. Now it looked over his head.

No choice. Gotta cross it. He dug his feet into the stirrups. "Come on, Lightnin'. You can do it," he coached, moving the horse forward.

Hesitating for a brief moment, Lightnin' stepped into the creek. Within two steps the bottom had dropped off, and the horse was swimming.

Larry held onto the horse's mane, pushing the branches away that came rushing toward them. "Keep movin' . . . keep movin'!" he shouted. But Lightnin' was caught in the rush of the river.

Then they both saw it coming toward them. A nest of snakes, caught in the crotch of a scorched tree, bobbed down the river. The horse saw the snakes and panicked.

"No . . . no . . . keep goin'!" Larry shouted.

There were at least twenty hissing snakes in the nest. Three started out in the waters toward them. Larry kicked at the branch and snakes, trying to keep the horse from shaking him off.

I need somethin' to hit them with, he screamed inside. Then a straight stick floated in front of him. Larry grabbed it and beat back the snakes. Suddenly, the horse's hoofs caught hold of the opposite bank, and Lightnin' pulled himself forward.

Larry held on as well as he could as Lightnin' clambered up the bank and back onto the road. As they crested the hill, Larry saw the train in the distance. Crews were working to clear the trees that blocked the tracks.

Sherry's medicine is just down there, Larry told himself, kicking the horse to speed. As he raced down the muddy hill, jumping the fallen trees, the mist parted on the distant granite cliffs behind him.

"Hey, mister," he shouted as he came up to the train "which one's the car carryin' packages?" he asked the engineer.

"Second one from the end," the man pointed.

Larry raced alongside the tracks and skidded Lightnin' to a halt at the train car. A man leaned against the open door, smoking a pipe.

"You got a package in there for Dr. George of Mansfield?" Larry asked.

"You don't look old 'nough to be a doctor," the salty old train man said, blowing a cloud of smoke at Larry. "You look like a kid whose been playin' with mud pies."

"I ain't the doctor, but there's a package with some medicine that'll save my sister's life. Dr. George needs it."

"Then tell him to come get it himself. Go on home, kid."

"Mister, I rode all the way from Mansfield to get it, and I ain't leavin' without it."

"Yes, you are," the man said, reaching up to close the door.

Larry kicked Lightnin' in the flanks until the horse stood against the train. Before the man could stop him, Larry grabbed hold of the door handle and pulled himself in.

"You can't come in here!" the man said.

"I can and I did," Larry said defiantly, pulling himself up to his full ten-year-old height. "Now listen to me," he said, trying to catch his breath and keep his nerve up. "My sister's gonna die unless she gets the medicine that's in the box."

"What's wrong with her?" the man said, eyeing the pistol stuck in Larry's belt.

"She might have rabies. And if she does, then she'll die without the medicine. You understand?"

The ornery train man considered the situation for a moment, then looked again at the pistol. "What's your name? You think you're some kind of reincarnated Billy the Kid?"

Larry saw that he was staring at the pistol and smiled slyly. "You never know. Now find me that package."

"Think you're tough, don't ya, kid?"

"Tough enough . . . now please find that package."

The man considered the situation, then said, "Oh, what the heck. You just sign for this doctor and you can take the danged package."

Larry thought his heart would jump through his chest while he watched the man root through the pile of packages. "Dr. Hinkins? No, that ain't it. Dr. Wesley? No, you said it was a Dr. . . ." he turned to Larry.

"Dr. George . . . Dr. George of Mansfield, Missouri," Larry snapped.

The man dug around some more. "Everythin' just fell all over when we came to a stop on account of those trees," he grumbled. "Ah, here it is!" he said, straightening up.

"Give it to me," Larry said.

"Not so fast, kid," the train man said. "Sign this," he said, pointing to the package log on his stand-up desk.

Larry scribbled quickly. "Now let me have it." The box was marked

"Extremely Fragile," but the train man didn't notice. He tossed the box to Larry who gasped.

The box seemed to take forever to reach him, rolling over and over in the air. Larry steadied himself, and reached for the box. But it slipped from his grasp, and he bobbled it all the way to the hard wooden floor, barely managing to save it with his fingertips.

"Good catch," the man laughed.

Larry turned to leave, then looked back. "You shouldn't have done that. It made me mad."

"Too bad, kid," the man sneered. "Now get outta here."

Larry shook his head, then jumped from the train car onto Lightnin' and rode with the wind back to Mansfield.

"Stupid boy," the train man said, picking up the log. "Thinks he's real tough, carryin' a gun . . . probably don't even know how to use it."

Then he saw what Larry had signed, and he went to the door to watch Larry ride off. On the log was written: Billy the Kid.

45

Breakout

Dr. George sat by Sherry's bed, putting another wet cloth on her head. Eulla Mae stood in the corner. "Isn't there anythin' you can do, Doc?"

Dr. George shook his head. "Only hope now is if Larry can reach that train."

"But it's up at Seymour and he's just a boy and—"

Dr. George turned. "That boy's doing a man's job . . . what I should have done."

"But—" she began.

"Listen, we were waiting for the world to take its course, sitting around, complaining about the mud. But Larry, why, he just decided to take the world into his own hands and see if he could speed things up."

"I'm prayin' for that boy," Eulla Mae said quietly. "I'm prayin' for Sherry . . . prayin' for Larry . . . prayin' they hunt down that big sick dog and—"

"Heck, woman," Dr. George said, "pray for all of us. We're all in this thing together."

"Will Sherry live if he gets that medicine?" Eulla Mae asked, looking down on the fevered little girl.

"If that boy brings it back, it's the one chance for life she's got. Without it, she's not going to make it."

Downstairs, Rev. Youngun paced the kitchen, waiting for word from the sheriff about Larry. Terry sat at the kitchen table, wanting to do something, but not knowing what to do.

Finally the phone rang out. It was Sheriff Peterson. "Any word about Larry?" Rev. Youngun asked sharply.

While his father talked, Terry slipped out the back door. "Gonna check the animals, Pa," he said quietly, wanting to tell the truth as much as possible about what he was going to do.

"Fine, Terry, fine," his father said. "Now, Sheriff, tell me about that big dog."

Terry went out to the barn and looked at Crab Apple the mule. "I don't want you to give me no trouble," he said, holding a bit in front of the mule.

Crab Apple hee-hawed. T.R. the turkey came gobbling up, looking for a handout.

"Get away!" Terry said loudly. "Oh, jeesh," he mumbled, looking over at Bashful the fainting goat who had just lived up to his name.

Terry managed to stand on the stall rails and get the bit into the mule's mouth. He thought about putting a saddle on, but he knew Crab Apple might kick down the barn if he wasn't in the mood.

"Gonna ride you bareback," Terry said, leading the mule out the back of the barn.

Standing on the pig's trough, he looked at the mule. "Now, don't move or I'll get wet," he ordered. Crab Apple hee-hawed and bucked. Terry grabbed onto the mule's mane and teetered back over the water trough.

Crab Apple bucked again, and Terry pushed off with his toes and climbed up onto the mule's back. "Now git, 'fore I find a stick 'n switch you for what you jus' tried to do."

Terry didn't have a real plan. All he knew was that he wouldn't be able to live with himself if he didn't try to save Dangit.

As he trotted off toward town across the Springers' fields, Maurice noticed Terry riding alone. "Think I better just see what Mr. Trouble is up to," he said, getting onto his wagon seat. "Come on, girls," he called out to his mules, "follow that redheaded woodpecker."

Gordo had eluded the sheriff and his men all night. They'd almost trapped him at the south ridge, but the cagey dog had managed to slip through the rocks.

Now he lay just west of town on a small cliff above the road that

Larry was traveling on. Gordo was burning with fever. The sores on his body had begun to fester.

Death stalked through his veins, and there was nothing he could do except wait for it to come . . . unless someone or something else came into view.

The sheriff looked at the map on the wall. "John, you sure you covered the area up by Devil's Ridge?"

John rubbed his earlobe and nodded. "I covered every foot of mud. Checked all my traps too. Had three more sick 'coons, but no sign of that dog."

The sheriff poured another cup of coffee. He hadn't really slept in two days and the signs of fatigue showed on his face. "I think we ought to put out some poisoned meat."

John hesitated. "Might kill a lot of other animals."

"What's more important," the sheriff asked, "a few animals or a couple of people?"

John didn't answer. He knew the answer but wished there was another way.

"And now we got that Youngun boy ridin' all alone," Sheriff Peterson said, tracing Larry's route on the map. "Scales got a telegraph that said someone picked up the vaccine that was comin' to Dr. George."

"Someone? Wasn't it Larry Youngun?" John asked.

"Most likely." The sheriff chuckled. "But the boy signed for the package as Billy the Kid and . . . " the sheriff stopped. His face was ashen.

Without explaining himself, he cranked the phone and got Beatrice, the phone operator. "This is the sheriff. Ring up Rev. Youngun for me."

When the minister answered, the sheriff got right to the point. "Rev. Youngun, just want to let you know that I think Larry got that medicine for Dr. George from the train and—"

Rev. Youngun's shout of joy was so loud that even John could hear it. "But, Reverend, I need to know somethin'." Sheriff Peterson paused and John listened intently. "Do you still got that pistol I left you?"

"Pistol?" John repeated.

Rev. Youngun looked and didn't find it.

"You don't! Heck, Reverend, I told you to put it in a safe place. You think Terry took it with him? Maybe? Well, does he maybe know how to use it? All right, 'bye," he said, hanging up the receiver angrily.

"You think that Youngun boy took a pistol with him?" John asked.

The sheriff rubbed his eyes. "'Fraid so. Now we got some armed kid, ridin' out there, probably scared half to death, with a loaded pistol in his hand." He hit his fist against the wall in frustration. "Hope he doesn't blow his fool head off."

Wonder where he's goin'? Maurice thought as he followed behind Terry and Crab Apple. Terry kept to the side of the road after crossing the Willow Creek Bridge, making it easier for Maurice to follow him, but the conditions of the road made traveling slow.

"Hi, Granddoc," Maurice called out, as he came upon her buggy moving slowly up the muddy road.

"Good morning, Maurice. Just did a good deed for a friend of yours back at the county animal farm."

"What's that?" Maurice asked.

"It's a surprise. You'll hear 'bout it soon enough."

Bet that's where Terry's goin', Maurice decided. A mile down the road, he found he was right and pulled his wagon to a halt outside the county animal disposal farm.

Terry had tied Crab Apple up in a stand of trees alongside the road and was sneaking through the tall grass toward the cages. Maurice shook his head. *He's goin' to get Dangit. I should have known.*

He waited on the wagon bench. *Think I'll stick around and wait for the fireworks to begin. There's no tellin' what will happen when that kid sets his mind to somethin'.*

He scratched his head. *Wonder what Granddoc's surprise is?*

Terry crept forward, trying to spot J.J. *He's gotta be around here somewhere,* Terry thought, eyeing the cages.

There's Dangit! He beamed with excitement. The dog sat with his nose pressed against that of a short, squat brown dog in another cage. But then Terry saw J.J. swing the door open from the shed behind the barn. The door banged hard against the outside wall.

"Sorry, old girl, but the law's the law," J.J. said to the poor collie he was dragging by a rope. "Ain't no health certificate for you."

Terry's eyes welled up as the dog resisted, barking and howling. J.J. pulled the dog into the shed and closed the door.

He's not gonna shoot Dangit, Terry thought, standing up and running toward the cages. Dangit saw him coming and began jumping up against the sides of the cage and barking.

"Quiet!" Terry whispered.

Working as fast as his shaking hands would allow him, Terry yanked hard on the lock. "Where's the key?" he said to Dangit and himself.

Then he saw the ring of keys hanging from the barn wall and pushed an old feed crate under it. It was still just above his reach, so he put a bucket on top of the crate and reached for the keys. But as he grabbed the ring, the bucket slipped and he crashed down.

The shed door banged open. "Who's out there?" J.J. hollered. Not seeing Terry behind the crate, J.J. went back into the shed.

Terry ran to Dangit's cage. "Which key is it?" he moaned, fumbling with the lock. Dangit jumped up and down against the cage, wanting to be let loose.

"I'm hurryin'," he grumbled, but none of the keys seemed to work. Then he noticed the number two above Dangit's cage and saw a number two on a key. "Maybe this one," he said, and the lock fell open. "Come on, boy, let's get outta here."

But then all the other dogs in cages began barking. "Hush . . . quiet . . . he'll hear you," Terry said, flapping his arms up and down to shush them.

Trying to think of a way to calm the dogs down, he picked up the feed buckets and began tossing food into the cages. Then he noticed a group of six dogs of all sizes locked in a cage together next to Dangit's. A crudely written sign said: Healthy dogs. No owners. Destroy Today.

The dogs sat moaning in front of Terry. "Oh, jeesh, don't look at me that way," he said, trying to cover his eyes. Dangit nudged his hands with the key ring, then put his nose against the brown, pudgy dog.

"What are we goin' to do with 'em?" Terry asked.

The healthy dogs started whining, and the stubby brown dog started jumping around. Terry began trying the keys on the ring. "Can't find the right one," he said to the dogs who were trying to lick him through the cage.

The other dogs were still barking, and J.J.'s voice boomed out, "Shut up or I'll shoot you all today!"

Terry saw the dogcatcher coming. He looked at the number three above the cage and then at key number three on the ring. "How stupid can I be?" He inserted the key and the lock opened.

"Come on!" Terry said, and was knocked over by the dogs fawning all over him. Dangit and the stubby dog jumped all over each other.

"Hey, kid! You with the red hair! What you doin'?" J.J. shouted.

Terry didn't bother to answer. He took off across the field with Dangit and the six dogs following behind, barking up a storm. He looked over his shoulder and saw the dogcatcher shaking his fist. *What am I gonna tell Pa?* he wondered.

Maurice watched them coming through the tall grass and shook his head. *He's in trouble now. He might just get hisself a wuppin' for this one.*

Terry untied Crab Apple and climbed on. Then he saw Maurice. "Mr. Springer!"

"That's me," he chuckled, "and that's the dogcatcher comin' after you."

Terry turned to see J.J. hitching up the team on his animal wagon. "What am I gonna do?" he asked.

"You should have thought 'bout that 'fore you went off breakin' into the dog pound." Dangit and the six dogs ran over to Maurice's wagon. "Don't be lookin' at me. I don't want no six dogs fleain' up my house."

"But they're gonna be killed and—"

"And it ain't my problem," Maurice said. "Now you just take Crab Apple and get outta here."

Dangit and five of the six dogs jumped onto the back of Maurice's wagon and crawled under the tarpaulin cover. The sixth, the short chubby dog, kept jumping, trying to get up, but couldn't make it.

Maurice looked at the wet noses sticking out from under the tarpaulin and down at the chubby dog. He got down and lifted up the dog, who scooted quickly under the cover with the rest of the dogs.

He looked at Terry. "Now you ride across the fields toward town, then double 'round and meet me at my house. You gotta throw him off your trail and give me time to think of what to do."

"Thanks, Mr. Springer," Terry said. "I owe you."

"Don't thank me," Maurice said. "I don't want nothin' to do with these dogs."

Maurice pulled the wagon around. The mules pulled hard to get it through the first mud rut, then headed back toward the farm. Terry rode across the fields as instructed. Within a few minutes, J.J. came barreling down the road behind Maurice, his wheels almost flying above the mud.

Maurice said to the dogs behind him, "You bark, woof, or whine and he's gonna find you. Don't be sayin' nothin', you hear?" A couple of small yips answered him.

J.J. pulled his wagon to a halt alongside Maurice's. "You seen a redheaded boy and some dogs ridin' this way?"

Maurice considered how to answer without lying and nodded. "Saw a redheaded boy ridin' up across the field toward town."

"Thanks!" J.J. said, taking the fork in the road to Mansfield.

Maurice giddiyapped the mules. "Don't be thinkin' I'm gonna feed you mongrels. I ain't runnin' no pound."

He turned to see six heads panting up at him, and Dangit snuggled his head in Maurice's lap. "Lord's probably got a special place for children 'n fools. Guess I qualify, don't I, Dangit?"

Gordo

Gordo smelled the horse long before he could see it. Lightnin's labored breathing and scent came on the breeze. From his position on the ledge above the road, Gordo stared down the isolated dirt road that cut through the forest like a ribbon.

The moist sand under the dog had kept him cool, but now he felt the strange feeling coming over him again. Snapping at the air, the sick dog struggled to his feet, then fell over.

Gordo couldn't understand why his legs were stiff. Why he was burning with fever. Why he couldn't see straight.

But he had caught the scent of a human and a horse. The odor in the air was unmistakable and growing stronger every moment. Looking around, he saw nothing. But he could hear the clumping hoofs, hitting the isolated hard patches of road. Then he saw the boy on the horse coming toward him and focused on what he wanted to do.

Gordo pawed the ground and waited.

Larry held the package under one arm and clutched the stained leather reins in the other. "Come on, Lightnin', we're almost home," he said, trying to encourage the exhausted horse to keep going.

Larry's hands were slick with sweat, and he was more tired than he'd ever been in his life. His thoughts were jumbled. About Sherry and Dangit and sometimes about the sky warrior.

The road from Seymour had never seemed this long before, but he'd never ridden it alone on horseback either. And traveling through the mud made the hard journey harder.

He thought about the early French trappers, crossing over the land, building their lean-tos from the blackjack oaks and sumac trees. He remembered reading about Lewis and Clark's crossing of Missouri, and their finding hundreds of turkeys, white pelicans, and huge flocks of Carolina parakeets in the timbered areas.

Wonder what a Carolina parakeet looks like? Larry puzzled, moving his fingers to get a better grip on the box.

He rode so hard with sweat dripping into his eyes that the woods seemed a blur. He could see the forest but was blind to the individual trees along the road.

All he could think of was getting home. Getting the medicine to Sherry. Getting a hot meal and a bath.

The thick woods gave him chills. Always before when he'd gone out riding, he could see neighbors' homes or the buildings of Mansfield. But they seemed so far away now.

"We're gonna make it," he whispered to Lightnin'. He kept his vision focused straight ahead, not caring that he was covered with mud from head to toe.

Gordo froze in place and sniffed the air. His mangy body poised at rigid attention, ready to attack.

Drops of sweat had gathered at the back of Larry's neck. His shirt clung to him. He looked up and saw the big dog just before he leaped off the ledge at him. Larry flattened himself against the saddle and could feel the hot breath of the dog as it grazed his shoulders.

"No, Lightnin', no!" Larry screamed, trying to keep the horse from rearing up. The horse slipped in the muddy edge of the road.

Gordo had crashed into a large rock on the side of the road and staggered back to his feet. Covered with mud, the dog faced Larry, baring his teeth and growling deep in his chest.

"Come on, Lightnin', don't panic," Larry whispered, trying to calm the baying horse.

Gordo moved closer, pawing the ground. A thick drool dripped from his left cheek through his mud-crusted coat. The deep silence of the dense woods seemed to stifle the air, as if the whole world held its breath.

A swarm of gnats crossed in front of Larry. He waved them away, with the hand that held the reins. Lightnin' stepped backward as the dog advanced.

Larry knew the dog was sick with rabies. He clutched the box and felt panic overtaking him. Then, from somewhere in his soul, a burst of courage sprang forth.

He held the box tightly and gripped the reins. "Lightnin', forward now. We're gonna get outta here."

Gordo took two steps up and snapped at the horse's ankles. Larry put the package in his lap and pulled the pistol from his belt. Letting go of the reins, he cocked the pistol and aimed it at the dog.

He pulled the trigger and was caught off guard. He'd never fired a pistol before in his life and wasn't prepared for the kick. Lightin' reared up at the blast that knocked Larry out of the saddle and into the mud.

"The medicine!" he cried out. But the mud was so soft that the precious contents did not shatter.

Then he heard Gordo. The shot had missed.

Gordo snarled and charged toward him. Larry held the pistol with both hands and pulled the trigger again as the big dog jumped.

The bullet twisted the dog in midair. He landed in the mud, tried to stand, then fell over. Gordo was dead.

Larry climbed slowly to his feet, covered with mud. He stood wearily over the dog. "Weren't nothin' else I could do," he mumbled.

He picked up the box and mounted Lightin'. "Let's go home," he shouted, swatting the horse's flanks.

As he rode away from the rabid dog's body, he thought, *Almost home. Nothing can stop me now.*

As he galloped through Mansfield and passed Mr. Palugee's, he saw Willy sneaking through the bushes. *Bet he's goin' for that string ball. Guess we'll get blamed again,* he thought.

But he had something more important on his mind: saving his sister's life.

47

Hide the Doggie

Terry was waiting for Maurice when he pulled the wagon in front of the farmhouse. "What took you so long?" Terry asked.

Maurice shook his head. "Bad roads and Sausage," he said, nodding to the stout, short dog.

"Sausage? You already named him?" Terry laughed.

"Didn't know what else to call him. Had to stop two times so he could do his business. He's too fat to get off and on by hisself, so I had to play nanny and lift him up and down."

"What about the dogcatcher?" Terry asked.

"He was followin' you," Maurice said.

"I didn't see him," Terry said, then dropped his jaw. J.J. was riding up along the back road toward the farm.

"What are we gonna do?" Terry asked.

"What you mean *we?*" Maurice said. "You take these dogs and skedaddle."

"But he'll catch me and—"

Maurice looked at the animal wagon and then at Dangit and the six dogs. "Already got my foot in the water," he mumbled, "so might as well get all the way wet. Come on," he said to Terry, "we got to hide these dogs."

Maurice took them into the barn, and he and Terry stuffed the dogs into feed drawers and bins, in the haystack, and under the rag pile.

"That looks pretty good. He'll never suspect anythin'," Terry beamed.

"You're forgettin' somethin'," Maurice said.

"What's that?"

"Your hair, carrottop," Maurice chuckled. "Now you crawl into the haystack and don't come out till I tell you."

"Maurice, are you 'round?" J.J. called out from the drive.

"In here, J.J. What you want?" he asked, walking to the barn door.

J.J. got off the animal wagon and stepped through the mud. "I think that boy rode across your farm. Might be hidin' 'round here someplace with them dogs."

"You think so?" Maurice said. "I don't even own a dog."

From inside the barn, Sausage barked.

"What was that?" J.J. asked, looking around.

"What you talkin' 'bout? I didn't hear nothin'."

Sausage barked again. "Maurice, I heard a dog bark. Inside your barn," he said, striding into the barn.

"Hold on there, J.J. Hold on," Maurice said, stepping after him.

The dogcatcher didn't stop. "I know there's a dog in here . . . I can hear him."

Maurice stood over by the feed bins while J.J. nosed around the stalls. "Ain't no dogs in here, no sir," Maurice said. *Just some mutts. That's what I should have said.*

Then Sausage stuck his head out of the feed bin. "Get back in there," Maurice whispered, pushing his head back down.

"You say somethin', Maurice?" J.J. asked.

"No, just mumblin' to myself."

Then a brown and white mutt stuck her head out from the haystack behind J.J. Maurice saw that J.J. was going to turn around, so he acted quickly. "Look up there," he called out, pointing to the hayloft.

"What? Where?" J.J. asked, falling for the distraction.

Maurice pointed up toward the loft while he managed to push the dog back into the haystack. "Thought I saw an owl," he said.

"An owl?" J.J. exclaimed. "I ain't lookin' for owls. I'm lookin' for some dogs and a redheaded kid."

Sausage stuck his head out again, and Maurice rolled his eyes. Going behind J.J.'s back, he managed to shove the dog back into the bin.

"I still think there's dogs 'round here," J.J. said, looking around. Then he saw them. Three tails stuck out from the bottom of the hayloft, and Terry's red hair was exposed.

J.J. looked at Maurice. The game was up. Maurice had seen the tails and red hair at the same time.

"Sorry, J.J.," Maurice began.

J.J. held up his hands. "I'm sorry too. You and that fool boy, wherever he is," J.J. said, "made me come all the way over here to tell you that Granddoc came by this morning and filled out a health certificate on the Younguns' dog."

"She did?" Maurice asked.

"She did?" Terry said, sticking his head out from the hay.

"That's right, she did." J.J. repeated. "But those other dogs are the problem. Seems they don't have anyone who wants them and I've got to dispose of them this afternoon."

Sausage whined from the feed bin. "I'll get you outside in a minute. Don't wet on the feed," Maurice grumbled.

"Now, Maurice. Seein's that there's a fine for takin' dogs from the disposal farm without askin' and seein's that you don't have any dogs of your own, I'd be willin' to waive the fine if you were to say that you made a mistake by not askin' and came and got the dogs to keep 'em for your own."

"But I didn't and—"

J.J. held up his hand. "And it's cheaper to keep them and find them homes on your own than it is to pay the fine. And seein's how I don't like havin' to kill dogs, I think this all works out just swell."

Ten minutes later, J.J. drove his wagon away. Terry looked at Maurice. "Now you got your own dog." He beamed.

"Dogs, you mean," Maurice grumbled.

Sausage barked from the bin.

"Okay, okay, just hold it, I'm comin'," Maurice said.

Terry saw the look on his face when Maurice picked up the dog. "You did your business on the feed. I told you not to do that," he said, frowning at the squat, fat dog.

"Thanks for everythin', Mr. Springer," Terry shouted, getting back onto Crab Apple and riding home. Dangit raced ahead barking gratefully. Maurice locked the dogs in the barn and followed Terry home.

Tell the Truth

❖

By the time Terry and Maurice arrived, they found everyone gathered in Sherry's room. Dr. George was giving Sherry her first shot of the vaccine. Eulla Mae was praying, Rev. Youngun was praying, and Larry was nodding off to sleep against the wall, still covered with mud.

Maurice sat down on the other side of Sherry's bed and held her hand while the needle went in. "It'll be all right. Maurice is here to help you."

Terry went over and hugged his brother. "Hey, mudball, you did it!"

Larry barely opened his eyes. "What 'bout Dangit?"

"Look!" Terry smiled, pointing to Dangit who was lying under Sherry's bed, wagging his tail.

"Saw Willy sneaking up to Mr. Palugee's," Larry said quietly.

"Bet he's goin' to steal his string ball and blame us," Terry grumbled.

The idea dawned on them both at the same moment. "Let's go," Larry said.

"Where you boys goin'?" Rev. Youngun asked.

"We just gotta tie up some loose ends, Pa," Larry said.

"Don't you think you need to take a bath? You're covered with mud."

Dr. George put a wet cloth on Sherry's head. "The boy just saved Sherry's life. Let him take a bath when he feels like it. He's a hero."

Sherry smiled weakly from the bed, her arm dangling over the edge. "Thanks, Larry."

"Just get better," Larry answered.

"Is Dangit here?" she asked, then felt his wet tongue on her hand. "Oh, Pa, thanks. I'm so happy!" she said.

"Don't thank me; thank Terry," Rev. Youngun said.

Sherry looked at her brother. "You saved Dangit?"

Terry nodded. "Maurice helped," he added.

"Naw, it was his idea. I just was along for the ride," Maurice smiled.

Eulla Mae trudged up the stairs, carrying a package and an envelope. "Sherry, you got a package from . . ." Eulla Mae read the return address and looked at her husband, who winked slyly. "From heaven," Eulla Mae whispered.

Sherry looked at the box. "Open it, Pa . . . open it!" she exclaimed weakly.

Rev. Youngun opened the box and took out the red shoes. Tears came to Sherry's eyes. "Little Wings," she cried. "Little Wings got me my shoes!"

She clutched the shoes to her heart and looked at the adult faces around her. "See. I told you, Pa," Sherry said. "Little Wings is real!"

Dr. George laughed. "Give her a week, and she'll be running around like nothing happened."

Eulla Mae handed Rev. Youngun the envelope with no return address. "I don't know who it's from, but it smells like bacon and eggs."

Rev. Youngun looked at it questioningly. "I'm not expecting anything." Then he opened it. Inside was Hambone's five-dollar bill. "Praise the Lord," he whispered. "We've got food money."

The phone rang in the kitchen downstairs, and Maurice went to get it, leaving Rev. Youngun and the adults to wonder at the magic of the moment. On the line was Shiny Wilson of the marriage license bureau.

"Tell Rev. Youngun to get ready. I just sent over five mountain brothers with five women all wantin' to get married at the same time."

"I'll tel¹ him!" Maurice laughed and ran back upstairs.

Larry was dead tired from the ride, but he ran as fast as he could behind Terry, holding the wires to the fish shocker. "Don't you turn the handle."

"Tell me that you believe in Chief Pinchafanny," Terry laughed devilishly. Larry refused and Terry turned the handle once.

"Ouch, stop it!" Larry screamed.

"I just wanted to keep you awake."

They took the back trail, avoiding the mud holes, and came up to the rear of Mr. Palugee's property. They saw him sitting on his "throne," surveying his junk.

"Mr. Palugee," Larry said, marching boldly up to the stilted chair.

"I don't want you or Red here on my property," Palugee said. "You ought to go home and take a bath."

"Willy's plannin' to steal your string ball and blame us," Larry said.

"My string ball!" Palugee exclaimed.

"Yup," Terry said. "He's probably gonna roll it down the hill and you'll never see it again."

"Oh, no. He can't do that," Palugee said, getting weak in the knees at the thought of wasting so much string.

"You gotta trust us," Larry said. "We can stop him."

"Why should I trust you?"

"Don't you think it odd that every time somethin' happens, he's around?" Larry said.

Mr. Palugee thought for a moment, then said, "What you got in mind?"

The boys told him their plan to make it look like the long wires hooked to the fish crank was the end of the string ball. They didn't tell him what they intended to do.

"You think those wires will catch him?" Palugee asked.

Terry smiled. "These wires are special. He won't be able to let go."

Palugee looked at the fish shocker, seeing only a part of a phone. *Looks like good junk,* he thought. "What are you gonna do with that thing if you catch him?"

Terry looked at him and grinned. "I don't know. Some things are worth keepin'."

Palugee smiled. "You're a sly kid, you know it?"

Larry stepped between them. "We'll give it to you if you call Mrs. Bentley and tell her what happens."

"You got a deal," Mr. Palugee grinned, and let them in through his back door.

"What a junk heap," Terry whispered, looking around.

"Just hush and wrap the string around the wires real good," Larry said.

Keeping out of sight, the boys rolled the string ball toward the front door, and left the string-wrapped wires at the doorstep. Larry told Mr. Palugee to open the door. "Just walk out like you're goin' to town and leave the door open."

"And watch from the bushes," Terry said, "and you'll see some hair-raisin' truth right before your eyes."

Mr. Palugee did as instructed, and moments later, Willy Bentley came sneaking up to the door, grabbing at the ends of the string ball.

"Man oh man," he mumbled, "them Younguns have had it now."

But as he grabbed the string-wrapped wires, Terry cranked it up and Willy got the shock of his life. "Owwwwww!" Willy screamed.

"Tell the truth, you wart!" Terry shouted, cranking the handle as fast as he could.

"Stop, Terry," Larry said, worried about the pained look on Willy's face.

"No," Terry said, cranking even faster. He saw Mr. Palugee standing behind the boy, shaking his head. "Willy, you tell Mr. Palugee that you've been lyin', blamin' us for what you did."

Terry slowed his cranking down. "Tell him!"

"But . . . but . . . " Willy stammered, his hair rising.

Terry cranked it fast again. "Tell him!"

"I've been lyin'!" Willy screamed.

"Say you done it all!" Terry demanded.

"I done it all! I lit the doo-doo bag. I dumped the trash. I tried to steal the string ball."

Terry stopped cranking. "Good. Now go home and get outta here."

Willy stood up, rubbing his hands. He sneered at Larry and Terry. "I take back everything I said. And Mr. Palugee didn't hear it anyway."

Palugee tapped him on the shoulder. "Come with me, young man," he said, taking Willy by the belt loops on the back of his pants.

"Where you takin' me?" Willy cried out.

"To see your mother," Mr. Palugee said, then he turned and looked at the Younguns. "I owe you boys an apology. What can I do to make it up to you?"

Larry thought for a moment. "Just tell Willy's mother to fix our roof."

Secrets of the Ozarks

❖

Acold snap came in early fall to the Ozarks, killing the remaining animals with rabies that the people of Mansfield hadn't trapped. What could have been a disaster had been avoided as the people worked together to fight a common enemy.

Some say the thick forests and hills of the Ozarks keep secrets better than any lock and key. But they don't know the people of Mansfield.

Lafayette Bedal never revealed that Maurice had bought the red shoes for Sherry, though Rev. Youngun suspected it. Dr. George never let on that he was the one who paid for the medicine that saved Sherry's life. And Shiny Wilson at the marriage license bureau never told Rev. Youngun all he went through to convince those five brothers to marry at the same time. They were just simple acts of friendship that didn't need to be bragged about. That's what good neighbors did for each other.

Of course, some things can't be kept secret, like Maurice having to explain to Eulla Mae how he came to have six dogs in the barn. But working together, they found homes for all of them except Sausage, who just stayed on as the Springers' family pet.

After Willy confessed all to his mother, not only was the Younguns' roof fixed, but the piano key was repaired and a new sofa was delivered. Their house was even painted! Rev. Youngun received a public apology from Sarah Bentley at the next church supper and with her blessing, the Ladies Aid Society voted him a raise.

Rev. Youngun suspected that the five-dollar bill in the unmarked envelope was sent by Hambone. He gave Hambone a wink and mouthed "thank you" at church, and Hambone mouthed "you're welcome" back.

Little Wings stayed Sherry's secret. She never again talked about her, though her father suspected that the angel was still around because sometimes at night he'd hear Sherry whisper to her.

Life took on a more special meaning for the people of Mansfield. They showed it by being kinder and more caring to each other. And in the fall school play, Sherry danced her heart out in her new red shoes, making everyone appreciate just how precious life is.

Even Mr. Palugee brought over a string-wrapped present to apologize to Larry and Terry. He didn't even ask for the string back.

Inside the gift box they found two shiny silver dollars and a note that read: "Some things are worth keeping." From that day forward, he always waved to the Younguns and never minded when they sneaked through his yard to examine the new junk he had found. When they stopped to think about it, some things *were* worth keeping.

If you get back to this part of the Ozarks, you might just stop and listen for the rustle of little angel wings. Or look into the mists of the morning that shroud the hills, and maybe you'll see a sky warrior chipping at his dart point.

Folks say that if you look closely at the trees in the hills, you can still see some of John's Bible carvings on the trees. They also say that he and Cody are together again in heaven, but that's kind of hard to prove.

About the Author

Thomas L. Tedrow is a best-selling author, screenwriter, and film producer. He prides himself on stories that families can read together and pass on to friends. He is the author of the eight-book series, The Days of Laura Ingalls Wilder, the eight-book series, The Younguns, and such new classics as *Dorothy—Return to Oz, Grizzly Adams & Kodiak Jack,* and other books and stories. Tedrow lives with his wife, Carla, and their four children in Winter Park, Florida.

An excerpt from *Frankie and the Secret,*
Book Two in The Younguns series:

Something moved in the bushes behind the burned-out Sutherland house. Larry peered into the last light of day, trying to find it again.

"Did you see anythin'?" he asked his brother.

Terry shook his head. "Nothin' but nothin' out there."

Larry wasn't sure and had a thought that was strong enough to worry the warts off a frog. *I hope it's not Missouri Poole sneakin' up again,* he thought. *I don't want her jumpin' on me again.*

Missouri, the pretty hill girl who had a crush on Larry, had vowed to kiss him before the summer was out. Said she had itchy lips which only Larry could scratch. And Larry knew she was bulldog stubborn.

Ever since she'd jumped out at him when he was walking in town, putting her arms around him and trying to kiss his lips, he'd been afraid of her.

If I see Missouri comin' out, I might just have to shoot, he thought, shaking his head at the chilly thought. *Ain't gonna let no girl kiss me if I don't wanna.*

He couldn't understand why he got the chills thinking about it or why he felt attracted to her. *Why'd God have to give girls itchy lips anyhow?*

"General Jackson," Terry called out, using his brother's soldier name, "I think I see some cookies out there."

Larry turned with a questioning look. "Some what?"

Terry coughed. "Er, I think I see . . ." He peered out again. "Enemy soldier comin'!"

Larry looked over the dirt embankment they'd put up near the ruins of the Sutherland homestead, trying to see what his brother was pointing to in the twilight.

"I don't see nothin'," he said.

"Right there," Terry pointed. "Where them gumdrop lookin' rocks are."

"Use soldier talk," Larry said, disgusted.

Then Larry saw the shape in the bushes. Something was definitely there. "You're right General Stuart," Larry answered using Terry's soldier name. "Sound the battle cry."

Terry let out his best rebel yell, then shouted, "Yankees attackin'!"

Larry tapped his stick rifle on top of the fort's hospital. "General Barton," he shouted to his sister, "blow out the candle and come grab a weapon!"

Sherry crawled out from the pine bough lean-to they'd made for their headquarters. "What's wrong?" she cried, nervously clutching her dolly as thunder boomed.

Sherry was Fort Mansfield's chief nurse and only nurse. She went by the war name General Clara Barton after the famous nurse. Her dollies served as the battle wounded.

Terry pointed over the dirt wall as thunder pounded overhead. "Enemy. Hear their cannon?" he asked. "They're hidin' out there in them bushes waitin' to drop mortar shells on us."

"Where?" she whispered, looking over the wall with one eye closed.

"Twenty yards that away," Terry nodded.

"Up where?"

"Up near the Yankee graves," he said, pointing toward the graves of Jack and Caroline Sutherland.

"Can they get through?" Sherry asked, worried more about the graves than about the imaginary Yankee troops they were always fighting.

"Naw," Terry said, shaking his head. "We've built enough traps, holes, and trip ropes to stop the entire durn Yankee army."

Sherry looked out again, feeling better. "No Yankee will get in here," she said to herself.

"And even if they do," Terry said, puffing his chest, "any Johnny Reb worth his salt can stand blindfolded and hog-tied and still lick ten Yankees." He patted the walls that he'd help build. "Fort Mansfield is what the Confederates needed. Had this and they'd have won the war."

"What war?" Sherry asked.

"The Civil War, you dummy."

"What was the war about?" Sherry wondered.

"How the heck should I know? War is just war." Terry shrugged. 'Don't ask so many dumb questions. It's just a game."